This novel is dedicated to my parents,
Frans and Lony van Heugten, who fought in the
Dutch resistance during World War II.

In their early twenties, they risked their lives
for what they believed in.

Their spirit and courage has inspired
me in every endeavor.

They will always be my heroes.

PREFACE

We have no milk, no bread, no potatoes—just rotten peels. The boys now have to go far into the fields to pull frozen tulip bulbs from the ground. We grind the pulp and make thin soup and watery porridges from them. They are bitter, practically inedible, but we choke them down because otherwise we will starve.
—*Anonymous Dutch housewife, circa 1944*

During the Hongerwinter in 1944, a railway strike was ordered by the exiled Dutch government to further Allied liberation efforts. The Germans retaliated by placing an embargo on all food transports. Gas and electricity were cut off during one of the harshest winters in history. Potatoes and vegetables were long gone. There was no meat, milk, butter, coffee or sugar and not enough bread to feed one person, let alone a family. There was only one thing left to them in the barren fields. Tulips.

Four and a half million people were affected by the famine.

Over 20,000 starved to death. This represents the nadir of the war—Dutchmen forced to forage and choke down their national flower to stave off starvation. It is one of the great ironies of the Dutch occupation.

I

Nora balanced the grocery bag on one hip and inserted her key into the lock of the door leading from the garage into the house. This was the best moment of every day. *Rose.* Her beautiful baby—almost six months now. Every little thing she did was a revelation. How she raised her tiny hand to Nora's face as she held her. How her wide eyes, the deepest of blues, reacted to the slightest change of tenor in Nora's voice. How the warmth of her small body nestled into Nora's when she took her into her arms. When she held Rose, Nora didn't know where her own body ended and her daughter's began.

"Mom?" she called. No response, but that was normal. This was usually when her mother put Rose into her tiny, ruffled bathing suit and swirled her around in the pool. Moving back from Amsterdam to live with her mother had been a blessing. The thought of Anneke and Rose at home playing while she worked filled her with gratitude—and today was no exception. Contentment warmed her as she thought of the love she and Anneke shared in caring for Rose. Grandmother, mother and child. Life was perfect.

Nora shifted the groceries higher onto her hip and glanced at the pile of mail on the entryway table. Nothing interesting. The newspaper lay open. She scanned the headlines. *Iranian Phantoms and F-5 Tiger IIs Attack Iraqi Airfields Near Basra.* Nora shook her head. It was already 1980. Would the Middle East ever right itself? Her eyes flicked down the page. *Los Angeles, Comedian Richard Pryor Badly Burned Freebasing Cocaine.* Big surprise, she thought.

She looked through the living room window and caught a shimmer of water from the pool. Joy flooded her. She would take the groceries into the kitchen and then put on her bathing suit. She couldn't wait to hold Rose in her arms. Every evening it felt the same—as if she had been gone for days. That first touch of baby skin revived her spirit, calmed her soul.

She stepped into the living room, still holding the groceries. She heard them crash to the floor and then her own scream. "Mom!"

Anneke lay prostrate on the thick white carpet, her beautiful hazel eyes gaping at the ceiling, a single bullet hole through her forehead.

"No!" screamed Nora. She ran into the living room, fell to her knees and feverishly searched for a pulse. Her fingers pressed again and again into the soft skin of her mother's neck, but there was nothing, *nothing!* Darkness exploded within her as she stared into Anneke's vacant eyes. Nora's heart leaped when she heard ragged breathing, until she realized that it was her own. "Oh, God, Mom!" she moaned.

Nora bent and cupped her mother's face with shaking hands. As she pressed Anneke's cold cheek against her own, Nora felt her heart slamming against her ribs, her breath now in hoarse gasps. Moaning, she closed her eyes, hoping wildly that when she opened them, this would all be a nightmare. But when she looked again, all she could see was a sickening stream of dark, ugly blood that ran from the gaping hole in Anneke's forehead in a jagged path down her pale cheek. Then she released her mother's face and saw the same slick blood on her own palms. Vomit rose up, but she fought it down. She stared at this face she loved. "Mom," she whispered, "please, please don't leave me!"

Half-choking, she looked at the blood on her shaking hands. Then she smelled it—a metallic odor of copper and rust—one she recognized all too well from the operating room. Her own mother's blood on her hands! Bile rose in her again.

She studied the bullet hole. Scarlet blood had stained her mom's silver hair, turning it a grisly purple, the flesh around it charred and black. The odor made Nora gag when she realized it smelled like burnt pork.

Moaning, she sat and clutched Anneke's limp body and rocked her back and forth. Anneke's slight frame swayed with the movement. Then Nora noticed that her gorgeous gray hair had been hacked off in ugly clumps, leaving stark patches of white scalp. She looked wildly around. Tufts of silver hair all over the carpet—feathers from a bird shot from the sky. "Why?" she cried. "Why would anyone do this to you?"

She drew back to shift her mom's body onto the carpet. Anneke's head lolled to one side. Nora screamed. The bullet had blasted a large hole through the back of her head. Nora felt faint. Gray brain matter mixed with blood hung out of Anneke's skull. Nora tried to push the gray lumps back into her mother's skull. They felt like buttery worms and smelled like spoiled eggs.

"Mom! Oh, Mom!" Gasping, she saw nothing but the hideous remains of her mother's head and the slippery blood and brain matter on her own hands. The monstrous sight gripped her. She struggled up onto all fours and heaved waves of green bile onto the white carpet. Then she knelt, taking huge breaths, trying not to pass out. The silence felt endless. She heard only the ticking of the grandfather clock across the room, a relentless metronome to the macabre scene before her.

She roused herself. Her next thought was an iron spike into her brain. "Rose!" she cried. "Where are you?" Adrenaline shot through her as she jumped up and ran to the bassinet. *No Rose!* She raced into the nursery. The room was dark, the crib empty. "No!" Panic surged within her.

She rushed back into the living room and ran past her mother, desperate to search the other rooms. Running toward her bedroom, her heel caught on the rug and she fell. Pain seared through her right ankle.

Sobbing, she rolled over and found herself face-to-face with a total stranger. A man lay on his stomach, his right arm outstretched. His head was twisted toward her, right cheek pressed into the carpet. She screamed and tried to move away, but her ankle felt on fire. His face was so close that she could have felt his breath on hers—if he were alive. His black eyes looked as dead and cold as her mother's. Then she saw the gun, dark and sinister, inches away from his outstretched arm and gloved fingers. Nora gasped, her heart in her throat. *Who was he? And where, oh God, where was Rose?*

She got to her feet, wincing at the pain in her ankle, and rushed into each of the other rooms. "Rose!" she cried. "Rose!" She limped back and knelt by her mother, sobbing. "Where is Rose, Mom? Where is the baby?" She appealed to Anneke as if she could still give Nora an answer. Anneke's blank, unholy stare never moved from the ceiling. *What in God's name had happened?* She rose unsteadily, favoring her ankle. Her body still shook. *Who was the dead man? Why had he killed her mother? And Rose? Why would anyone kidnap her baby?*

Ignoring the pain in her ankle, she ran to the front door and flung it open. She saw no one in the street, no one in the neatly groomed front yards. "Rose!" she screamed, as if her darling could answer her. She slammed the door and went back inside. Something on the carpet now caught her eye. As she knelt down and picked it up, she moaned. It was Rose's tiny yellow hair band. Its cheerful flower had been ripped off and lay a few feet away. Then she knew. Rose was really gone. She clutched the flower to her breast and sobbed. One thought now pierced her mind.

Was Rose still alive?

2

Nora limped into the kitchen. As she dialed the operator, her sobs strangled her. *Ring. Ring. Ring.* "Come on!" she shouted. "Answer the goddamned phone!"

"Operator, may I help you?"

"Yes—*please!* There's been a murder, my baby is—"

"I'm putting you through to the police," said a nasal female voice. "Please stay on the line."

Nora felt as if an eternity passed before she heard a slow Texas drawl finally come through. "HPD—Brody."

"Officer—my mother, my baby!" she cried.

"Hang on," he said soothingly. "What's the problem?"

"My mother—she's been murdered!" Terror scrambled her words. "Dead man…on floor…my baby…kidnapped!"

"Slow down now," he said quietly. "Is the perpetrator still in the house?"

Nora wished she could reach through the line and throttle him. "No!"

"Name?"

"Nora—Nora de Jong."

"Address?"

"Four eleven Tangley. Get someone here—now! Rose could be anywhere—someone could have killed her...."

"Yes, ma'am," he said quickly. "I'll send an officer right over. You sit tight. Don't touch anything, don't do anything. You understand?"

Nora sobbed. "Yes, yes! Just please hurry!" She slammed down the receiver. *God, what should she do? Call Marijke.* Her Dutch girlfriend visiting from Amsterdam was giving a speech at Rice University on European economics. *She would help!* Nora scrabbled through the notepad on the kitchen counter, finally locating the number Marijke had written down that morning. Her hands trembled so she could barely punch the buttons. With every ring, Nora grew more frantic.

"Professor Sanford's office," said a bland female voice. "Miss Mitchell speaking."

Nora took a deep breath. "I need to speak to Marijke van den Maas immediately."

There was a pause and then she heard a rustling of paper. "Dr. van den Maas is giving a lecture now. I can't interrupt her. Are you a student?"

"No, I'm not a student!" Nora could hear her own hysteria. "I'm a friend of Dr. van den Maas's. This is an emergency!"

"Name?" The woman's unruffled tone sounded as if students called with emergencies all the time. *Stupid, asinine woman!*

"Nora de Jong!" Another sob escaped her. "You have to find her and have her call me immediately. My—my mother has been murdered—"

"Oh, my God!" The wooden voice came to life. "Give me your number."

"She has it," Nora sobbed. "Hurry, please!"

"Don't worry, she's just across the quad. I'll run over there right now."

Nora now heard the hollow dial tone. She sat on the kitchen stool, stunned. She could not face going back into the living room. The silence was eerie, malevolent. As if she were in purgatory, suspended in agony. All she could think about was Rose. *Rose.*

She wrung her hands and struggled to breathe, trying to focus. *If the dead man killed Anneke, then who took Rose?* There had to have been someone with him. How would the police even begin to find him? Her thoughts darted to horrible scenarios. Rose clutched in the arms of a killer or madman racing down I-10—out of Houston, out of the U.S.—never to be seen again; Rose held for ransom and tortured to scream through the phone; Rose thrown into a Dumpster where she would be eaten by rats; Rose screaming and shaking, her tiny face turning blue while large hands strangled her.

"No!" she told herself fiercely. "Stop it! You don't know anything. She's fine, she has to be. They just want money. That's it, that's got to be it!" But her words sounded hollow. She shut her eyes to keep away the horrible visions.

After what felt like hours, the phone rang. Nora picked it up on the first ring. "Marijke?"

"What happened?" Nora heard the astonishment in Marijke's voice. "Your mother—she's dead?"

"Marijke," she cried. "Please come home—now! It's too terrible. My mother's been murdered—" Then a strangled sob. "Someone took Rose! She's gone—I can't find her anywhere!"

Marijke's voice came through clear and firm, a voice Nora had always trusted. "Listen to me. You have to calm down. Did you call the police?"

"Yes, but they're not here yet." She burst into tears.

"Okay, I'm going to talk to you until they get there and then I'll come right away."

Nora began sobbing so that her wailing was the only sound she heard.

"Nora?"

"Yes," she said, feeling faint.

"I'm here," said Marijke. "Just hang on until the police come."

Nora took a deep breath. "You're right. I have to keep it together, for Rose."

The front doorbell clanged. "They're here!" Nora dropped the phone and sprang to her feet, forgetting about her ankle. With a sharp cry, she ran to the door. Three officers stood there with grim faces. One stepped forward. He was forty-ish, tall and square-jawed, with intense brown eyes and short-cropped hair. No wedding band, but the pale ring of flesh on his left hand showed it had not been long since it had been removed. With his blue suit, white shirt and polished black shoes, Nora thought he looked more like a politician than a policeman.

"Ms. de Jong?" he said. "I'm Lieutenant Richards."

Nora flung the door wide-open. "Please...please help me!"

Richards nodded at the other two men and walked in. They followed.

"There!" She pointed at the living room. "My mother, that...*man* on the floor...the gun." She tried to walk with them into the room, but Richards held her back with one of his large hands.

"I'm going to have to ask you to step aside, ma'am," he said. "We have to keep the crime scene undisturbed." He nodded to the two officers. "Gloves and footwear. No moving anything, no touching the bodies."

Nora wrung her hands and sobbed. "My baby! Someone took her. She's only six months old!"

Richards took Nora by the shoulders and focused his dark eyes upon hers. "Ms. de Jong, I have to ask you to calm down. I need to get as much information as I can, especially since your daughter appears to have been taken."

Nora took a deep breath and forced herself to be still.

"That's better," he said softly. Nora noticed that he had a tic in his right eye. It distracted her. *Was he nervous now or was it something he did all the time?*

One of the officers walked over to them. "I radioed the station," he said. "CSI and the M.E. are on their way."

Richards nodded and turned back to Nora. "First, is there anyone I can call for you? Your husband? A friend or relative?"

Nora shook her head, her eyes tearing again. "No," she whispered. "I've called my friend who's visiting from Holland. She'll be here soon."

"What about your father?"

"Dead. Three years ago. Cancer."

"No one else you'd like here with you?"

"No." There was no one. Since she'd returned to Houston, she'd been swamped with her job and then Rose's birth. The friends she'd had here had scattered to the winds during the two years she'd been in Amsterdam. Anneke had been her only friend—her best friend.

Richards put on latex gloves and pulled paper booties over his shoes. As he stepped into the living room, Nora saw Marijke walk into the foyer. She stopped and clapped her hands to her mouth as she took in Anneke's mutilated body and the dead man on the floor. Nora rushed to her and Marijke threw her arms around her. Nora sobbed uncontrollably as she felt Marijke's comforting grasp tighten. *"Nee, nee,"* she whispered, *"het komt goed—echt waar."* No, thought Nora, *it will never be all right!* The lilt and accent of her voice sounded so much like Anneke's that it made Nora cry even harder.

Nora saw Richards cross the room and nod a silent greeting to Marijke. His tic had stopped. "Ladies, I'm afraid you can't come in here. We have to let the crime investigators do their work—search for evidence while the scene is still fresh."

Marijke nodded at Richards and took Nora's arm. "Come with me."

"No, I have to know if they find anything!"

Richards shook his head at Marijke, who then tugged gently on Nora's arm and led her through the kitchen to the nursery. Sweet baby smells assaulted Nora as she stepped into the room—the silken scent of baby powder, freshly laundered clothing, one yellow wall covered with photos of Rose.

Nora clutched the empty crib and fell into the rocking chair beside it, shaking. "Who is that monster?" she asked. "And why would he do such a thing?" She looked up at her friend, tears still streaming. "Oh, Marijke, none of this makes any sense! Who took Rose? What has he done with her?"

Marijke knelt in front of her and put her strong hands over Nora's trembling ones. She looked steadily into her eyes. "Start from the beginning."

When she finally managed to speak, Nora could hear the frenzy in her voice. "I came home from work and called for Mom— Oh, God..." Marijke squeezed Nora's hands. "I went into the living room and there she was." Nora stopped. Telling the story made it too real, but she had no choice. She forced herself to continue, making Marijke's warm eyes her focal point. "There was blood everywhere. The back of her head, her brains. I...I tried to put them back...."

"Enough," said Marijke softly. She stood and pulled Nora out of the chair, wrapped her in a warm embrace and let her cry.

When Nora had exhausted herself, she lifted her eyes. Gratitude filled her. "I don't know what I'd do if you weren't here."

Marijke gave her a small smile. With a firm arm around
Nora's waist, she walked her to the bed. Nora stopped and put
her hand in her pocket.

"What is it?" asked Marijke.

Nora handed her the bright yellow headband and its pitifully crumpled flower. Nora felt her stomach turn, rushed to
the bathroom and vomited. Using the tiled counter for support, she watched Marijke grab a washcloth and run water over
it. Nora closed her eyes and let Marijke gently wipe away her
tears. The washcloth felt cold. Nora never wanted to move,
never wanted to see what she had seen, never wanted to believe that Rose was gone. She walked back into the nursery,
pacing. She spoke in Dutch. "Marijke, they've got to find her!
I can't bear it!"

Nora watched Marijke go to the couch and pat a place next
to her. *"Kom."*

Nora sat down and let Marijke still her trembling hands
again. Nora felt some of her strength return. "I have to stop
this," she said firmly. "I can't help my mother. All I can do is
work with the police to find Rose." She met Marijke's brown
eyes and felt fire in her own. "I just have to believe that Richards and his men will find her."

Nora stood and stared at the corner of the room. The paint-
ing she had begun of Rose rested on an easel, half-finished.
Her heart lurched. Would she ever see her again? She felt
haunted by Rose's luminous blue eyes, staring at her from
the canvas—so happy, so trusting. She felt as if a limb had
been ripped from her body. She smelled Rose's baby smell,
felt the delicious weight of Rose in her arms and the pull of
her womb as Rose latched on to her breast. *Would she ever feel
those things again?*

3

After what felt like hours, Richards came into the nursery. "Ms. de Jong? Could you come with me?"

She stood but felt dizzy and stumbled. He caught her. She felt his strong arms around her. When she steadied and he let her go, she yearned for someone she loved to hold her, to shelter her from this torment.

"You all right?" She nodded. He grasped her elbow and led her into the kitchen, avoiding the living room.

Marijke followed and patted Nora's shoulder. "I'm going to make you a cup of tea," she whispered.

Richards pulled out a chair from the table. Wearily, she sat. Her eyes felt as if they were swollen shut from her tears. *How long had it been? How long since she'd walked through the front door and her life had stopped?*

Richards took a chair opposite and pulled a worn notebook and a stubby pencil out of his shirt pocket. She watched as he rubbed his right eye. When he lowered his hand, the tic started again. Nora couldn't stop staring. She tried to focus on his good eye as he nodded at her. "Tell me everything you know. Let's start with Rose. I'll need a photo that we can give to the press and TV stations. We'll also send it to the FBI."

Numbly, Nora got up and walked to the counter and picked up a framed photo of Rose in her christening gown. Anneke had wanted this picture of her in the dress even before the actual event. Rose was an angel in white, her toothless smile beaming. Nora's fingers ached to touch the down of her pale red curls. She removed the photo from the frame and handed it over silently. He took it from her and walked into the hallway. She saw him hand it to one of the officers, then return.

"What was Rose wearing? Does she have any distinguishing birthmarks?"

Nora shook her head. "No birthmarks. This morning she was wearing a pink ruffled top and her diaper, of course. She wore a yellow hair band my mother bought for her—it had a flower on it." Marijke took the tiny band and its crushed bloom from her pocket and handed it to Richards. Nora cringed at the memory of her mother holding Rose in her lap after she had put the headband on that morning. How they had laughed at Rose's surprised expression as Anneke had clapped Rose's tiny hands together.

She made herself look up at Richards. "What will you do to find her?"

"Three officers are combing the neighborhood to find out if anyone saw something unusual," he said. "If so, maybe someone got a good look at the kidnapper's face. If we get lucky, we might get enough of a description for a police artist to work with. I called the regional FBI emergency response unit that deals with kidnappings before I got here. A CARD team has already been alerted."

"What is that?"

"Child Abduction Rapid Deployment. They get on these right away." He glanced at his notes. "What do you do for a living?"

"I'm a doctor, a pediatric surgeon."

Richards raised an eyebrow, impressed. "Where do you work?"

"Methodist." She turned to Marijke. "God, I've got to call Bates. I have two surgeries scheduled tomorrow and five more this week."

"I'll do it." Marijke walked over and picked up the receiver. "What's his number?"

"On the wall. Tell him I don't know when I'll be back." She couldn't think about work now.

"Is there anyone at Methodist who might be holding a grudge against you?" asked Richards. "A former lover perhaps? A disgruntled coworker?"

"No," she said. "I don't date or socialize at work. No time."

Richards scribbled a few notes. Nora glanced up. Men in white coveralls walked slowly by the kitchen doorway in thin gloves and booties. One held the dreadful gun she'd seen near the dead man's hand. It was in a plastic bag. "Who are they?"

"CSI," he said. "They're going through the house with a fine-tooth comb. They'll be here awhile."

Nora nodded, but felt her panic return. "Isn't there anything else we can do? What about my mother? And who is that bastard in there on the floor?"

"These are all questions we'll try to answer, but our first step is to get the wheels in motion to find your daughter." A tic twitched his other eye. He rubbed it wearily. It seemed to Nora that its constant motion must be dreadful. He looked up at her. "Now that we've put that into gear, we'll focus on the rest."

Marijke walked quietly to the table. "Bates sends his condolences and says he'll cover for you as long as he can." Marijke slid a cup of hot tea in front of her and gave her a quick hug. Nora whispered her thanks.

Richards flipped to a blank page in his notebook. "What was your mother's name? Can you tell me a little about her?"

"Anneke," whispered Nora. "Anneke de Jong. She is—was—Dutch. She and my father, Hans, immigrated here from the Netherlands after the war."

"Do you know any of their friends or acquaintances? Someone your mother knew who might have disliked her? Did she belong to any organizations? Was she politically active? Anything like that?"

Nora shook her head. "She was a very private person," she said softly. "After my father died, my mother isolated herself from the few friends they had. I think she found being with people too painful."

"Are there any relatives we can talk to?"

"No. They didn't keep in touch with their family in Holland. I never knew why."

Richards scribbled on his pad. "What did your mother do?"

"She was a housewife." Her voice trembled. "My mother was a warm, loving person. She spent all her time taking care of Rose." An old thought seared her brain. Was it her fault? If she had stayed home instead of going to work, would any of this have happened?

"How old was your mother?"

Nora cringed at his use of the past tense. "Sixty."

"And your father?"

She had to think. "He would have been sixty-two last month."

"What did he do?"

"He was a literature professor at St. Thomas University. The classics."

"Did he have any enemies that you know of?"

Nora shook her head and then felt a well of panic rise. "Shouldn't you focus on finding Rose?"

He must have sensed her hysteria, because he reached across the kitchen table and squeezed her clenched hands. Nora was surprised. She had not expected the police would openly offer comfort to a stranger. She felt a bit calmer. "Thank you," she whispered. *A nice man, a good man. He will help me.*

"We've done all we can for the moment," he said. "We'll see what the investigators come up with once they've gone through the house."

Nora felt a tap her on the shoulder.

"Drink maar op," said Marijke.

"Dank je wel," whispered Nora. She wrapped her trembling fingers around the hot cup, took a small sip and put it down.

Richards looked up from his pad. "Ms. de Jong, did you disturb the crime scene in any way when you came home?"

Nora hesitated. "I don't know. When I saw my mother on the floor, I ran over to her."

"Did you touch the body?"

She nodded. "I looked for a pulse. I held her in my arms."

"Did you touch anything else?"

Nora felt her eyes fill. "Her head—her brains…"

"That's all right." He gave her a moment. "And the man?"

"I tripped over him looking for Rose."

"Have you ever seen him before?"

"No."

"Did you touch his body?"

She put her head into her hands. "No—no! I didn't want to get near him. And then I saw the gun on the floor…"

Richards's eyes narrowed. "Did you touch it?"

Nora thought and then shook her head. Richards straightened his blue tie and made a few notes. His pencil was down to the nub. He muttered as he tossed it aside and drew out a pen from his jacket pocket. As he fired more questions, it seemed to Nora as if he were a journalist on a hot story. *What time had Nora left the house that morning? Had she noticed anyone or anything out of the ordinary in the neighborhood? What time had she gotten home? Did her mother care for Rose all day? Was there a housekeeper, gardener or anyone else who had access? When had Nora last spoken to Anneke?*

"I left around eight in the morning and got home before five," she said. "I didn't notice anything unusual in the neighborhood. No one else has a key to the house. I spoke to my mother after lunch. She sounded...happy." She realized then that she would never speak to her mother again. Her grief felt unbearable. Then one of the crime scene investigators walked into the room.

Richards stood. "I'm going to see what they found. You wait here."

"No, I'm going with you."

Richards studied her. "All right, but first you have to put on gloves and shoe covers." He glanced at Marijke. "Same goes for you."

"Of course," said Marijke.

One of the CSI men handed over gloves and booties. "Don't touch anything," Richards warned. "Just look."

They quickly donned their gear and followed him into the living room. The M.E., a slight man with graying hair, had apparently arrived while Nora was answering Richards's questions. He stood next to Anneke's body. Nora could not help but stare at her mother's forehead, the hideous bullet hole and the blood that had leaked from it, now coagulated into a thick black stream. Pitiful remnants of what used to be Anneke's beautiful silver hair lay strewn in clumps on the floor. A pair of scissors with its blades wide-open lay partially hidden by the locks of shorn hair. It struck her again that the killer must have chopped off sections of her hair. *Why in hell would he do that?*

Nora watched as the M.E. knelt and examined the man's body, first studying the eyes. "No petechial hemorrhaging here."

"What does that mean?" asked Marijke.

"No burst veins," Nora explained.

"Means he wasn't strangled." The M.E. pointed at tiny red marks that crisscrossed the man's cheeks. "See the hemorrhaging there? Indicates heart attack, maybe stroke." He pulled a thermometer from his bag and nodded to one of the investigators, who pulled down the man's pants, exposing his buttocks. He inserted the thermometer, his eyes on his watch. Nora felt sick.

"Time of death?" asked Richards.

The M.E. wiped the thermometer and gave it a quick glance. "Probably four, five hours ago." He held up one of the man's arms. It was stiff, doll-like. "Rigor's begun."

"Cause?"

The M.E. shrugged. "Stroke, heart attack, like I said. Can't confirm till the autopsy." He struggled to his feet, nodding to the investigator, who pulled the dead man's pants up.

Nora looked away. Marijke moved next to her and held her hand, their fingers entwined. Nora's eyes riveted upon her ravaged mother. "Can't you at least cover her?" she asked angrily. "A sheet, anything?"

The M.E. glanced at her, his eyes sympathetic. "I'm finished. When the investigators give us the green light, we'll move her to the morgue."

Nora's eyes fixed again upon her mother and she caught a glint of silver around Anneke's neck. Of course, she thought, her locket. She bent over Anneke and reached for it.

An investigator grabbed her shoulder. "Hey! You can't do that!"

Nora pulled back. "That's my mother's necklace," she said in a strangled voice. "Could you please take it off? She was never without it and I...need it."

He shook his head. "We haven't dusted it for prints yet."

"Then do it now." She absolutely had to hold it in her hand—the last earthly thing that had been warmed by her mother's body.

The investigator nodded at one of his men, who walked over and dusted it. The powder left a black ring around Anneke's neck, as if it were a noose. The investigator then examined the markings on the necklace and compared them to the fingerprints they had taken of the murderer and Anneke. He nodded at the head investigator and handed the locket to one of his female assistants. The woman carefully wiped the soot from the necklace and handed it to Nora. "It's clean," she whispered. "I'm so sorry."

Nora nodded numbly as she held the silver orb in her hand. It felt smooth and delicate. She turned it over. Inscribed on it, in fine, ornate script, was the letter A, but barely visible, as if Anneke had rubbed it so often that it had almost vanished into the silver. Nora smoothed the metal until it was warm, as if it had lain only moments ago upon her mother's skin. *Her suprasternal notch,* thought Nora. The beautiful hollow in the front of her throat. Nora fastened the chain around her neck, tucked it into her blouse and felt it swing gently into place. It emanated grief and loss, but also love and remembrance.

Nora walked to the window and stared into the backyard. She couldn't bear the men picking over her mother's body, like vultures over their kill. Marijke followed and put her arm around Nora's waist.

Richards finally nodded at the M.E. and Nora watched as

two police officers raised Anneke's body, her limbs hanging askew. Her head lolled to one side, her hazel eyes wide, staring at nothing. Struggling, they got her into the chasm of a black body bag. Another sickening wave of grief rushed through Nora. *It was impossible!* Marijke held her while she cried and then released her with a soft kiss on her cheek.

Richards moved closer. "Can you think why someone would hack off your mother's hair like that?"

"I have no idea."

Richards took her arm and walked with her across the room where the dead man lay on the floor. "And you're sure you've never seen him before?"

Nora forced herself to study the crumpled form and then shook her head. She watched as one of the officers traced a crude, white chalk outline on the carpet around his body. She glanced back to where her mother had lain. That empty space now encircled by the rough drawing struck her like a hammer blow. It was all that was left of her mother.

Nora turned to the dead man again and shuddered. His navy sport jacket, white polo shirt and khaki pants struck Nora as weekend golf wear, not the attire of a killer. He still lay as she had first seen him, his black, hawkish eyes staring up at nothing, his body sprawled, right arm outstretched. *Where was the gun?* She scanned the room and saw it in a plastic evidence bag on top of the sofa, next to another bag that contained the scissors. She walked over and stared at the gun, fighting a compulsion to pick it up. Maybe if she held it in her hand, felt its heft, then she might accept that her mother was really dead.

After a long moment, she turned back to the officers, who now had formed themselves into a U shape around the stranger's body. She joined them. Someone had removed the black glove on the man's right hand. Then something caught her eye. "What is that?"

"Fingerprint ink," said Richards.

She felt her breathing quicken. "Will you be able to identify him?"

"If he's committed a previous crime, there's a good chance. Or if he was ever arrested. His prints are already on their way to the lab. They'll find a match if there is one."

She saw one of the investigators now walk in, an older man with a bone weariness about him. Nora wondered if years of seeing mutilated bodies had scored those wrinkles on his face. He stuck his sun-spotted hands into the worn pockets of his uniform and then raised bloodshot eyes to Richards. "Here's what we know so far," he said in a raspy voice. "No evidence of forced entry or defensive wounds on the victim's body."

Richards nodded. "So she let him in."

"Them. There's another set of footprints besides the dead guy and the victim."

"But my mother would never have let strangers into the house," Nora gasped. "She was always careful, especially when she was alone with Rose."

The investigator nodded at one of the other officers, who brought over a bouquet of large, broken tulips, brilliant red and yellow, their petals hanging pitifully over shiny, silver wrapping. "He apparently posed as a delivery man," he said. "We found them in the dining room, behind the door."

Richards nodded. "Bag it. What else?"

He nodded toward the sofa. "The gun. We're taking it to the station."

"Let me look at it," said Richards. The older man walked to the sofa and returned with the pistol. With gloved hands, Richards opened the bag and took it out. He peered at it, turning it over and over. Nora noticed that now both his eyes were steady and focused. "Second World War, German. Looks like a Luger."

Nora squinted at the black gun. "How do you know?"

Richards shrugged. "My father was a collector. He was in the war." Nora saw Richards turn it over with an admiring look. "It's in great condition. Looks like the original finish."

Nora stepped back, repulsed. She couldn't bear to look at it any longer. She stared at the dead man on the floor. "Do you think he's German?"

Richards shrugged. "He may have gotten it in the war. Or could have been a collector, too." He peered down the barrel. "Doesn't look like it's been fired much." He opened the chamber. "Only two bullets missing."

Nora winced. Her stomach threatened to betray her again.

Richards put the gun back into the bag and handed it to one of the officers. "Put it with the other evidence. Once the CSI guys are finished, take it to ballistics. Confirm the make and model." Richards turned back to the investigator. "What else?"

He shrugged. "We've searched the entire house, dusted all the prints we could find and looked for anything that would indicate a struggle." He pointed at a lamp near the stairs that had fallen to the floor. "That's all there is on that score." He exhaled. "I think the killer got in fast, killed her fast. We bagged everything we could, but my gut tells me we haven't found much to help us."

"Anything that indicates who the second perp might be? The kidnapper?"

The investigator shook his head. "The dead guy wore gloves. I assume his partner did, as well."

"What about the child?" His voice was grim.

Nora held her breath. *Please,* she thought. *Let there be something.*

The investigator slowly shook his head. *"Nada."*

"Nothing at all?" she cried.

"At this point we got zilch." Then seeing the look on her face, he spoke more gently. "But in a while we'll be getting back stuff on the prints and fibers from the lab." He made a note on a grimy notepad. "By the way, could you look around and see if you notice anything unusual? Furniture misplaced, valuable objects missing—anything like that?"

A thought struck her. "What about by the pool? My mother usually swam with Rose in the afternoon."

He shook his head. "Looks like they never made it there."

Richards bent over and studied the dead man's body. "Have you searched him?"

"You told us to wait."

Richards looked at Nora and Marijke. "Don't touch anything and stay back." They nodded and huddled a distance away. The man lay as Nora had found him—on his stomach, right arm outstretched, head twisted to the left. Richards put on new gloves and knelt, as if genuflecting. With gentle fingers, he folded back the front of the man's jacket and felt the inside pockets.

After a few moments of probing, he slid something out—a small photo. He studied it and then rose and handed it to Nora. She looked at a worn sepia photo and stared at a slender young man holding on to the handlebars of an old bicycle, smiling boldly into the camera. He had dark, expressive eyes. Nora turned the photo over. Only a date: *1940.*

"Ever seen him before?" asked Richards.

"Never."

"Anything strike you at all?"

She flipped the photo over and looked at the man again. "No."

He nodded at the investigator, who slid the photo into an evidence bag. Richards then dug into one of the man's back pockets and pulled out a folded card. "Shamrock Hotel, room 1154." He handed it to one of the officers. "Get over there. Find the manager and search his room. Find anything you can that might tell us who he is and who was with him. Maybe they left something behind." The officer turned on his heel and left.

Richards searched the other back pocket. He shook his head. "No wallet, no driver's license, nothing," he muttered. "Damn." Moving to the side of the body, he lifted the man's left shoulder up and rolled him onto his back. His head bobbled to the right, the dead eyes now staring fixedly upward.

Marijke clutched Nora's arm and pointed at the stranger. *"Nora! Kijk eens!"*

Nora followed Marijke's index finger to the man's left front pants pocket. Something glittered gold and yellow, barely visible. "Lieutenant, there, in his pocket!"

Richards turned from the officer he was speaking to and stared. He slid the piece of paper from the pocket. It tugged a little before coming free. Richards stared at the bill with its bright colors and odd gilding and then looked up. "Some kind of foreign money."

Marijke stepped forward, her cheeks flushed. "It isn't just any money." She and Nora exchanged excited looks.

Richards looked at Nora. "You recognize it?"

Nora nodded, stunned. "It's a Dutch twenty-five guilder note." She looked down at the dead man's face. "He was Dutch? Why would some Dutchman want to kill my mother? Or kidnap Rose?"

"Hold on," said Richards. "He could be anyone. Dutch, German, American—who knows? Maybe he's just someone who traveled there recently and that's why he had guilders in his pocket." He handed the bill to the investigator, who bagged it. "Check it for prints."

Nora leaned closer. She pointed. "Lieutenant, what's that?"

Richards dug farther in the man's right pants pocket. As the item came free, Nora caught a glint of silver and saw shock on Richards's face. Her heart quickened as she stared at Richards's upturned hand. A pistol. "Jesus Christ," he muttered. "I can't believe this."

He turned it over and examined it. He held it up, looked down the barrel, sniffed and shook his head. "Looks brand-new. And it hasn't been fired today."

Marijke and Nora gave each other confused looks.

"If this is *his* gun…" began Marijke.

"Then whose gun is that?" finished Nora, pointing at the black gun on the sofa.

4

Anneke de Jong grasped her trowel more firmly as she peered through the bay window into the sunken living room. She could see Rose sleeping peacefully in the wicker bassinet Anneke had bought when she was born. It stood close to the window so Anneke could check on her frequently while she worked in the garden, as she did every afternoon. She peered at her watch. *Twelve-thirty.* Rose would sleep at least another hour.

As she straightened, she felt a pain in her back. *Sixty.* The thought amazed her. In her mind's eye, she saw herself as forty—not a day older. She knelt next to the pool and glanced at her reflection. A slight woman with shoulder-length silver hair stared back. In the calm water, she could even see her hazel eyes and the wrinkles etched in their corners. *What had happened to the young girl with jet-black hair and endless possibilities?*

Walking back to her garden, she refused to think of the different choices she could have made. *It doesn't matter. At least the cancer is gone.* She remembered the look in the doctor's eyes when he'd told her that she had malignant tumors in both breasts. *Gone,* she now thought. *All gone.* She still felt the phantom of their softness until her silver locket brushed against the empty places where her breasts used to be.

She held up the trowel to shade her eyes. The sun was blinding, the humidity oppressive. Even after all her years in Houston, she had not gotten used to the searing summers, the air swarming with mosquitoes that increased tenfold after every rain. Here it was, early November, and the afternoon temperature was still seventy degrees. She closed her eyes and imagined Holland's rows of brilliant tulips in the spring. She was that girl again—laughing on her bicycle with her girlfriends as they rode down green-leaved lanes, the air so crisp. Or swimming in the shocking cold of the North Sea in January when no one else dared go in. She opened her eyes and sighed. *The past was the past.*

She knelt, dug a small hole in the hard ground and reached for one of the rain lilies she had bought yesterday, flowers that could withstand the blistering Texas sun, blooming only after a rainstorm. She'd bought them in honor of Rose, who had also come after a great storm, one in Nora's life. Anneke put the plant gently into the ground, filled the hole with potting soil and tamped it firmly with the trowel. As she reached for the next flower, she heard the doorbell.

"*Verdomme,*" she muttered as she took off her dirty gloves and walked inside. Deliciously cold air hit her at the door, causing her to shiver slightly. She stepped to the bassinet and bent to give Rose a kiss. Her baby scent made Anneke smile. It was even better than the rain lily's blooms. The doorbell rang again.

"Coming!" She hated her quiet afternoons with Rose to be interrupted. It was a golden, sacred time, not to be broken by some lost deliveryman who needed directions or, worse, a zealot who wanted to lead her to Jesus. At the door, she looked through the peephole, opened it and clapped her hands. "Flowers! Oh, how wonderful!" She saw a tall man with white hair and a craggy face holding a brilliant arrangement of tulips— yellows, reds, whites—looking as if they would burst from the silver paper wrapped around them.

As she reached for them, the smile on the man's face disappeared. He threw the flowers inside and lunged for her. In seconds, he had gloved hands around her neck. He kicked the door shut and forced her backward.

Terrified, Anneke opened her mouth to scream, but no sound came. His hands were tourniquets. She couldn't breathe. She felt herself passing out, but then he released his grip. She stumbled, fell to the carpet and took deep, hacking gulps of air. Her mind reeled in horror. Who was this monster? What did he want?

The man stood over her. "Look at me, you bitch!"

Gasping, Anneke slowly hauled herself up and stared at the furious man, his white hair and black eyes. *Dutch! He was speaking Dutch!*

"Don't you recognize me?" He grabbed her shoulders and then shook them—hard. When she did not respond, he shook her again in a wild rage.

"Please," she whispered hoarsely. "I don't know you."

"Speak Dutch to me, you bitch. Or have you forgotten that, too?" He yanked her toward him and then shoved her down onto the living room floor. She tried to scramble away, but he was quick and kicked her fiercely in the ribs.

Anneke screamed and writhed on the white carpet. Her heart slammed in her chest, her legs would not obey her. "Stop!" she cried in Dutch. "Take what you want. My purse is on the counter! Just please, please, don't hurt the baby!"

As if she knew what was happening, Rose began wailing. Anneke held up her arms, as if to ward off another blow. The man moved quickly to the bassinet and picked up the baby, swathed in a soft yellow blanket, and stood grinning at Anneke. "And who is this? The grandchild of a whore?"

"No!" *He had the baby— Oh, God!* She struggled to her feet and tried to wrest Rose from his arms. Rose's screams became screeches. Every cry was a spike into Anneke's heart. *Rose! I have to get her—now!*

The man blocked Anneke with one arm, holding the baby just out of reach of her desperate arms, taunting her with crazed black eyes. He thrust the infant high above him. Rose howled even louder, her face a florid red as the blanket fell to the floor. He then yanked off the baby's yellow hair band and threw it onto the carpet.

"Stop!" Anneke fell upon him, her fists pummeling his arms and head, but her blows were futile. The man struck her across the face. It was as if a hammer had slammed into her jaw. *God, he wasn't going to stop until he killed them both!*

"Get out of my way." He pushed Anneke aside and dumped Rose in her bassinet.

Anneke rushed to the baby, who was purple from screaming, and clutched her precious Rose to her breast. *I have her safe—in my arms!* She whirled around and felt fury rise in her. "What is it you want! If it isn't money, then what?"

He smiled at her, a twisted grimace. "I've waited for this moment for over thirty years." His voice was soft and cruel. "You know me from the war. Can you guess now?"

Anneke quickly laid Rose in her bassinet, trying to breathe. *Who could he be?* "I don't—really, I—"

He glared at her. "Isaac."

Feeling shocked and confused, she stared at him. And then it hit her. "Isaac? Can it be?"

He smiled at her, a twisted grimace. "Remember me now?"

Her hand went to her throat. "Abram's brother," she whispered.

"Don't even say his name, you Nazi! You and your husband." He laughed. "What a shame he's already dead. Killing him would have been a true pleasure."

"What are you saying? I *loved* Abram—"

"You're a goddamned liar!" He shook his fist. "You've always been a liar. Hiding here like the assassin you are, *Mrs. de Jong*. Your filthy name is *Brouwer*. And your husband—his was *Moerveld*." He strode closer and stopped a foot away. "You ran away. You knew you'd be arrested for the traitor you are. Your neighbors would have hacked off your hair, marched you down the street in disgrace and thrown you into prison!"

"No!" she cried. "That's not true!"

He pulled out a pair of scissors from his jacket pocket. "And that's exactly what I'm going to do to you now."

Anneke ran, but he thrust his foot out and tripped her. When she hit the floor, she screamed and scrabbled to fight him off, but he knelt on both of her arms. She was a pinned butterfly, desperate to escape.

With one hand, he grabbed her hair. With the other, he clutched the scissors and began savagely slicing off clumps of her fine, silver hair. With each cut, he threw the locks up into the air like a madman.

"Stop! Oh, God, stop!" she shrieked, watching her hair snow down around her. The more frantic his motions, the less precise his cuts. Black terror consumed her. She felt shooting pains as he gouged her scalp. Blood ran into her eyes as she screamed and tried to twist away. As if in communion, Rose began wailing from her bassinet.

As he hacked, Isaac ranted on. "No, dear Anneke, you

tricked Abram into falling in love with you and then you be-trayed him—and my entire family."

"I did not!" she cried. "You, of all people, know I would never do that! I loved Abram *and* your family! I tried to help in every way I could—"

Isaac threw down the scissors and stood. Anneke tried to get up but fell back, sobbing. Struggling to her knees, all she could see were bloodied clumps of her hair strewn across the white carpet. She sat and cradled her head in her hands. When she pulled them away, they were covered in blood.

"Isaac!" She moaned and held up her crimson hands. "What in God's name have you done?"

Isaac stood above her, pulled the pistol from his pocket and spat upon her. Anneke recoiled, sobbing. *He was mad! What would he do to her—to Rose!*

"Now admit it, all of it!" He pointed the gun at her head. His eyes speared hers, his voice molten metal. "Including what that bastard of a husband of yours did."

"Hans?" Anneke looked up, unable to stem her tears. "He married me and brought me here. I was so numb and hope-less about Abram that I didn't care where I went, as long as it was out of Holland."

"You married your lover's murderer!"

"Are you crazy?" she cried. "Abram was killed by the Nazis. Hans had nothing to do with it!"

"Can you truly sit here in front of me and deny it? Your boyfriend was jealous and shot my brother between the eyes. All the neighbors heard them raging at each other—over you."

Anneke raised her bloody hands, imploring. "You're wrong, Isaac. Hans could never hurt anyone. Yes, he was jealous of Abram. And Hans wanted me to love him. But I didn't."

"No, no, he killed my brother and you turned us all into the *Groene Politie*."

"No! I was there!" she cried. "Abram and Hans were fighting, that much is true. But the police shot Abram—not Hans. I came running to try to stop them—"

"Stop lying!" His voice was a razor cut. "Your lover killed Abram and you brought the police with you in case that son of a bitch didn't finish the job."

"Isaac, I don't know why the police were there!" she sobbed. "They must have followed me. You have to believe me."

Suddenly he slapped her so hard she fell. It felt as if a bullwhip had sliced her face.

"How stupid do you think I am? We had witnesses! They came running when they heard that bastard of yours threaten to kill my brother if he didn't leave you alone. By then Abram was dead." Anneke put her bleeding head into her hands and moaned.

"What they did see was you standing there with the *Politie* by your side. Did you know that two days after Abram was murdered all of us were arrested, thrown on a train and shipped to *Mauthausen?*" He wiped away his tears with a rough gesture, his other hand still pointing the pistol at her. His voice was broken. "My whole family was gassed. Amarisa and I made it out."

"Amarisa," whispered Anneke.

"Yes," snarled Isaac. "My brave sister. Would you like to hear what they did to her?"

"I can't—"

"Can't what? Hear that she was raped every day? That they smashed her leg when she took too long in the food line? That they slit her face from lip to ear?"

Anneke felt vomit rise in her throat. "Oh, God, Isaac, please believe me—"

He grabbed her by the collar with his free hand and pulled her up until her eyes were level with his, now pressing the cold gun barrel against her forehead. "Don't you talk to me of love! You seduced my brother, promising you would find a way to get him out of the country." He shook her hard. "'Foul spawn of a Nazi,' my father said. 'Apples don't fall far from the tree, especially rotten ones.'"

She tried to pull away, but every wound he had inflicted had left her in agony, helpless. "Isaac, I wasn't lying to you, or them! Why would I do such a thing?"

"Because you were a Nazi, just like your father. You haven't forgotten about Joop, now have you?"

She sagged in his arms. "No," she whispered, "that part is true. My father was a Nazi."

He flung her onto the couch. "All you good Dutchmen kissing the Nazis' boots. In 1940, there were 140,000 Jews in the whole country. Lucky for you and your SS father, almost all of us were rounded up in '43 and forced to live Amsterdam. Like shooting fish in a barrel."

Anneke hung her head. "But I'm innocent."

"You know damned well that you went to every Dutch Nazi rally, every march, wearing your brown NSB shirt and swearing allegiance to that maniac! Pretending to steal coal and food from your SS father for us, when all along you were just reeling us in for the kill."

"No, no!" Her eyes searched wildly around. She felt that her shame must be stamped in her eyes. "I was in the NSB and did go to the rallies," she whispered. "My father made me."

"And did he make you go out with charming *SS* officers?" His snarl was a cobra strike. "Don't bother to deny it. I saw you myself, walking with some gallant German killer."

Anneke hung her head. When she raised her eyes, she felt only dullness and defeat.

"Enough. You're a liar and a murderer and you're finally going to get what's coming to you."

Anneke fell to her knees. Hopelessness filled her. "Do what you want to me. I don't care. Just please, please, don't hurt the baby."

Isaac pointed the pistol at her and shook his head. "No, I'm not finished with you yet. I want you to imagine my father starving in that miserable camp after you betrayed him." He stepped closer, lowering the gun barrel until it touched the top of her head. "Do you know how we even knew he was alive? He got messages to us from a cell he shared with fifteen other men! Fifteen men with only one bucket to piss and shit in! He wrote on lousy scraps of toilet paper that he sewed into the lining of his filthy clothes. The laundry girl passed them on to us."

Isaac choked up and then pressed the barrel harder against her head. "And do you know the first question my brother always asked when I snuck into whatever hellhole you found for him to hide in? 'Where is Anneke? Is she all right? Tell her I love her.'"

"Oh, Isaac, I loved him, too—you must know that! And I protected you. What about the day you were walking down the *Singel* and were stopped by the *Groene Politie?* Don't you remember?"

"You wore the NSB uniform, that's what I remember," he snarled.

"No, you know what I'm talking about. I pretended to fall off my bicycle and the *Duitsers* ran over to help me—"

"Because they saw your uniform and knew that you were a filthy Nazi, too."

Anneke looked into his angry eyes. *She had to make him understand!* "No! I did it to distract them so you could get away. And you did!" Isaac still glared at her, but said nothing. "What about the food I brought your parents every week? And in the winter of '44, when your mother was so sick, I brought medicine for her that I stole from my father."

"What I remember about your Nazi father is that he turned in four of my friends. Shipped them off. Dead now. And we all know why you pretended to protect us, feed us and even made Abram fall in love with you."

"Why?" cried Anneke. "Why would I have done that if I didn't love all of you?"

"Because it was all part of your plan to turn in a Jewish family to win more NSB medals to pin on that Nazi outfit you wore. We were just another notch in your belt."

"You don't understand any of it."

"I understand perfectly." Then Rose wailed from her bassinet. Isaac picked her up and walked to Anneke, baby under one arm, pointing his pistol at her with the other. But Rose kicked and cried in his arms. He tried to switch her to his right side, but she screamed louder. "Shut up, *godverdomme!*"

Anneke saw her chance and sprang up. She kicked out at Isaac and caught him in the knee, grabbed Rose and ran. Off balance, Isaac recovered quickly, shoved the pistol in his pocket and dashed after her. Anneke bolted up the back stairway, adrenaline erasing her pain, and hurtled breathlessly into her bedroom with Rose under one arm. Hands shaking, she slammed and locked the door and then flung open a drawer on the night table. *Where was it?* Her hand closed around the cool metal.

Isaac banged on the door. "I'll break it down, you bitch!" he yelled. "And when I do, I'll kill you with my bare hands— and that child!"

Anneke flung the door open. With Rose on her hip, she moved toward him. Isaac lunged forward, his hands reaching for her throat. But when he saw what she held, he stopped cold.

"Get your hands behind you." She pointed her pistol at

the spot between his eyes. She waved its barrel gently up and down. A deadly calm filled her. When she spoke, her words sounded like silk. "I know how to use this, as you are well aware."

Isaac's face contorted with rage. "A Luger!" he shouted. "And you say you're not a Nazi? You lying whore!"

Anneke gave him a small, bitter smile. "Shut your goddamned mouth," she said softly. Then she saw him frantically try to free the pistol from his pocket. She clicked off the safety. Isaac froze. "Put your fucking hands behind your back."

"No."

Anneke hiked Rose higher on her hip and trained her eye down the sights of her pistol. "I never enjoyed killing. But you are threatening me and my family. If you don't do as I say, what happens will be your fault—no one else's."

She saw the artery in Isaac's neck bulge with each ragged breath he drew. He was clearly calculating his odds, but finally did as she said. *The bastard was listening to her now, wasn't he?* "Turn and walk slowly down the stairs." Rose began to whimper and struggle, but Anneke shushed her, jiggling her as they followed behind him.

Isaac quickened his descent, tensing as he glanced sharply behind him. Anneke jabbed the gun barrel into the back of his neck. "Run and I'll kill you."

As they neared the foot of the stairs, suddenly Anneke heard the front door open and someone burst into the front hallway. "Papa! Papa, are you here? It's Ariel!" a man called in Dutch.

Anneke shoved the barrel into Isaac's neck—hard. "Don't move!" she said with deliberate calm. Isaac halted like a marionette whose string had been jerked.

She heard this Ariel's voice coming from the dining room. "Papa!"

"Walk." Anneke's voice sounded like the slice of dueling

swords as she prodded Isaac with the gun barrel. They crept farther down the back stairway in silent tandem. "Say one word and I'll kill you both." He gave her a deadly glare, but obeyed. At the bottom step, Rose slipped on Anneke's hip and cried out. Isaac whirled around and managed to grab the baby and wrench the Luger out of Anneke's hand.

"Rose!" Anneke leaped forward to wrest away the baby, but Isaac grabbed the pistol and shoved her aside. Then he turned and pressed the black barrel into Rose's pink cheek. The baby twisted and screamed, but Isaac held her fast. Now he smiled.

"You! Walk here!" His voice was an evil whisper as he pointed the gun at her. "Slowly, very slowly."

Horror gripped her as she saw the black pistol sink farther into Rose's cheek. Then she saw the younger man, Ariel he called himself, on the far side of the room. "Help us!" she pleaded.

"Papa!" he cried. "Put down the gun!"

Barely breathing, Anneke continued her careful approach, trying not to hurry, to alert Isaac. But when she was a few feet away, he pressed the barrel against Rose's temple so hard that the baby screamed. "Stop!" he thundered.

Anneke halted as he backed away from her. "Isaac!" she screamed. "Don't!"

Ariel rushed toward them but stumbled on a small rug. By the time he righted himself, Isaac was on the far side, away from him and Anneke. "Ariel, don't move!" he shouted.

"Papa, I can't let you do this...."

"Stop right there!" he bellowed, swinging the barrel from Anneke to Rose and back again. "Or pick which one you want to die."

"No!" he cried. "Neither!"

Isaac gave him a hard look. "Why the hell are you here?"

Out of the corner of her eye, Anneke saw Ariel inch closer to her. She felt a wild hope. *Maybe he could stop him!*

"I went to your apartment and couldn't find you," he said. "Then I saw the plane reservations and I knew—"

"Enough! Let me do what I have to do!" He clutched Rose tighter and pressed the barrel to her temple.

Anneke fell to her knees, sobbing. "You can't kill her!"

"Now you will see what it is to watch a member of your family murdered." His voice was a deadly whisper. "First her, then you."

"No, please!" *She had to do something.* And then it hit her. "Wait—you don't know!"

"Oh? And what don't I know?"

"The baby..." Anneke choked on her sobs.

"Spit it out. It will be last thing you say before I kill you both."

"Rose, she's—" Anneke, still choking, uttered her next words. "She's Abram's granddaughter."

"What?"

Anneke, racked with sobs, collapsed onto the carpet. "I was pregnant before Abram died," she whispered. "I had Nora, his daughter...."

"Get up!" yelled Isaac. "This is just another one of your lies! You'd say anything to save her."

Anneke struggled to her feet and stood shaking. She looked at Rose, still writhing in Isaac's arms. *Doomed. My darling Rose is doomed—because of me! And Nora—how will she—*

Suddenly, Ariel sprang over the couch, but when he recovered his balance, Isaac had already taken aim at Anneke. The gunshot roared through the air. Anneke's body jerked backward as blood spurted from her forehead.

"No!" shouted Ariel. He ran to her, knelt and felt wildly for a pulse. Her blood sluiced his hands, slick and hot. He looked up at Isaac. "You killed her!"

Isaac, still holding Rose, dropped the Luger as his knees buckled. Rose tumbled onto the white carpet, still wailing. Ariel saw Isaac's eyes widen as he clutched at his throat and gasped for air. He fell to his knees, his face contorted.

Ariel rushed to him and cradled his head, moaning. "Papa? Papa, no!"

"My heart—" His voice was a strangled whisper. "Medicine...hotel."

Frantic, Ariel looked around and then saw the phone on the end table. "I'm going to call for help." He started to stand.

Isaac grabbed his son's arm and pulled him down, spittle foaming at the corners of his mouth. His eyes were fading as color drained from them. "Too late for me," he whispered. "The baby, take the baby!"

Ariel sobbed, holding his father close. "Papa, please!"

Isaac shook his head and held Ariel's weeping face between his hands. His eyes struck Ariel like an army commander dying in battle. "She's Abram's...take her home, raise her Jewish. Promise me!"

"I can't do that, Papa!"

"Yes, you can," he said hoarsely. "You can and you *must*."

"Please don't make me!"

"Promise me!"

Ariel sobbed. "All right—I promise. I promise!"

Isaac nodded and dropped his hands from Ariel's face. A half smile played upon his lips. "Abram..." he whispered.

Ariel watched as he convulsed and then was still. Ariel thrust his fingers into Isaac's neck, digging for a pulse. *Nothing.* "No, no," he moaned. Ariel stared at him and at Anneke, horrified, until he realized that Rose was twisting on the carpet, howling. Softly sobbing, he picked her up.

Then he heard the sound of a garage door churning. "Oh, God, what do I do?" He clutched Rose to his chest.

Then ran as fast as he could.

5

Nora stood in the blistering Houston sun at Anneke's freshly dug grave and watched as her coffin was lowered. The funeral ceremony had been a dreary blur. Her black blouse and skirt, damp and clammy, clung to her like wet leaves. Feeling suffocated, she only half listened as the priest recited the Catholic rite. The priest had never known Nora or her mother. She had had to provide him with the highlights of Anneke's life so he would have something to say.

After Hans died, Anneke had stopped going to church. Her mother had never told her why, nor did Nora ask. Nora had gone only for her father. He would have been crushed if she told him that she didn't believe in the Pope. She still lit a candle for him at St. Anne's—on his birthday and on the day he died. She tried to pray after lighting the candle. Just sitting in the silence, surrounded by the glow of stained glass that cast down prisms of color, she always felt restored.

She stared at the coffin in the ground. More candles to

light, another dead parent to pray for. Nora glanced around her. It was pitifully sad. She now realized how rarely her parents had strayed outside the world of two they had built and then guarded from outsiders. Other than Marijke, a few colleagues from the hospital stood awkwardly around the grave, telegraphing bleak looks in her direction showing that they were clueless about what to say. *How do you comfort the daughter of a brutally murdered woman?*

If it hadn't been for Marijke holding her up, Nora knew she would not have gotten through it. So many times she had thought she would faint, run or scream.

The aching that filled her now made her realize that she had been unable to truly mourn Anneke's loss because of her terror for Rose. Now her mind flooded with memories: Anneke's cool hand on Nora's hot forehead as she lay in bed with the flu when she was eight; Anneke's eyes shining with pride at Nora's graduation from the University of Texas; Anneke's joy-filled face when she first held Rose in her arms. *Her mother.* The only person in the world who had known her completely. Now she would know what it was to be an orphan, lost and alone.

She bent to clutch a fistful of dirt and let it fall from her hand onto the coffin. It hardly made a sound. That made her heart clench and then she felt dizzy. Marijke wrapped her arm firmly around Nora's shoulders. Nora took a deep breath and turned from the grave. Nothing she could do for her mother now. After receiving hushed condolences from the few attendees, she and Marijke walked toward Nora's car.

"Are you all right?" asked Marijke.

"Don't worry. Once we get home, I'll be fine."

Just as they reached the car, someone called to her. "Ms. de Jong?"

It was Richards. He loomed above her. She felt confused. What was he doing here?

As if reading her thoughts, he nodded at the last of the mourners heading toward their cars and shrugged. "We always go to the funerals. Sometimes the murderer—or, in this case, his accomplice—shows up or watches from a distance."

Nora felt sick. "I...see." She saw Richards glance quickly at Marijke and mouth, *Wait here.* Marijke nodded and got into the car. Richards took Nora's elbow and walked with her to a nearby oak tree. The lush green leaves against the cloudless sky seemed so damned peaceful. Nora felt anything but. He released her elbow and stopped. She didn't like something in his eyes. Her breath caught. "What is it? Have you found Rose?"

"No, no news on that front yet, I'm sorry to say."

Nora felt tears come to her eyes. She wiped them away.

"Did you see anyone here today you didn't know?"

She thought and then shook her head. "Just old friends of my parents. My boss, a few colleagues, that's all."

Richards nodded. "Well, we have found out a few things I'd like to tell you about." He pointed to a concrete bench by the oak. "Let's sit."

Nora suddenly felt so exhausted she wondered if she could manage those few steps. She wished she could just curl up under that huge, leafy tree and go to sleep. And never wake up.

She sat on the hard bench. Richards sat, reached into his suit pocket and pulled out a pack of cigarettes. He shook one out and lit it with a silver lighter.

"I didn't know you smoked."

He gave her a half smile. "Goes with the job."

She nodded. Yes, that's all she wanted, small talk. If it wasn't about Rose, then focusing on Anneke's murder would require more energy than she could muster.

Richards took a deep drag and then exhaled. "We have

something to tell finally. The perpetrator checked into a Motel 6 the day before the murder and never checked out. My men were able to get into his room."

Nora felt some of her energy return. "Was there anything to help us find Rose?"

Richards put up a hand. "Hang on. Let me run through it all first. We found a passport." He took out a small notepad and read from a worn page. "The fingerprints match those we took from the dead man. Dutch Immigration confirmed yesterday that his name was Wim Bakker, born in Amsterdam, address Westerstraat 453, fifty-seven years old." He gave Nora a sharp look. "Have you ever heard that name?"

Nora shook her head. "But that doesn't mean anything. My parents never talked about their life in Holland. All they told me was that they had family there, but that they were estranged and did not want to discuss their past. When I lived in Amsterdam, I tried to find them, but never did. The name 'de Jong' is very common in Holland." She shrugged. "I suppose they could have known this Bakker before they came here, but how would I know?"

"You're absolutely sure you've never heard of him?"

"Yes, of course." Impatience rose in her. "Who was he? How did he know my mother? Do you have any idea why he killed her?"

Richards shrugged. "We asked the Dutch police to obtain a warrant to search his home, which they did yesterday. All they found was a bed and a few chairs. Looked like he hadn't been there in a while."

All she wanted now was to jump up from the bench and run—*somewhere!* It was maddening getting these useless bits of information in drips and drabs.

She stood and paced. "Are they going to find his family? He must have children, friends, maybe an employer. Someone will know why he did this and who was with him. And who took Rose!"

Richards flicked his cigarette on the ground and looked up at her. His eye twitched. Nora stopped. She remembered that twitching when he first saw her mother's body on the floor. When she was hysterical about Rose and he tried to calm her down. "What is it? What aren't you telling me?"

Richards avoided her eyes. "It looks like we're at another dead end."

"What do you mean?" She made him meet her eyes.

"We just got another call from Dutch Immigration," he said quietly. "Apparently the 'Wim Bakker' whose information was on the passport is not the man who killed your mother."

"But that doesn't make sense!"

"The Dutch police have confirmed that Wim Bakker is a heroin dealer who was arrested when he went through Immigration in Amsterdam six months ago. He is now in prison."

Nora shook her head several times. She needed the puzzle pieces to fit and they didn't. "But how would this man who killed my mother get his hands on a fake passport?"

Richards stubbed his cigarette out on the grass and straightened. "Dutch Immigration says that because of Bakker's incarceration, the killer could have gotten it anywhere. When a Dutch citizen is wanted for arrest, the typical protocol is for his passport number and photograph to be placed on a list for the Immigration agents to check in case the criminal tries to leave or enter the country. If the agent finds such a number on the list, they're supposed to confiscate the passport and immediately alert airport security so the suspect can be taken into custody."

"So why didn't that happen?" Nora was furious. "Why was he permitted to go to Schiphol, waltz through Immigration, take a transatlantic flight and enter the U.S.?"

"Because he had an excellent forgery. He replaced his photograph with that of Wim Bakker, but he didn't change the fingerprints."

"But wasn't the passport number the same?"

Richards shook his head. "One digit was altered."

"How could that happen? Are they just idiots? People must try to get away with this all the time."

"They told us that the forgery must have been done by a professional."

"The black market?"

Again Richards shrugged. "They don't know. Whoever did it had specific knowledge of the special papers and symbols used, the particular sequence of numbers and precisely what information was required."

"Are the Dutch police going to figure this out?"

"It's out of their jurisdiction. Immigration is in charge and they're looking into it."

Nora sat and felt her shoulders sag with hopelessness. "That's the Dutch way of saying that they've done all they're going to do."

Richards stood. "I wish I had better news."

Nora turned away, forcing herself not to cry. She heard her voice come out in a defeated whisper. "Me, too."

They walked silently back to her car. Before Richards turned off the path toward his own vehicle, Nora grasped his arm. "What about prints? Did the crime investigators find any?"

Richards shook his head. "We have the killer's prints, obviously."

"No, no! I mean the kidnapper. He didn't necessarily wear gloves, did he? Surely he touched something—the front doorknob, the furniture, maybe even Rose's bassinet."

"Well, if the killer wore gloves, we have to assume his accomplice did, too. Besides, we've dusted the entire place," he said wearily. "We did find a few latents, but the FBI isn't ready to say anything until they've run them through Quantico."

"And when in hell will that be?"

Richards looked at her, surprised. "Soon, Nora. We're pressuring them."

Nora thought a moment. "What about footprints?"

"It appears that there was a struggle and movement on the staircase to your mother's bedroom, and other footprints in the entryway and dining room."

She looked up at him, feeling almost hopeful. "Maybe they were looking for something. Maybe that's why they were all over the house?"

Richards shook his head. "We combed the house thoroughly taking prints, seeing if anything seemed to be disturbed. But other than the furniture that was in disarray, nothing else was tossed. When you confirmed that your mother's jewelry and other valuables were still in the house, it might fit the profile of a robbery gone wrong. That might account for your mother's murder, but it doesn't explain the kidnapping. The last thing a robber caught red-handed would do is to take off with an infant."

"Maybe they didn't find what they were looking for and the struggle got out of hand before they could."

"Who knows? It still doesn't make sense that the accomplice didn't steal *something*."

"Except my child." She shook her head. "I can't imagine that my mother would let Rose out of her sight or out of her arms, no matter what the struggle." She looked up at Richards and finally let her tears fall. She was furious to feel so helpless.

Richards took Nora's shaking hands into his own. They were warm, but Nora drew no comfort from them. *He probably does this for every mother with a missing child,* she thought.

She withdrew and began pacing again. If she kept her feet moving, maybe something else would come to her. Something *had* to come to her.

"Once the FBI processes the prints we found in the house, we'll send them on to the Netherlands. Maybe the killer had a record and they are on file. Maybe the partials we found— they must have belonged to the accomplice—will turn something up, as well."

"You told me it was unlikely that latent prints would do us much good."

"We'll see."

"'We'll see, we'll see.' That's all I ever hear from you people."

She stood and started to walk to her car. She flung a look back at Richards and spit out her next words. "I'm sick of this. No one is doing enough. You don't have one damned lead about my daughter and she's been gone for three days. I'm going to figure this out for myself." She flung open the car door and started to climb in.

Richards held the door open. "Nora, wait!" His voice brooked no argument. "You can't do that. You don't have the resources to track this down and you'll just do more harm than good."

Nora yanked on the door, but he held it fast. "Let go," she said in a menacing voice.

"Obviously, this isn't the time for us to continue this conversation," he said tersely. "We'll discuss it later. But there's one last thing you need to keep in mind. You have no choice right now but to stay at home."

"And why is that?"

"Because you have to be there if the kidnapper calls."

Nora got in and slammed the door closed. She felt a cold resolve as she rolled down the window and met his hard glance.

"You know as well as I do that if that bastard wanted a ransom, he would have called days ago." She refused to give way to tears. "I'm going to find my daughter. You tell your people to lead, follow or get the fuck out of my way."

6

Late that evening, Nora sat in the living room with Marijke. Both were exhausted after the funeral and Richards's discouraging news. The police were tapping her telephone, but no call had come from the kidnapper.

"I don't think I can take any more today," mumbled Nora.

Marijke poured Nora a glass of cold white wine and then one for herself. "Maybe we should try to sleep."

Nora glanced at the clock on the wall. "It's only ten. I'm too wound up. How can I sleep when Rose is still out there?"

"Nora," said Marijke softly. "You've been through so much today. The funeral, Rose, Richards…"

"I know, I know." She joined Marijke on the couch and sipped her wine. Instead of calming her, it made her more anxious.

Marijke suppressed a yawn. "I think I might turn in."

Nora noted the dark circles under her friend's eyes. "You should. You've been shoring me up for three whole days."

"I got a call from the nursing home. My mother isn't doing well. After two strokes, I'm not sure how much longer she can hang on."

"Oh, God, Marijke. I've been so selfish. How old is she now?"

"Eighty-five." Marijke sighed. "I'll have to go back soon."

"Of course. Don't worry, I'll be fine." *No,* she thought sadly. *I won't.*

Nora stood and patted Marijke's shoulder. "Go to bed and get some sleep. We'll both feel better in the morning."

Marijke yawned. "Don't stay up too long."

Nora summoned a smile. "I won't." After Marijke said good-night,, Nora paced for an hour, waiting for something. *Someone. For Rose.* Her wandering was useless, but she couldn't face her empty bed and the nightmares she knew would come. She sat on the couch, staring at the Sony Walkman that Anneke had given Nora on her birthday, a wildly extravagant gift at two hundred dollars, the first gadget of its kind. Anneke had known how much Nora loved listening to music while she jogged at Memorial Park.

Nora stood and continued her pacing. As she passed the front window, a dark, official-looking Ford pulled up to the curb. A man got out and strode up the walkway. Nora looked through the peephole and opened the door before he could ring.

"Lieutenant?" Panic rose in her throat. "Have you found something?"

Richards shook his head. "Not yet." He stood awkwardly on the doorstep. "May I come in?"

"Of course." She stepped back and led him into the living room, avoiding the thick blue blanket she had spread over the bloody carpet. She couldn't bear the sight of it.

When they sat, Nora turned to him. "I'm confused. Why are you here?"

He gave her a sheepish look. "I thought I'd drop by after you chewed me out this afternoon."

Nora felt her color rise. "Oh...that. I was completely out of line."

"No, I was thinking like a cop. I can't imagine what you're dealing with, even though I've seen so many parents go through it."

"I owe you an apology."

"No, no, I have a daughter, too. I can't imagine how I would feel if the same thing happened to her."

"Where is she now?"

"With her mother." He loosened his tie and sighed. "Melissa's autistic. It's been a hard road."

"Oh, God, I'm so sorry." Nora felt terrible as she watched him stare at the floor. "How severe is it?"

He looked at her with pained eyes. "She's nonverbal, has been since birth. Now she's seven and things aren't much better. She needs round-the-clock care. I couldn't be there. My schedule." He shrugged. "My wife couldn't take it anymore and left."

Nora didn't know what to say. She held up a wineglass. "Red or white?"

He smiled. "Whatever you're having."

She waited for him to settle back and take a swallow. "I just realized I don't even know your first name."

"Nathan."

She nodded. "Well, you didn't have to come over so late just to apologize."

"I just wanted to make sure that you're okay," he said. "But you're right, it's late. If you want me to go—"

Nora shook her head. "Oddly enough, I don't. I'm terrified."

"I hope you believe me when I say we're doing everything we can."

Nora felt a catch in her throat. "You don't think you'll find her, do you?"

"It's way too early to think like that."

"But how can I think about anything else? No witnesses. A murderer no one can identify. A kidnapper who hasn't called for a ransom. My baby gone, maybe forever." Her head fell into her hands.

She felt his arm around her shoulder. She shook her head and sobbed.

"Hey, it's going to be all right."

"I don't know what I'll do if I lose her," she whispered. "She's my whole life."

"I know. We'll find her, I promise. You should try to get some sleep."

They sipped the rest of their wine in silence and then she stood and walked to the foyer. Richards followed. "I'm going to do everything I can to bring Rose back to you."

Nora felt a rush of gratitude. "I know you will. And I want to thank you—for caring."

She watched him walk to his car, get in and drive away.

7

Nora held a steaming cup of coffee in her hands. She had slept fitfully, alternately waking in a cold panic without knowing why until the terrifying realization washed over her that Rose was really gone, maybe hurt, maybe dead. Interlaced with those terrors were images of her mother, bloody and battered, begging Nora to help her.

She glanced at the clock, her vision blurred, as if her eyes were filled with sand. Eight o'clock. She sipped the hot coffee gratefully, hoping that it would give her the strength to make it through another day. She looked at Marijke, calmly knitting on the couch.

The phone rang. Nora went to the kitchen and picked up the receiver. "Hello?"

"Nora? It's John Bates."

Oh, God. The hospital. Her job. "Hi, John."

"Nora, how are you? I can't believe it. Your mother, your daughter—it's awful."

"I know, I know. And I'm sorry, but I just don't know when I'll be back. I have five surgeries this week, but—"

"Don't worry. I've already covered them for you."

Relief swept through her. "Thank you, John. I know how shorthanded you are."

"I've told Personnel you're on a leave of absence for a while."

"I pray I'll have Rose back soon, but I can't even think about work now."

"It's a terrible situation." There was an awkward pause. "You know I'll give you as much time as I can."

"I understand." Nora closed her eyes. He couldn't promise to keep her job open. Residencies like the one she had were rare. There were scores of young doctors who would kill to take her place. "John, how long a leave do I have?"

"I've bought you two weeks so far."

"Thanks. I appreciate it."

"Call me when you hear anything. We're all thinking about you."

"Please thank everyone for me. I'll call as soon as I know anything."

"Of course."

Nora hung up and stared across the room. She had completely forgotten about work. God, was it only a few days ago that she had operated on Rita? Nora's eyes felt gritty and raw as tears welled up and coursed down her cheeks. She remembered her dismay when she diagnosed the three-year-old with a brain stem tumor. And although she would have preferred a less dangerous course of action, the magnitude of Rita's tumor forced Nora to perform a surgery that might kill her. She'd had no choice but to go in and pray that she could sufficiently debulk the tumor and give Rita a fighting chance.

Nora could still feel the nausea that had gripped her when she had opened Rita's tiny skull. The cancer had spread, its evil tendrils wrapped around the ganglia of the lower hemisphere of her cerebellum and had already crept through the opening to her spine. There was nothing she could do. Then, as Nora began to close, Rita's frail heart simply stopped beating. In her mind's eye, she saw the monitor flatline. Her stomach clenched. She would never get used to the dread of that long walk from the O.R. to the waiting area. The mother had rushed toward her, had taken one look at her eyes and wailed—a keening that filled Nora's ears even now.

And what about Michael, a seven-year-old whose malignant brain tumor had returned? The brave little boy had made Nora promise that she would do his operation. Then there was Alana, a teenager, terrified by the blindness caused by a tumor pressing on her optic nerve. Nora dreaded letting them down. *But if she didn't have Rose, she didn't care about her job, about anything.*

Her coffee was now cold and she felt too tired to pour herself another cup.

Rose, Rose. Each day that passed without a sign or information of her abductor meant that the chance she'd be found decreased dramatically. Thinking that Rose might be one of those kids, sought for years and then lost for all time, made Nora desolate. "We can't just sit here," she said through clenched teeth.

"What else can we do?" Marijke asked. "We have to let the police here and in Holland do their jobs. I know you hate this, Nora, but we have to be patient."

"I'm sick of waiting." Nora stood and paced.

"Then let's do something productive."

Nora heard the very Dutch, let's-get-on-with-it tenor in her voice. "What do you suggest?"

"Have you thought about whether you want to stay in this house when Rose comes back?"

Nora sank to the floor in her old jeans and T-shirt, surprised by her friend's question. "I haven't given it a moment's thought."

"What do you think you will do?"

"I never want to live here again. I couldn't bear it."

Marijke put down her knitting needles and stood. "So maybe we should just start packing things up? Wouldn't that be more positive than just sitting here feeling trapped? Besides, I'll have to go home soon and I don't want you to have to do this alone."

"God, Marijke, I'm so sorry. Of course, you have to go back. Is there more news about your mother? Is she worse?"

"She's the same, but there's also my job." She poured herself another cup of coffee. "The director has subtly informed me that I must return soon. He knows I'm up for tenure, so I can't risk disobeying him."

"Damn. You told me you couldn't stay much longer, but I didn't want to think about it. It'll be hell for me without you here."

Marijke looked stricken and Nora forced a smile. "No, I'll be fine. I always pull through. And I'll let you know the moment I hear something."

"Surely there must be someone you can call when I go?"

"Well, it's embarrassing, but the answer is no." Now she hesitated, avoiding Marijke's gaze. "When I came back to the States, I was still broken-hearted about Nico."

She hated hearing the sadness in her voice. Nora thought briefly of her two years in Amsterdam, the happiest of her life, and her fellowship with Dr. Jan Brugger, one of the world's top researchers in brain cancer. It had been intense, thrilling, each day more fascinating than the next, and she somehow had become the superstar of his program, the reason that John Bates had contacted her to come work for him in Houston.

Nico. Falling in love with him, living together in perfect happiness. Until it all fell apart. She had so tried not to dwell on him and their tortured breakup, his refusal to move to Houston with no future for himself in America. Nora still felt a stabbing regret. She glanced at the silver ring of his she still wore, its tulip design delicate, lovely.

"Nora?"

Nora returned to the present. "I didn't want to be around anyone except my mother. And she understood that I needed to be left alone until I could get my life back on track. Then just as I started meeting people, I found out that I was pregnant. What a shock! But so exhilarating. It eclipsed my life. I didn't have time for anything else."

She saw Marijke give her a sideways glance. "You're still in love with him."

Nora avoided her gaze. "No, I don't think about him anymore."

"Hmm," murmured Marijke. Nora was relieved when she said no more about it.

She glanced at the silver-framed photograph on the coffee table. Rose's newborn face was red and scowling, as if birth had not been the liberating experience it was cracked up to be. She stared out with her big eyes and fierce wisps of copper hair. Nora felt comforted. It made Rose look as if she had come into the world a fighter, a survivor. Like herself.

Marijke slipped her knitting into her bag. "So, if you're not going to stay here, why don't we start packing up boxes?"

"Not Rose's room."

"Sure. But we can work here and then tackle your mother's bedroom."

Nora was so deathly sick of waiting and of the adrenaline rushes that plagued her that Marijke's words brought her a welcome sense of purpose. She stood and dusted off the seat of her jeans. "All right. You start here. I think I've got some empty boxes in the garage."

"Fine." Marijke stood.

"Wait a minute," said Nora. "Do you suppose the killer and the kidnapper might have been looking for something?"

"Like what?"

"I don't know. But the investigators said there seemed to be a struggle—footprints up and down the stairs." She rubbed her chin, thinking. "What if killing my mother wasn't the only thing they came for? And we still have no idea why they'd take Rose."

"Nora, maybe you're just grasping at straws."

"But what can it hurt? We're going to pack up all of this stuff, anyway—why not search for a clue?" Possibilities rushed through her mind. "Something my mother had that they needed? Something that could give us insight into why this nightmare happened?"

Nora thought she saw Marijke bite her lip. "We have to pack up everything, anyway, and if we do a thorough job, who knows what we'll come up with?"

"There must be a link between my mother's bizarre murder and that man on the floor. But what?" Her eyes now fixed upon Rose's bassinet, a cruel reminder that pierced right through her.

Marijke returned to the couch and motioned for Nora to sit, but Nora remained standing, energized by her theory. "Look, the police searched the house, but how much time did they really spend looking? Their objective was physical evidence, not motive. And one guy said he could tell by the footprints that two people went upstairs. Maybe that's what we should focus on."

Marijke shrugged. "If the FBI and all those policemen can't find a connection, how can we?"

Nora felt excitement for the first time since that terrible evening. "Look, we're going to search every nook and cranny of this house. We'll go inch by inch until we find something—anything—that might shed light on the murder."

"Nora, even if we do find some motive, how will that help us find Rose?"

"Because the two have to be linked. Mom was Dutch. The forged Dutch passport, the Dutch money on the killer—these aren't coincidences. Maybe the accomplice panicked, grabbed Rose and then ran away, not thinking of the consequences."

"But even if we find out why your mother was killed, how will that explain why his accomplice would risk kidnapping Rose? And why wouldn't he already have called demanding a ransom?"

Nora saw Marijke react to what must have been Nora's look of disappointment. "But," said Marijke kindly, "anything is worth trying at this point." She stood. "Tell me what you want me to do."

Nora hugged her, the most positive reaction she had mustered since that awful day. She went to the kitchen counter and picked up a pad of paper and a pen. She chewed on the plastic cap, her brow furrowed. Then her eyes cleared and she wrote furiously on the pad. She tore off two pages and handed one to Marijke.

"Here's a list. You start in Mom's bedroom. I'll look downstairs. Even if we don't find anything, it will give me something to do instead of sitting by the phone going crazy."

Marijke glanced at the page Nora had handed her. "What am I looking for?"

Nora shrugged. "I don't really know. Anything. Old papers or letters, documents, something hidden away. If there's anything at all, it won't be sitting out in the open. I'll start down here with the oldest files in my father's study. Who knows where they would hide things?"

Marijke stood and folded her arms. "Nora, do you really think they would have kept incriminating documents?"

"Maybe not, but what else can we do but try?"

"*Vooruit!* I will begin." She disappeared down the hall.

Four hours later, Nora, still sitting on the study floor, looked at the cardboard boxes now packed with books, files of financial papers and tax returns, small Delft Blue plates and figurines. The sad detritus of over thirty years—all she had left of her mom and dad. She looked around her. In a way, it was the souls of two people she was packing into those boxes, fragments of two lives not only unfinished, but unlived. She had found nothing relevant from their past, but every object had evoked a memory. In her mind's eye, she saw her father's wide, gentle hands holding a thick book with a look of pleasure on his face. The needlepoint pillow nestled into her mother's chair, its profusion of roses like the ones Anneke had tended so passionately in her garden.

Nora stood, her legs cramped from sitting cross-legged while poring over her father's files. She glanced outside. The fiery Houston sun was setting in a bath of surreal colors. Probably pollution, she thought. She walked to her father's desk, picked up a framed photo and studied it. A dark-haired, beautiful Anneke stared out at her, a quiet smile on her face. The photo, she knew, had been taken in 1946, the year her parents married. She studied the background. *Was it Holland or Houston?* The sepia backdrop and faded black-and-white figures told her nothing.

She studied her father's expression—proud and happy. He had been the affectionate one, a disciplined academic with one soft spot—his daughter. She'd never known him to be anything other than patient, kind and fair. She stared at the smaller photo next to it, Hans pulling a red wagon up the hill at Her-mann Park, while a five-year-old Nora waved and smiled.

Her eyes blurred with tears. Her mother had had terrible bouts of depression, often emanating an all-consuming sad-ness. Sometimes they would make her angry; other times she'd withdraw to her garden or stare out of the small bay window next to her bed. Nora's poor father had never seen Rose, had never known the relaxed woman Anneke had become dur-ing the years after his death.

As a child, whenever Nora would try to touch Anneke's arm or awaken her from what seemed to be some kind of trance, Anneke would not react, as if her mind were elsewhere and her soul had fled. It had frightened Nora as a child and even more now.

Where had Anneke disappeared in those moments? Could it have something to do with the man who killed her? Why didn't she ever tell me? How will I bear it if Rose never comes back to me—if I've lost both of them without any answers? Nora heard a keening cry, an animal in the wild, lost by its pack, howling in the dead of winter. Only after she had heard the piteous noise did she realize it had come from her.

She looked over at the door to Rose's nursery and walked into the dark room. Rose's sweet smell, which had permeated the house, had started to fade. Nora panicked. *What if she for-got what Rose looked like? The tiny details of her chubby cheeks, the unique spectrum of blues in her eyes...would they fade, too? Would she forget all the features that made up the Rose she adored, the min-ute, vital things that no one knew but her mother? And if she forgot those, would Rose—wherever she was—know instinctively that her mother's image of her had faded, feel it and then give up?*

"No!" She grabbed a photo of Rose and, through blurred tears, studied each of her features—every crinkle of her smile, every shade of her flushed cheeks, every pixel of color that made her eyes the only ones Nora believed in.

She would find Rose. Rose would be safe. Her baby would come back to her. To think anything else was a black road to madness. Taking a deep breath, she walked into the dining room and stared at herself in the huge mirror over the china cabinet. The light of dusk that sifted through the plantation shades cast a fading glow. Nora felt she was looking at herself in a different century, like the wedding photograph of her parents, which had branded itself in her mind.

In the photo, Anneke sat without smiling, her dark, long hair and eyes somehow resigned, the terrible fragility of her thin body, her white skin a sharp contrast to the dark hair and eyelashes. A second look at herself in the mirror told Nora that she was her mother, her coal-smudged eyes set in skin too-pale, paper-white.

Turning away, she wondered if she should have acceded to Anneke's pleas that she live with her. If she hadn't agreed, at least her mother would be alive and she would still have Rose. No, she could not have done otherwise. When she saw her mother's radiant face as she'd exited the blurred Customs door in Houston, she'd known that there was no other choice. Her mother's piercing look of longing and love had overwhelmed her.

And Nora did need her. When she found out that she was pregnant, it had sealed their commitment to each other, walking the ancient path of life: mother, daughter, granddaughter.

She wiped away her tears and looked at the dining table, so dark, heavy and worn. Four plain chairs surrounded it, the fourth rarely hosting a guest. Although born in America, Nora was raised in an undeniably Dutch home. Dinner at six every evening—meat, potatoes, gravy and applesauce— vegetables optional. And canned, never fresh. Family meals passed through her mind, the quiet murmur of Dutch as they related the small details of their day. The house always spotless, the *stoep* scrubbed every day with her mother's hard bristle brush and a cake of old-fashioned soap. Work was work, duty was duty, family was private.

As she walked through the downstairs hall, it struck Nora that Anneke had changed nothing since Hans's death. Every object on the walls and tables, every stick of furniture, every candlestick and piece of silver, was precisely the same as it had been when Hans drew his last breath. *Did it give her comfort to keep everything the same? Did she love him?*

The banging of opening and closing drawers from upstairs brought Nora back to the present. Marijke had taken her instructions to heart.

Opening the hall closet, Nora pushed the winter coats aside and looked at the floor. *Nothing.* She ran her fingers down the row of jackets and suddenly felt something familiar, the coat Anneke had bought for Hans only months before he died. His cancer had made him so weak that he was freezing all the time. Nora tried to imagine what that felt like—to have Siberia in your bones. Raising the thermostat to its highest setting hadn't helped. Anneke had abandoned the Dutch rule against extravagant spending and bought him a full-length navy cashmere coat. From the moment he slipped it on, Nora knew that he would never take it off. On the morning he died, it was wrapped tightly around him, as if he had created his own shroud to avoid further troubling his wife or daughter. She crushed her face into the soft sleeve, wishing he were here now to help her.

An hour later, she was finished. And not one step closer to any discovery than when she began. She felt too exhausted to cry. She heard footfalls as Marijke came downstairs and into the hallway. Marijke looked at her and shook her head.

Nora closed her eyes. Maybe she should take a nap. She hadn't slept more than a few hours at a time since that horrible day. And Marijke must be dead tired, too. As Nora watched her open the door and walk into the garage, she felt a stab of guilt. *Had she had taken terrible advantage of the fortuitous visit of her dear friend?* If her mother died, Marijke would never forgive herself for not being there. Well, a few hours' sleep might give them both the strength they needed to carry on.

But then she thought of the attic. She hadn't been up there since she was a small girl, playing hide-and-seek with Hans. She went into the hallway and looked up at the trapdoor, its worn rope dangling from the ceiling. Despite Nora's height, it took her two attempts to grab it and yank it down. The old wooden stairs finally released and lowered, groaning as dust and dirt fell onto her head.

Nora wiped her eyes, stared up into the dusty abyss and then went into the kitchen. She opened the drawer where her father had always kept the flashlight and then walked back to the rickety ladder that hung with an air of crooked despondency. She picked her way carefully up, waving the flashlight back and forth as soon as she entered the murkiness of the attic.

The light traveled over rose-colored insulation and, through dust motes, the fetid air clutched at Nora's throat. Almost immediately, rivulets of sweat ran down her face. *It must be over a hundred up here!* Once her eyes adjusted to the dim light, she spotted a row of old cardboard boxes. She opened every one, sneezing at the dust that rose from them.

Their contents were unremarkable. Her grade school records, baby clothes and photos of her with her parents in Galveston in summer. Her heart lurched as she saw the happiness on both their faces. *Gone, gone.*

When she closed the last box, she stared at her filthy hands as sweat streamed down her back. Weary and disappointed, she took another look around. She saw nothing other than the boxes she had already opened. In typical Dutch fashion, her mother had stacked them neatly against the wall, had even organized them chronologically.

She took a final glance at the marshaled nothingness around her. This was getting her nowhere. And the attic had been her last resort. *Surely this was where secrets would have been hidden if they existed at all?*

She swept the dim light around one last time. It fell upon a broken chair, an old broom and a pair of heavy work shoes, the kind favored by her father. She pointed the faint beam into every corner, but saw nothing except disabled toys, crippled furniture, old mattresses and torn boxes that revealed their useless contents with an almost defiant air.

She knew why her mother had saved these things. It was the Dutch way—the conviction that the moment anything was thrown away, it would be needed again. Well, it was all just junk.

She turned to go back downstairs. Her feet felt leaden, her mind reduced to dull panic. At ground level, she would call to Marijke, only to learn that she, too, had found nothing. And then she would fall into her bed and try, try, try, to make another plan—no matter how crazy—to do something to find Rose.

Thoughts tumbled over in her mind like laundry in a dryer. *Why hadn't she found even a hint of why this son of a bitch had come? Surely there had to be something that would give a clue as to what she should do next!*

She again pointed the beam into every corner, but saw nothing. She had turned to go back down when the flashlight shifted in her hand and reflected something metallic in the far corner. She pushed aside a few empty boxes and looked. On the dusty floor was a small container about the size of a toolbox. She wiped the dirt off of the label. Blank. Probably empty. She picked it up. It rattled.

She sat on the broken chair. It wobbled, but held her weight. She put the metal box on her lap. Its clasp was broken, as if it had been smashed long ago. She struggled to breathe as she pulled back the lid and aimed the wavering light at its contents.

Nora stared into it, afraid of what she might find. *Could this be it? Could it contain the clue that would connect the dots to these horrible events?*

Hands shaking, she cradled the box in her lap and aimed the light down. A sheaf of papers—yellowed onionskin with battered edges bound by a green ribbon. She untied it and spread the papers on her lap. She realized she was holding her breath. She stared at the green ribbon as it fell to the floor, a satin spiral. *Would it be a clue, a Pandora's box, or worse—nothing?*

She took a breath, picked up the flashlight and pointed it at the first page. It was thick paper that seemed to be an identification document. The name at the top was "Anneke Brouwer." A small black-and-white photograph of her mother stared back, unsmiling. Nora felt almost dizzy. Her mother's maiden name, as far as she knew, was *de Bruin*. Moving her index finger slowly down, she peered at the card more closely.

"Damn!" Her hands shook so that the beam of light skittered wildly. She gripped it tighter and looked again. The card was dated July 1945 and stated that Anneke was born in 1920. It had an arresting illustration at the top, a black-and-red flag with a triangle in the center. The emblem of the Dutch lion with sword and arrows stood in front of a blue-and-white shield. Nora felt confused. She knew what the Dutch flag looked like, and this was not it. But it was the words in flamboyant print underneath that caused her to gasp. *"Nationale-Socialistische Beweging."*

"What?" she whispered. "The *NSB?*" She knew enough

Dutch history to know that during the war, this was the reviled organization of the Dutch Nazis. "No!" she cried out.
"It can't be!" She dropped the stack of papers as if they were
coiled rattlesnakes.

Her mother an NSB-er? A Dutch Nazi? The one thing Anneke had told Nora when she had asked about the war was
that she had fought for the resistance. Nora strained to process
this new information, to see where its edges might fit into the
puzzle about Anneke's murder and Rose's kidnapping.

She snatched up the documents and peered at the card again.
It was incomprehensible! The print before her eyes shimmered
and rippled, a mirage in the desert. Dizziness filled her head
as she felt the flashlight slip. Her sweaty forehead fell into her
filthy hands.

She sat back and stared at the brown dust that had sprinkled
over the documents, the lockbox and her hands. *What did all
this mean? Who was her mother? A hero fighting the Germans or a
fanatic Dutch Nazi carrying out Hitler's version of the New Order?*

Moments later, she raised her head. She had to go on. With
shaky hands, she laid the first page on the floor and picked up
the second. It bore an ornate wax stamp. She picked up the
flashlight and examined it, some kind of legal document so
translucent and brittle it could have been an ancient scroll. The
bloodred seal cracked in two as she raised the paper into the
watery beam of light. A small photo of her father as a young
man was stapled to the right corner. Unaccustomed to the le-
galistic Dutch, it took her a while to make out the gist of it.

In the Name of Her Royal Highness
Queen Wilhelmina of the Netherlands,
This action is hereby brought against the Dutch Citizen
hereinafter named
HANS ALBERTUS MARTINUS MOERVELD

For the Murder of
ABRAM DAVID ROSEN
By virtue of the Complaint sworn to before
The Royal Court on this
Sixteenth Day of September
In the Year
Nineteen Hundred and Forty-Five

Nora gasped. Her eyes flew to the middle of the page, where the charge was stated in bold print, along with the *Oordeel,* the Court's decision. Only two words.

WAR CRIMINAL

And the *Vonnis,* the sentence.
DEATH.

8

―――

Nora stared at the paper, the words blurred. Finally, she calmed herself enough to focus. Her father's real surname must have been *Moerveld*. And the paper stated he had been tried in absentia for murder. Tears of disbelief fell onto her cheeks. Her father—a *murderer? Of a Jewish man during wartime?*

"No, Papa, no!" she whispered. It couldn't be. Imagining him, she saw a gentle smile on his face as she sang "Twinkle, Twinkle Little Star" for her first-grade class at Poe Elementary; felt his strong arms pick up her bruised body from the street the first time he tried to teach her to ride a two-wheeler; the cozy comfort as she sat on his lap as he read *La Fontaine* to her. Whoever the man described in this document, it was not—could not—be her father.

And Abram Rosen, who was he, and why would Papa be accused of killing him? The attic air choked her. *No, no, no!* She could not accept this. Wiping her eyes, she looked at the last line of the document and that one, black, irrevocable word: *Death*.

She glanced through the remaining papers and then folded them into a clumsy parcel. She would take them downstairs to Marijke. She felt a new stab at their import, but also something electric. This had to be the "something else."

As she started to put the papers back into the metal box, she peered into it. Something was stuck to its metal side. She scrabbled her fingernails against it until it came free. A small booklet, a Dutch passport. A stern, younger version of her father stared back at her. Underneath was the name "Hans Moerveld."

Why had he changed his name to "de Jong"? And when had he and Mama decided to abandon their true identities? If the documents were true—and how could she dispute them—then they both had urgent reasons to flee. Papa must have whisked Anneke away to avoid arrest.

Nora thought back to her college days, when she had embarked on a self-made path to learn about her parents' lives during the war. Neither would speak of it. They each insisted that she not ask more questions. Their admonition had, of course, fueled her intention to do precisely that.

She'd learned that after Dutch liberation day on May 5, 1945, known NSB-ers—men and women—had been dragged down the streets and jeered at by their neighbors and countrymen. Many were paraded around with shaved heads to further demonstrate how reviled they were. Some were pelted with rotten fruit, tied up and beaten.

Could that be why the killer had hacked off clumps of Anneke's hair? God, what other reason could there be? Her mother a Nazi and her father a murderer?

And this killer—whoever he was—maybe he had come back for revenge. Maybe he'd also meant to kill Papa but didn't know he was already dead.

Nora's head spun. *But why did this bastard wait thirty years? And even if Mama had been an NSB-er, what could she have done that would warrant such a long-held hatred and brutal death?*

9

Clutching the metal box, she clambered down the folding attic stairs and ran into the living room. "Marijke!" she cried. "Come quick!"

Marijke hurried in from the garage with a sheaf of papers in her arms. "*Wat is er?* Are you all right?"

Nora grabbed her arm. The papers Marijke held fell as Nora pulled her down onto the couch next to her. Hands shaking, she put the metal box onto Marijke's lap.

"What is it?"

"It's insane! It's about my parents, the NSB…during the war, my mother, their names—" She tried to catch her breath. "Everything I ever knew about them was a lie!"

Nora saw Marijke's eyes widen as she stared at the box. "What do you mean? Where did you find this?"

"In the attic, in a corner. It doesn't matter. Read!"

"Okay, okay, I will!" Marijke pulled the sheaf out of the box, placed it on the floor and stacked the papers on her lap.

"For God's sake, Marijke, hurry up! It's so awful, I can't stand it!"

Marijke held up her hand. "*Wacht even,* Nora. I want to read these carefully." Minutes dragged like hours. Nora felt like jumping up and pacing, but she didn't want to miss the moment when Marijke finished reading. Other than her widened eyes, Marijke didn't say a word. When she finished, she sighed and turned to Nora. "You had no idea about this? They never mentioned any of it?"

Nora gave a harsh laugh. "Would you tell your daughter that you were a Dutch Nazi? Or that you killed a Jewish man and were wanted for murder? That you fled the country and changed your name?" She raised her hands. "Of course they didn't tell me!"

"But what could all this mean?" asked Marijke. "For your mother's murder? For Rose's kidnapping?"

Nora rose and paced, clenching her hands into fists. "I don't know, but it's all connected. I'm sure of it. What if this killer was related to this Abram Rosen?" She suddenly stopped. "But that doesn't make sense, either. If Papa killed this man, then why did the murderer kill my mother? What had she ever done to this Rosen? And if Mama was a Dutch Nazi—" she turned to Marijke as she felt a hot flush on her face "—which I still can't get my head around, then what role could she have played in all of this?"

"Nora, stop pacing, for God's sake. You're driving me nuts. Sit down and let's try to think this through."

Nora let herself drop into a chair. Nazis, NSB, murderers and kidnappers raced crazily around in her mind. What if it was all true? "Tell me what you think. I can't connect the dots."

Marijke sat back and took out a cigarette. She lit it and

inhaled. Nora watched blue smoke escape her lips and spiral away.

"Okay. Let's assume everything you found in that box is true. We'll start with your father. His papers show he changed his name before he came here, so I think we can assume he fled either because he killed this man or there was enough evidence to accuse him."

"I don't believe it. He would never kill anyone!"

"Nora, we have to take these papers at face value so we can try to link them to your mother's murder and Rose's kidnapping."

"Okay, okay."

"So," continued Marijke. "It seems logical that someone has taken revenge."

"But why would that bastard wait over thirty years? That's crazy!"

"Crazy, but not impossible."

"What if the killer couldn't find my father?" she asked. "He'd changed his name and covered his tracks. There had to be a lot of confusion after the war. No easy way of tracking him. But wasn't it hard to enter the U.S. back then? Didn't you have to have a sponsor? A job?"

"Then how did he do it?"

"No idea."

"And how would Anneke figure into this?" asked Marijke.

Nora drew a deep breath. "The only document of Mama's shows that she was an NSB-er. So no matter how badly I don't want to believe it, the fact remains that along with Papa, she changed her name and ran away after Liberation Day. And you know what happened to those women after the war. It would explain why her hair was shorn."

Marijke nodded, her face grim.

Nora rose and began pacing again. "Okay. So he's accused

of murder, whether he did it or not, and she's an NSB-er who will surely be arrested. They change their names and somehow end up in Houston."

She saw Marijke tap her cigarette against the side of the blue ashtray that had been Papa's and watched the ashes flutter. "So after they moved here, they somehow got jobs and left everything—their families and friends—behind."

"And then they had me," said Nora bitterly. "Whoever I am." She held out her hand in silent request for the sheaf of damning papers.

She saw worry on Marijke's face as she handed them over. "But we still come back to the same question. What could any of this have to do with Rose?"

"I don't know." *Would she ever?*

10

Ariel Rosen sat in a cramped motel room near Houston Intercontinental and stared out the window. Darkness had finally settled over this strange city. He checked his watch and gazed at the sleeping infant. How could this morning ever have happened? *Murder, his father dead!*

She lay next to him, swaddled in his jacket. He had managed to tuck her into its warm lining and zip it up so that it formed a crude but soft sleeping bag. Just her small head peeked out. Her calm face belied the hours of wailing that had racked her tiny body. Only faint tracks remained of the tears that had streamed down her face when he'd run out of the house and roared off in his father's rental car.

Panic struck him. Did Isaac use a fake passport before Ariel flew to America to find him? But what about the rental car, and a driver's license? If he had stayed in a hotel, the clerk would have insisted he provide a license plate number. Surely the police were already checking all the rental companies and hotels in town! Ariel calmed himself. Isaac had certainly forged the passport and license before he had left Amsterdam. His father was no fool. A customs agent for years, he knew all about forgeries. Besides, he had obviously planned this for over thirty years.

He took a deep breath. Houston was enormous. Even if the police eventually traced Isaac's passport to the rental company or a hotel, it would take time to discover that it had been forged. By then Ariel would be long gone.

He walked to the small sink, wet a washcloth with warm water, sat down and patted away the traces from the baby's soft, pink cheeks. *Rose.* She was aptly named.

He shut his eyes tightly as his mind replayed the past twenty-four hours with cruel clarity: the awful murder, his crazy, crazy father collapsing and dying, and now the bizarre fact that he had kidnapped a tiny, defenseless child. He felt wetness on his face, not realizing that he had been crying.

What could he have done to prevent this? He thought of the evening he had seen Isaac in his Amsterdam apartment before the murder. It was the last real conversation they ever had.

Isaac sat on his worn couch and stared at the carpet, as if lost in another world. Ariel studied his father's clenched, veined hands, rutted face, angry eyes. When Papa spoke, his words were rough river stones brought out again and again, rubbed, polished and then carefully put away—until the next time. Papa drew a ragged breath and began.

"It was during the war," he said. "It started in 1940. It took the Germans only five days to conquer our Dutch army, such as it was."

Ariel groaned and drained the glass of *genever* that he and Isaac shared during their weekly visits. "Papa, not again! Can't we talk about something else?"

"If you don't like the conversation, then leave."

It's always the same. Just shut up, get it over with, go home. "Never mind."

Isaac pointed his index finger, an eagle's claw. "You have to remember every detail. It is your heritage. I won't be alive forever."

Ariel rose, walked to the *ijskast* and opened the freezer. Shot glasses were lined up like frozen soldiers, a bottle of *oude genever* next to them, the silent general. Ariel poured two drinks, his hands burning from the cold. One wasn't enough. Not if he had to listen to the whole goddamned story again. He handed Isaac his glass and sat down. The first sip almost knocked him on his ass. Well, he needed it. Why did Papa insist on buying *oude* instead of *jonge?* He knew why. *Oude* tasted like gasoline, but the brand Isaac bought had the highest alcohol content. Took less to get him drunk.

Isaac bent over the table, supported himself with his palms and put his lips to the frozen glass, in the old way. Somehow the gesture made Ariel sad. There were so many old men sitting on bar stools doing the same thing—downing gin, reliving their pasts, telling Ariel's generation how they had it so easy. It was true, of course, but Ariel was sick of hearing it.

Isaac straightened, his cheeks flushed. "And then the Queen took her Cabinet and ran away to London. Everyone crowded around the radios, listening to her tell us to hang on. *Ha!* That stupid woman left without telling anyone to destroy the government records! The name and address of every Jew in Amsterdam at the Nazi's fingertips. Sitting ducks!"

"Papa, shall I tell you what happened at Immigration today? There was an arrest—"

"I worked there for thirty years—who gives a damn?"

"Papa, please—"

Isaac slammed his glass down on the old wooden table. "Tell me the names!"

Ariel felt anger flame in his cheeks. "Stop it!"

"Rachel, Sara, David—"

"I won't do this anymore!" He stood.

"You will sit! You will listen to your Papa!"

Ariel sat down and hated himself for it. *Weak. Just as Papa had always told him.*

"Continue!"

"Evan, Miriam, Levi," he whispered.

Isaac reached for the table, picked up his bag of *zware shag* and rolled a cigarette. Ariel was grateful for a few moments of silence. His heart was still pounding. Isaac lit the cigarette, took a heavy puff and began coughing and sputtering.

"Papa. You know what the doctor said."

Isaac shook his head and downed the last of his *genever*. "One heart attack. What do I have to live for, anyway?"

Me! thought Ariel. "Never mind."

Isaac watched the smoke rise into the air, eyes hooded. *Maybe he's thinking about his family in the ovens,* thought Ariel. *Maybe about his own ashes when he dies. I should be more patient.*

"Just five minutes. Is that too much to ask?"

Ariel now heard the slur in his father's voice. *How much had he had to drink before Ariel got there?*

"The world thinks that the Anne Frank story is how it was. *Ha!* By the end of the war there were 100,000 filthy NSB-ers, helping the Nazis every step of the way." He picked up his *genever,* staring into the liquid as if it were a window to the past. "Then they took us—even the babies—marched us to the *Concertgebouw.*" A harsh laugh escaped him. "Our marvelous concert hall—a jumping point to annihilation."

His cigarette had burned down and out, but Papa didn't notice. He still held it pinched between his nicotine-stained fingers. Ariel felt trapped. *How could he get out of there? He had to wait for the end of the story. Like every time before.*

Isaac droned on, his words slow, too deliberate. "At the end of the war, 120,000 dead—90,000 from Amsterdam—Auschwitz, Sobibor—" He looked at Ariel with tortured eyes, tears flowing freely down his craggy face. "Did I say that already?"

"Yes, Papa," whispered Ariel. "It's all right."

"Cousins, nieces, parents—all dead." His voice was a hoarse whisper. "Why *me?* Why did I survive? Or your *Tante* Amarisa?"

Ariel felt his heart wrench, as he did every time Papa told his hideous tale. Such a tragic waste of a life. He stood, sat next to Isaac and put his arm around him. The shoulders felt thin and pinched under his strong arm. "It's all right, Papa. I'm here."

Isaac's head fell into his hands. "I am sorry, my son. You deserved a better father. And my precious Agathe, living her life with a dead man." He looked up at Ariel with fresh pain in his eyes. "When she died, I begged her to forgive me." His voice trailed off.

"Papa," said Ariel softly. "You must rest. It's all over now."

Isaac gently removed Ariel's arm and looked up at him. The agony in the black eyes tore at Ariel's heart.

"No, my son," he whispered. "It will never be over."

Now another thought pierced him. *Amarisa!* What would she do when she found out that Isaac was dead? She had always terrified Ariel with her wild, black hair and deadly agate eyes, that hideous scar that sliced from mouth to ear. When angry, the twisted, ropy tissue turned a grotesque shade of purple.

Ariel felt cold sweat under his armpits. Isaac was everything to Amarisa, the only family he still claimed. She would go insane—wailing, furious, bereft. He imagined her charging across the room as fast as her crippled leg would let her, pummeling him with her fists, screaming at him for not saving Isaac, for being a coward.

He had felt her wrath all his life. She had had no use for Ariel, even as a child. She had never given him presents, even on his birthday or Hanukkah. He couldn't remember a single time that she had kissed or hugged him. When he was older, Amarisa had waved him away whenever she and Isaac talked about the war, nursing their bitterness and rage. "You're weak, just like everyone in your generation," she had sneered. "Living the good life while we watched our loved ones being marched to the ovens. Go into the kitchen with your mother where you belong." Ariel never understood how Isaac could let her speak that way to him, but he learned early that Isaac always let anything Amarisa said pass.

God, it wasn't just having to tell her, a filthy rich diamond merchant, as cold and calculating in business as she was in life. She had grudgingly given him and Leah a good bit of money over the years. He sensed that it was her way to control them and make them grovel, but his job didn't provide the money they needed to live comfortably in Amsterdam, even with Leah's job as a nurse. And now Ariel was certain that Amarisa would cut them off as soon as she heard about Isaac's death. *Where would they be then?*

Rose's cry snapped Ariel out of his reverie. Her face was red as she wriggled unhappily. *Oh, God, was she sick?* He felt her tiny forehead. It seemed hot. *What should he do?* He picked her up gently, rocking her as he walked around the small, airless room. She stopped crying and snuggled deeper into her down nest. Relief coursed through him. Maybe she was all right. Exhausted, he looked at the infant he carried and tried to focus. *What now? What had he done?*

After he had sped away from Anneke's house, he'd driven as fast as he could toward the airport. He'd had no plan, just desperation. He had driven around until he found a nondescript motel and checked in.

Rose wailed again. "Shh, it's all right, little one." He picked her up and then understood. *Diapers. How could he be so stupid?* He carried her to the elevator and went downstairs, cooing to her.

The woman at the desk smiled. Ariel couldn't help staring at her flashy red lipstick, fake eyelashes and blond beehive hairdo.

"'Ounds 'ike 'umbuddy ain' heppi." The drawl that dripped like honey from her lips strangled any hope Ariel had of understanding her.

"Excuse me?"

"You a furrener?"

"Ah—yes. German."

She leaned across the desk, her enormous breasts straining to free themselves from the prison of her low-cut blouse. She wiggled her fingers at Rose, her long red nails clacking against one another like shucked oyster shells. She raised her voice, as if Ariel were deaf. "I said, it sounds like somebody ain't happy."

Ariel felt his cheeks burn as he tried to wrest his eyes from her obvious endowments. "Oh—no, no she isn't. Can you tell me where the closest store might be? Where I can buy diapers and formula?"

The woman snapped her gum and pointed a cherry fingernail across the highway. "There's a FedMart right over there. They'll fix you up just fine."

"Thank you," he said.

"She all right?"

"She seems a little warm to me."

"Give her to me. I'm a granny four times over."

Reluctantly, Ariel complied. Rose quieted the moment the woman held her. She placed a confident hand against Rose's forehead. "Hey, darlin'," she crooned. "Got a little cold?" She handed the baby back to Ariel. "Baby aspirin. Fix her right up."

Relief coursed through him. "Thank you so much. I don't know very much about babies."

She gave him an amused look. "Where's her momma?"

Ariel jiggled Rose and summoned what he knew must have looked like a plastic smile. "In Idaho visiting her father. We're flying out tomorrow."

"You're a good daddy," she said. "Anybody can see that. Most men wouldn't fly alone with such an itty-bitty. How old is she?"

The words came from his mouth before he could stop himself. "I don't know."

The woman's dark, penciled-in eyebrows raised. "What?"

"I mean—" Ariel wiped the sweat from his brow.

She hooted. "Oh, you men! Never know nothin' about kids, not even if they're your own! We don't expect you galoots to count by minutes, hours and days like we do." She stroked Rose's fat cheek. "We don't need 'em, now do we, honey?" She spoke in the high, excited babble women always seemed to use when addressing babies. "Yes, ma'am! I'd say you're no more'n six, seven months old." She winked at Ariel. "Close?"

"Next month," he said quickly. "Now, I'm afraid we really must be going." He stepped back.

"If I was you, I'd be addin' some of that baby cereal to her feed. Don't want her keepin' you up on that long plane ride."

"I—I will."

"Be good now, hear?" One last red-nailed wave and she disappeared through the office door.

Ariel mumbled his thanks and almost ran to the car, Rose

bouncing in his arms. Dodging heavy traffic, he drove to the store. It was only when the cold air-conditioning blasted him and he got Rose settled into the cart that he drew an easy breath. *God, I've got to be careful! It's the simple things that will screw me.* He vowed to write out an entire history about Rose so he would know everything a normal father would.

Rose looked up from the cart's blue plastic seat and gurgled happily. Apparently the diaper wasn't bothering her now. He walked down aisle after aisle. It slayed him, America. These huge stores selling everything anyone could imagine. As he wandered up and down the aisles, a friendly Hispanic woman took pity on him and helped him pick out diapers, formula, a pacifier, baby clothes, blankets, a collapsible stroller and God knows what else.

All he knew was that by the time he checked out, he had racked up almost a hundred dollars' worth. Luckily, when he learned that Isaac had gone to Houston, he had raced to his bank and almost emptied his savings account to exchange guilders into dollars. He now had just over a thousand dollars in cash, not knowing how much he'd need to get Isaac back to Holland. There had been no time to get traveler's checks. Now he was glad he had cash. If he had used traveler's checks, he would have had to countersign them using his passport, putting him at further risk. Ariel wondered if any of it would be left when he got home.

Back at the motel, he put Rose on the bed, buffered by pillows, and hauled his purchases into the room, including a large suitcase he had bought. No way he could fit Rose's new wardrobe and paraphernalia into his overnight bag.

The first order of business was that diaper. He made short work of changing it and won a smile of approval from Rose. He warmed some formula on the stove, put it into a bottle and let it cool until a splash on his wrist let him know it wasn't too hot.

Thank God he did have some experience with kids. Leah had been heartsick when she found out that she couldn't bear a child. In the past few years, many of their friends had had babies. So she and Ariel had become babysitters. A bitter-sweet chore.

A few minutes later, he sat in an armchair with Rose in his arms. She stopped crying the moment he put the nipple into her mouth. She sucked greedily, all the while fixing him with her big blue eyes.

"What a good girl!" He held her up and laughed. "You're perfect, you know that?" When he lowered her into his arms, her sweet, milky cheek swept against his bristly one. He was shocked by the joy that filled him.

But guilt stabbed him as he thought of the grandmother—killed by his father's hand. It all flashed before him again: Isaac's humiliation of Anneke, her frantic denials, holding Rose to her breast, begging, begging for Rose's life. The bloody hole in her forehead, the fearsome scarlet blood on the white carpet.

Ariel tried to wipe away those images and held Rose even closer to his chest, as if to protect her from further harm. But she'd finished the bottle and fallen asleep. He rose and burped her. The sweet weight of her in his arms made him want to weep. Ariel buried his face into Rose's neck before he laid her back on his jacket.

But the promise! Papa's dying wish!

How could he fulfill it? His father had been crazed, in agony, near death. It didn't matter. He remembered Isaac's fierce eyes and his cold fingers clutching his wrist, the agony receding only when he had agreed to take Rose back with him.

"No!" he cried out loud. He must take this child and return

her immediately. He couldn't imagine the terror her mother must feel—his cousin, he now knew. He was not a criminal, someone who would steal a child and deprive it of its mother's love. He lay Rose back upon the sofa cushions.

So how in hell should he do this? Drop her off at a hospital with her name pinned to the pink blanket he had bought her? Or leave her here, call the woman at the desk from a pay phone and tell her who Rose belonged to? But now she could identify him and the police would think he was involved in the murder.

And Leah? How could he ever explain any of this to her? He looked at the phone by the bed. *Should he call her?* All she knew was that he had chased after Isaac. He thought back to what he'd told her. When he hadn't been able to reach Isaac all day, he'd let himself into his father's apartment, where he'd found the Houston address, Isaac's flight details and his passport. There was a hole where Isaac's photo should have been. Because of Ariel's job in Immigration, he knew instantly that Isaac had procured a black-market passport to travel to the U.S.

Leah had begged Ariel not to go. But he'd had to try to stop his goddamned father. Ariel remembered telling her he feared the worst. Who knew what Isaac would do to satisfy a lifetime of obsessive hatred? The last thing he remembered was the outpouring of love in Leah's embrace at the airport and the faint lavender of her perfume that stayed with him down the runway. No, he couldn't call her now. She would be frantic, even more worried when he told her what had happened. And what he had done.

A hunger pang returned him to the present. *Shit.* He'd forgotten to buy food for himself. But not now. He had to think this through.

Even if he gave Rose back, he'd still be arrested, charged, put away in prison for years. All he knew about American prisons was that they were terrifying. And who would believe he hadn't taken part in the murder? Or that he'd never dreamed of taking Rose? Damn it. He was trapped, as he always had been, in his father's life.

He rubbed his eyes and looked hard at Rose again. *Beautiful, heavenly child.* Maybe there was a way. It wasn't right. It wasn't fair. But this baby could be the answer to his and Leah's prayers. Could he possibly take her back to Amsterdam, make sure she was raised as a Jew, as Isaac had begged him to? After all, little Rose was family, Abram's granddaughter. There was a bizarre symmetry to it, despite the Nazi horror and tragedy that had spawned it. This sweet, precious girl could be brought back into the family. She had not only been denied Abram, but Isaac, as well. If he had lived, Rose could have eased Isaac's bitterness, seeing part of Abram live on, despite what her grandmother did.

His rationalizations rang hollow even as he thought of them. But he was scared. They couldn't stay in this country. Who knew what clues he may have left? Any minute the police could be at his door.

He bent over, kissed Rose lightly on her soft forehead and then stood. He crossed to his suitcase and pulled his passport from its side pocket. Sitting at the small desk, he opened it and scanned the lines on the page across from his photo.

He knew what to do. Under Dutch law, children under eight were not required to have a passport but could travel under a parent's. He ran his finger down to the appropriate box, then hesitated. He stared at the pen on the desk. No, he had absolutely no choice. He picked it up and filled in the space. *Jacoba Rosen.*

He sat back and breathed heavily. The die was cast. He was now traveling with his daughter. But they couldn't fly back to the Netherlands from Houston. Isaac probably had the false passport on him, which meant the police would be looking for a Dutchman flying from here to Amsterdam with a tiny baby. But what if the fake passport wasn't Dutch? They could be looking for a Romanian, a Russian—who knew?

He shoved everything he had brought with him into his carry-on, and then packed the things he had bought for Rose into his suitcase. He glanced at the collapsible stroller, satisfied with his purchase. He couldn't carry Rose everywhere he went.

He was glad he had taken a taxi to the woman's house until he realized that the police could already have tracked down the driver, who may have been able to describe him. His face could already be splattered all over the television, in newspapers: *Houston Woman Murdered, Baby Kidnapped, Artist Rendering of Suspect!* If so, surely the police had passed his likeness to Houston and Amsterdam Immigration.

First he had to ditch Isaac's car, rent another one and get the hell out of town. The documents in the glove box showed that the car had been rented from Hertz near the airport. Ariel called other rentals nearby. They didn't take cash, he would have to pay with a credit card. It was 1980, they said. Firm policy for the past five years. Ariel panicked. He didn't have one; no one he knew in Amsterdam used them. Finally he located a small company a block away from the Hertz lot. They told him they would take cash if he put down a three hundred dollar deposit.

When the sun fell over the towering Houston skyline, he woke a now-quiet Rose, put her, his suitcase and her small stroller into Isaac's car, and drove to the rental company. Rose looked up at him. He hated to do it, but he couldn't run the risk of taking her into the office. Even if they didn't have a description of him, the first thing the police would have done was to send Rose's photograph everywhere. Surely they would have alerted all rental offices to be on the lookout for a foreign man traveling with a six-month-old. Holding Rose with one arm, he put his suitcase on the front seat, zipped it open and snuggled her into his clothing. It wasn't a car seat, but it would have to do. He lowered the windows a bit to let the warm breeze in. She looked up at him, her blue eyes wide and curious. He kissed her again. "Be good," he whispered. "I'll be right back."

He pulled the brim of his hat low on his forehead and got into line. Someone at the far end of the counter was not happy.

"I don't give a *shit* what that machine of yours says," bellowed an angry young man in a white starched shirt, jeans and cowboy boots. "I reserved a Cadillac and a Cadillac is what you're goddamned well gonna give me."

The older female agent glared at him, pulled out a reservation form and pointed to a few lines of text. Her voice was sharp as cactus needles. "There it is—in black and white. We said we'd give you the car of your choice *if* it was available." She crossed her arms and smiled at him as if pleased to give him the news. "And it ain't."

The cowboy's face turned purple. "Listen, lady. I got a sweet little Mexican girl waitin' for me down in Nuevo Laredo and then we're hoppin' a plane to Acapulco. How do you expect me to drive that far in some shitty little compact?"

The woman looked him square in the eyes, held up a set of keys and shook them. "Guess you better get goin' then. You got about a six hour drive ahead of you to Laredo. Once you get there, you can just walk over the border, you know."

It was Ariel's turn. The young man facing him at the counter barely noticed him. His eyes were riveted to the argument. Ariel mumbled his request for a car—any car. The man nodded, looked at Ariel's drivers license and didn't seem to notice that it was foreign. When Ariel asked to pay cash, the agent waved the manager over. He glanced at Ariel's passport and then his face. "Three hundred deposit. You got that?"

Ariel fanned the cash on the counter, his heart pounding.

The manager turned to the agent. "Okay."

Ariel signed the rental papers quickly and had a sudden thought. "Where is Nuevo Laredo?"

The young agent looked at him curiously. "Not from around here, are you?"

"No," he mumbled.

The agent stamped the first page of the rental form, ripped it off and gave Ariel the copy and a set of keys. He reached under the counter and handed Ariel a map of Texas, and pointed. "It's a lousy town on the Mexican side of the Texas border. All it's got is booze, bad food and easy hookers." He jerked his head toward the cowboy, who was still arguing with the woman behind the counter. "Anybody can walk across the border and get some of what he's after."

"Without a passport?"

The clerk shrugged. "Nobody gives a damn who goes into Mexico. We just care who comes back. Lots of wetbacks tryin' to sneak in."

Ariel collected the rental papers and rushed back to Rose. *Was she still there? Was she all right?* He unlocked and opened the car door. There she was, sleeping, a soft smile on her face. Incredible relief shot through him. Before he lifted her out of Isaac's car and walked to the one he had just rented, he had a final thought. He used Rose's blanket to wipe off his fingerprints from the steering wheel, car handles and the keys, which he then threw under the driver's seat. "I am a criminal," he said softly to himself. But there was no time for moral reflection now.

Once in the car, Ariel turned the key and drove into the night. Just before they arrived in Laredo, he used a pay phone to make a reservation on the next Aeroméxico flight from Nuevo Laredo to Amsterdam via Mexico City. He would pay for the tickets at the airport.

The clerk had been right. He and Rose had just walked across the bridge from Laredo into Mexico with the other pedestrians. It was crazy. After the hour-long flight to Mexico City, they arrived at the airport. While he waited for the flight to Amsterdam to board, he placed a collect call to Leah.

"Ariel?" He heard the hysteria in her voice. "Where are you? Why haven't you called me?"

"I'm so sorry, sweetheart. God, I've never been so happy to hear your voice."

"Are you all right? What has happened?"

"God, Leah, I don't know where to begin."

"Did you find Isaac?" Her voice lowered to a fierce whisper. "Amarisa is frantic! She made me tell her where Isaac went and why."

Dread filled him. "Where is she now?"

"Here, in the other room," she said. "She says she's not budging until Isaac comes home. God, Ariel—*hurry*. You know how she is."

"Don't tell her anything."

"But you're bringing Isaac back with you?"

"He's—dead." The word choked in his throat. *"Dead?"* He heard the terror in her voice. "But how—"

"He killed—"

Ariel turned. A short young woman with two noisy toddlers in tow stared at him, her black eyes wide. She had obviously wanted to use the telephone but thought better of it and scuttled away as quickly as her entourage would permit. Ariel lowered his voice and whispered into the receiver. "I can't talk now—it isn't safe. I'm sorry, I know you're worried."

"But *murder?* Oh, God—"

Rose began to whimper. Ariel hoisted her higher on his hip. *"Niet huilen, schat."*

"Who is that? A child?"

"Yes," he said quickly. "I have to catch my plane. Will you pick us up? Eight tomorrow morning."

"Us?" she cried. "Who is us?"

"Leah, I'll explain it all later, I promise. Whatever you do, don't say anything to Amarisa. Just tell her I'm coming home and you don't know anything else."

"But—"

"Please, darling, do what I say. I'll handle her when I get back."

"I'll try, but—"

He heard his flight announced over the loudspeaker. "I have to go now, sweetheart. See you tomorrow."

"Just come home!"

He hung up. *How could he explain any of it?* Leah would freak out when he showed up with Rose in his arms. He hurried to the gate, struggling with his carry-on and jostling Rose, who seemed to think it was all very exciting. She gurgled and laughed. He glanced furtively around, expecting the police to intercept them at any moment. *God, just get me home!* He almost tripped in his haste to make it to the jetway. The stewardess relieved him of the stroller and he barreled down the aisle. Only when he and Rose were settled in and the plane pulled away was he able to take deep gulps of air.

After liftoff, the smiling stewardess offered him a refreshment. He ordered three tiny bottles of Scotch, poured them into a plastic cup with trembling hands and knocked them back before she fetched Diet Cokes for his seatmates. Her disapproving look was unmistakable. *A sweaty drunk slamming down drinks with a beautiful baby to care for!* He shut his eyes and let the fiery alcohol course through him.

During the flight, Rose alternately cried and slept, but quieted quickly after her bottle or a diaper change—no easy feat in the minuscule bathroom. He was grateful that the baby aspirin had seemed to work and that she was too young to stay awake long.

Ten hours later, they arrived at Schiphol. Bleary-eyed and exhausted, Ariel walked from the gate down the paths he knew so well and collected his luggage. His back and arms were killing him from holding Rose during the long flight. He realized he had forgotten to collect the stroller from the stewardess before deplaning. He felt so exhausted he thought he might collapse. Rose was awake and seemed to be taking in everything she saw and heard. His heart thrashed in his chest as he stood at the red line waiting for the next Immigration agent, hoping it wouldn't be anyone he knew. He gripped Rose tightly. Surely they hadn't come all this way only to be discovered now. He closed his eyes and prayed to God for the first time in years.

"Mijnheer?"

Ariel opened his eyes and looked at the agent waving him over to his cubicle. Fortunately, Ariel didn't recognize him. It was only then that he started to breathe again. He juggled Rose as he reached into his coat pocket and produced his passport. It felt as if the agent took years to examine it. The young man looked at the photograph and then up at him—twice. *Oh, God,* he thought. *It's all over. They must have found out who I was and put my name on the list.*

He knew that agents were provided daily with a list of passengers to be denied entrance. Most were wanted criminals. Ariel saw the young man pull the list out of a red folder. At that moment, his telephone rang. The agent picked up and spoke quietly. *"Ja, die is hier,"* he said. *"Kom maar."*

Ariel felt sick. *Who was coming? And why?*

A few torturous minutes later, two burly security guards walked up. He waited in dread. They would arrest him here and now. He would be deported and stand trial in Houston. They would take Rose away. He held her closer.

The agent handed the list to one of the men who ran his finger down the page and nodded to the other guard. Ariel shut his eyes. At least it would be over.

"We've got one on row ten," said the security guard to the agent. He turned to the other guard. "Let's go." They walked off.

Ariel almost wept with relief. The young agent shook his head and stamped Ariel's passport. "It's always something," he muttered. As he returned the passport to Ariel's trembling fingers, the agent nodded at Rose.

"Beautiful child," he said.

Ariel took a deep breath and managed a small smile.

"Mijn dochter," he said. *"Jacoba."*

II

Nora watched impatiently as Richards sat on the sofa. It was six in the evening. Early that morning, she had sent him all the documents she'd found yesterday by courier, including her translation. Richards called around nine. In a harried voice, he said he had just been called out on a double murder of a couple in River Oaks. He would come over when he could grab a few minutes. Nora called the police station around three to find out why he hadn't shown up. The intake officer told her that Richards was still at the crime scene.

So Nora cleaned the house. Then cleaned it again. Marijke went to the grocery store, she thought, to escape Nora's manic behavior. Not to mention that they had both been cooped up for a week now, tethered to the house. All Nora could do was to keep moving. The minute she stopped, fear for Rose filled her. Or she thought about her job and her patients. *Had Bryan, an eight-year-old with a medulloblastoma in his cerebellum, come through his surgery all right?* Bryan had held her hand and smiled when she told him not to worry, she would be there during the entire operation. She had promised to keep him safe. *How could she have promised such a thing? She couldn't even keep her own daughter safe.* She should call and find out, but did not. She couldn't handle more bad news.

Nora watched as Marijke brought Richards a cup of coffee. He thanked her and took a sip. Nora drew a deep breath, trying not to panic. She had racked her brain all afternoon to make sense of the awful things she'd found in the attic. She still could not believe it. Richards finally put his coffee cup on the table and sat back. His dark brown eyes met hers. They seemed preoccupied. *How much had the new murders diverted his attention from Rose?*

She couldn't stand it anymore. "Well? What did you find out?"

"Not a lot. Not yet, anyway."

Nora felt as if her entire body was a strung wire, rigid with fear and fatigue. She motioned to Marijke for a cigarette, something she had never done. Marijke raised her eyes, but pulled one from her pack, lit it and handed it to Nora. She nodded her thanks, stood and paced around, almost gagging as she drew the harsh smoke into her lungs. Six days of no Rose and no sleep had made her feel out-of-her-mind crazy. If she didn't find her baby soon, she wouldn't make it—she just wouldn't. "Who have you contacted about the information I sent you?"

"It's not as if we haven't done anything, Nora." She saw the frustration in his face. "Here is what we know so far. The FBI has conferred with the Dutch National Police, the KLPD, and notified the Dutch Ministry of Security and Justice, as well as the Dutch Ministry of Foreign Affairs." He took a deep breath. "We talked to Amsterdam Immigration about the false passport in light of the new information. The FBI's legal attaché to the U.S. Embassy in The Hague is also in the loop."

Why in hell didn't anyone realize that they had to act now—immediately!—or she might never find her Rose! She felt panic consume her. "And you sent everyone the documentation I gave you?"

"Yes, we did."

Nora stalked to her chair, sat and stubbed out the cigarette in Hans's blue ashtray on the table. *Her father, the murderer.* She shook off the thought. "What did they find out?"

Richards looked at her with his dark eyes, his voice calm. "Nora, you have to keep in mind that it's still very early in the case. I know it doesn't feel that way to you, but we're still processing the information from the crime scene and the FBI has taken both the murder and Rose's disappearance very seriously. Even though we don't have any hard leads yet, we can't simply drop that investigation and focus all of our energy on the documents you sent us."

"What do you mean?" She spit her words out as if shot from a machine gun. "Nathan, this is the first real evidence anyone has found that might link the murder and the kidnapping! Obviously that Dutchman—whoever he was—went to a lot of trouble to forge a passport and come here and kill my mother. He might even have been an assassin hired by someone to settle an old score. Or maybe he was an operative with one of the Israeli organizations who track war criminals." She stopped to take a breath.

She could tell that neither Richards nor Marijke seemed to embrace her logic, but she went on. "The real link here must be related to whatever my mother did as a Dutch Nazi and my father's murder of a Dutch Jew." Richards and Marijke listened in silence.

She spoke louder. "We have to find out who Abram Rosen

was, if his family is still alive, how my father knew him, why he would kill him, if my mother was really a Dutch Nazi, what she had to do with Rosen's death and how all of that may be connected to why she was murdered and why Rose was kidnapped—"

Richards held up his hand. "Nora," he said sternly. "You have to slow down—and calm down." Nora could tell he was waiting for a signal from her that she understood. To placate him, she took a deep breath and nodded. She had to appear rational. She sat on her hands to keep them from moving.

Richards continued as if he were teaching a child the first letters of the alphabet. "We have to think about this logically," he said. "You're talking about information that is over thirty years old involving people and events that occurred in a foreign country during wartime. Those records won't be easy to find, if they can be found at all."

"So you haven't found a single thing that might help us?" She dropped any pretense at being calm.

Richards's left eye began to tic. "Although the Dutch have promised to give the matter their attention, they told us that any records relating to Abram Rosen are probably long gone, packed away in archives or lost in the confusion after the war."

Nora felt stunned. "They have no way of tracking down who he was, where he lived or if he had any family we could try to contact?"

"They told us that there were too many Rosens in the Netherlands for them to move quickly. That it would take time."

"What about just in Amsterdam?" She could hear the flint in her voice. It was the way she spoke when a nurse handed her the wrong surgical instrument in the operating room. "Surely they can narrow it down and start from there." She picked up an empty wineglass and watched her hands shake as she poured claret into her glass.

Richards said nothing, but she felt him study her. He had to notice the trembling of her fingers and the black circles under her eyes. "They will," he said quietly, "but we have to be patient. We also contacted Dutch Immigration to see if there is some way to trace your parents' immigration into the U.S. They had nothing. Neither did U.S. Immigration. We're not even sure how they got into the country. And, again, I don't know how pertinent that information is to the murder or the kidnapping." Richards leaned forward. Nora noticed that his tic had stopped. She saw him watch as she took another shaky sip from her wineglass. He believed she had become unhinged.

"Your information may provide some insight into the murder, and it may not," he said quietly. "But in my professional opinion, we have a much better chance of finding Rose by working it hard from our end." He stopped and took a sip of his coffee.

"What about hiring a detective?"

"Good idea," he said. "I know an ex-cop—Williams. Used him before."

"Please call him."

"I'll fill him in and we'll go from there." He pulled his worn notepad out of his breast pocket and scribbled a few words. "But we still don't have the identity of the killer. Although he may have been Dutch, we can't even say that with certainty. It could be that he routed his trip through the Netherlands as a way to get into the U.S. Besides, anyone can buy a fake passport on the black market in any country in the world."

He paused and shook his head. "Even if we take what you found in the attic as true—that it is evidence of some link to what has happened—it still doesn't explain why the killer's accomplice would take Rose and not ask for a ransom. Why would he want to keep her?"

Nora brushed her hair back from her eyes and set the wineglass back onto the coffee table—hard. She had to keep her voice modulated, although her anger threatened to destroy the composure she had maintained so far. "Surely they must know something about the judgment out of The Hague condemning my father to death for killing this Abram Rosen."

"Again, they are looking into it. It seems that the bureaucracy over there is even slower than ours. I'm sorry, but this is going to take more time. You're going to have to be patient while we run all the traps. I know how you feel, but—"

She pointed a shaking finger at him and felt herself lose control. "Don't tell me how I feel! It isn't *your* daughter who was taken by some maniac almost a week ago! You aren't sitting here day after day, only to be told that the police—and the goddamned *F-B-I*—haven't found a single lead about who murdered your mother or whether your daughter is dead or alive!"

Marijke sat down next to Nora and patted her arm. "Shh," she whispered. "You have to stay calm. It won't help to get angry. We're all trying to help." She tried to take Nora's hand.

Nora shook it off. "No! I won't stay calm. I've been calm for almost six days! We finally have some connection to this nightmare and I want something done about it—now!"

Richards shook his head. Nora could tell her words had affected him, because both of his eyes were twitching madly. His voice, however, was smooth and low. "Nora, every possible line has been thrown into the water. We're doing the best we can. It's still far too early to write off the possibility of a ransom call. I've seen other cases where the kidnapper has let time pass to increase the panic and terror of the family in order to demand more money."

Nora stalked to the corner of the room. She took a deep breath, turned and then fixed on Richards. Her voice was deadly. "You know as well as I do that if we were going to get a ransom call, the son of a bitch would have contacted us before now. I told you that at my mother's funeral." Her throat felt thick and dry as she said her next words. "Every day that passes means it is more likely that Rose is gone for good—or dead."

"I can't tell you whether Rose is alive or not," he said softly. "What I can tell you is that we're following established police protocol for the murder and kidnapping. Everything has been done by the book. The course you want us to follow in the Netherlands will take a long time, if it turns up anything at all."

Nora sagged in her chair. He actually had said it. *I can't tell you if Rose is alive.* She could barely breathe. *Oh, God, now they're losing hope. Otherwise, he would never say that.* She forced herself to go on.

"That's exactly my point! This man—whoever he was—obviously went to a lot of trouble to falsify his passport, fly here and kill my mother. Don't you find it the least bit relevant that my parents lied about who they were, that my mother seems to have been a Dutch Nazi, and that my father apparently killed this Abram Rosen? Can you honestly sit there and tell me you don't believe that connecting those dots must be pursued?"

"I don't know, Nora. But the gist of your questions relates to the distant past. Even if we find your answers, it still doesn't get us any farther down the road to finding out why Rose was kidnapped. With the killer dead and no way to question him or to know his motive, can you understand how very tough it is for us to identify the kidnapper?"

Nora fell silent. What he said made sense. Her heart just

didn't—wouldn't—hear it. "But how could the kidnapper manage to be in the house and leave absolutely no trace?" she asked. "Surely there are fibers, fingerprints—something you can go on."

"As I told you before, the only fingerprints we found are your mother's and yours. And as I also told you, the killer's accomplice probably wore gloves." He sighed. "The latents haven't panned out. With respect to the fibers, there's nothing unusual. Carpet, clothing—nothing foreign."

Nora put her head in her hands. Every hour without hope exhausted her. She forced herself to meet Richards's eyes. He looked like Nora felt when she lost her first patient.

"As for your theory that the killer was an assassin or that your parents were the target of a revenge killing…"

"Go on."

Richards shook his head in a sad way. "Nora, it's too far-fetched. It's thirty years after the war. Who would wait that long?"

He paused, as if waiting for her to say something. When she didn't, he went on. "And if the killer was an assassin, why would a war crimes organization bother with one Dutchman who killed one Jew? I know it sounds harsh, but it isn't like your father was Eichmann or Goebbels."

Nora shook her head and stared at the wall. She knew that her connections were woven with the slimmest of reeds, but it was all she had. And now he was telling her that she was crazy. She felt tears fill her eyes.

Richards walked toward her slowly, as if approaching a deer that might take flight. She did not move as he walked behind her and placed a hand gently on her shoulder. His voice was even softer than before, a silken thread she felt a sudden urge to snap.

"Even if everything in those documents is true," he said

quietly. "Even if someone came back thirty years later to kill your mother, which sounds crazy to everyone but you, it still doesn't explain why, or who would take your daughter and keep her."

Nora turned and looked at him squarely. "You think she's dead already."

Richards dropped his hands and shook his head. "I'm not ready to say that."

"That's precisely what you're saying! We keep coming back to the same place. What other leads do you have? *None!* If you're telling me that I'm supposed to sit here by the telephone for weeks waiting for some idiotic ransom call and for all of those bullshit agencies to get their heads out of their asses, then you've got another think coming." She crossed her arms and glared at him. "I won't do it."

Richards stood where he was, his mouth slightly open. Nora whirled around and tried to compose herself. As her fury subsided, a plan suddenly bloomed. She took a breath. *Damn! Why hadn't she thought of it sooner?*

She turned back to Richards and heard the words shoot from her mouth. "You can all go to hell. I'm going to handle this myself."

12

As soon as Richards left, Nora marched into her bedroom and began pulling clothes from her drawers and throwing them wildly into a suitcase. She pushed aside her dresses and retrieved a heavy leather jacket. She yanked it off the hanger and threw it onto the bed.

Marijke appeared, her eyes wide with surprise. "What are you doing?"

Nora held up a pair of winter pants. "I wonder if these will be warm enough."

"Nora! Are you out of your mind? You know you have to stay here. There's nothing to be done. You heard Richards."

Nora folded the pants and stuffed them into her bag. "And I told both of you that I'm going to handle this myself." She saw the hurt in Marijke's eyes and then sat on the bed, patting the place next to her. Marijke sat and crossed her arms. "I know you think I'm insane, too," said Nora. "But I had a brainstorm while we were talking."

Marijke pointed at Nora's suitcase. "And what does that have to do with getting on an airplane?"

Nora smiled. She felt calmer than she had since that first hellish day. "I have a plan. I don't know why I didn't think of it days ago." She paused. "I'm going to Amsterdam—to RIOD."

"RIOD?"

Nora nodded. RIOD was the *Rijksinstituut voor Oorlogsdocumentatie,* the Dutch Institute for War Documentation. It was where Nico worked. "If there are any answers to be found, that's where they'll be."

Marijke sat silently. Nora noted her furrowed brow, but ignored it as she walked into the bathroom and gathered her toiletries. She walked to the bed and threw them into her bag. She wouldn't meet Marijke's eyes. She couldn't let anyone or anything deter her. Glancing now at the contents of her suitcase, she spoke quickly. "Thanks to Nico, I know every nook and cranny of that place, how it's organized, how to do the research—"

Marijke stood, put her hand on Nora's arm and held it fast. "What about your job?"

"I've got one week left of the two Bates promised me. I'll ask for another. That should give me enough time."

"Nora, I have something I must say." Marijke's voice was firm, laced with impatience. "I'm trying to help you get through this. Please know I can't even imagine how horrible this is for you, but you're completely losing control." She paused. "You're heading off on a wild-goose chase because you're terrified that if you don't do something—anything—you may have to accept that Rose may not be coming back."

"That's not true!"

Marijke shook her head. "At this point I have to agree with the lieutenant. You have to let him do his job. Regardless of what you now discover about your parents, how will any of that be either relevant or discovered in time to do Rose any good? We need to focus completely on the kidnapper right now—nothing else." Marijke sat on the bed and stared at Nora, waiting for a response.

Nora felt bitterly disappointed. It was one thing for Richards to think she was crazy, but if Marijke believed she was completely off base, then was she? Her mind spun. Yes, she knew what she was proposing was a long shot, but how could she accept that the solution was to sit and do nothing? If the ransom call came, they could contact her in Amsterdam as quickly as in Houston. She had given Richards her bank information the first day in the event a ransom demand was made and she wasn't available. Now she would further instruct the bank in writing that he was authorized to withdraw up to twenty thousand dollars. It was almost everything she had as a young doctor, but once her mother's estate was probated, there would be more. For Rose, she would beg, borrow or steal.

No, she had to go with her gut. "I'm sorry you feel that way. I hoped that at least you would believe in me."

Marijke shook her head. "Of course I believe in you! I believe that you're a wonderful mother who is grasping at anything that might, but won't, help her deal with a terrible situation."

"Marijke, you don't have children. You have no idea what this is like."

"You're right, and that is precisely my point. I bring a different, more logical perspective to bear on this. And I believe that the lieutenant is correct." She paused. "But let's put that aside. Tell me what you hope to accomplish with this plan of yours."

Nora zipped up her suitcase. She knew now what Marijke's real question was. "Yes, I'm going to call him."

"Who?"

"You know very well who." Nora reached under the bed and retrieved a long pair of boots.

"Nico?"

"Yes, Nico. He's the only one who can help me." Nora felt Marijke's eyes searching hers. "Listen, I haven't told you the truth about some important things."

Marijke stood, took Nora by the hand and led her into the living room. She pushed Nora gently onto the couch and walked to the small bar. She took two crystal jiggers, went to the freezer in the kitchen and brought back a bottle of Dutch *genever*. Nora felt she was back in another time, another life. *Holland. Nico. Dinner and drinks with friends.* She lost herself in that until Marijke put the ice-cold glass into her hand. Each raised a glass to the other. *"Proost,"* they said, and took the first bracing sip.

Marijke settled back into one corner of the couch, facing Nora. "So," she said. "What don't I know? You and Nico lived together for two years in Amsterdam. I know that—I introduced you."

Nora felt the cold gin slide down her throat and send out waves of warmth to her body. "What else did you know?"

Marijke shrugged. "I didn't see you two that often, you know. I was busy working on my thesis on the effect of European economics on the Netherlands so I could *promoveren*. All I knew was that you were doing an advanced fellowship in pediatric surgery and when the job in Houston opened up for you, you two broke up."

Nora nodded. It still hurt to think back on those agonizing weeks. She had tried again and again to persuade Nico to investigate the possibility of moving to Houston. Like the stubborn Dutchman he was, he refused to even consider it. His life was in Amsterdam at RIOD. He was determined to

become its director general. He believed that he had no serious prospects in the States.

Nora looked up at Marijke. "And," she said slowly, "you
knew that he wanted me to stay in Holland, get married and
have babies."

"I knew he wanted to marry you. It was obvious. He was
so in love with you and, from what I could tell, you adored
him. What I didn't know was that children were an issue."

Nora grabbed the *genever* and poured another shot. "*Jezus,*
Marijke, I was so naive. As crazy as it sounds now, I thought
I didn't want marriage or children. If I had agreed to stay in
Holland, it meant that I virtually had to do college and medi-
cal school all over again. Nine years! I felt I had no choice. I
had to go back to the States. That was where my future lay."
She sipped at her drink, reliving those endless nights of argu-
ing and pleading.

"So," said Marijke. "You broke up."

Nora nodded, the heartbreak fresher than she thought it
could be. "We agreed to part. And we did."

Marijke curled up on the couch and shook her head. "So
what didn't you tell me?"

Nora hesitated, her heart still heavy with the guilt of non-
disclosure, particularly toward so wonderful a friend. "Do
you remember when I called you from Houston a few months
after I got back?"

"Of course. That's when you told me you had gotten pregnant—a one-night stand with some resident at the hospital."

Nora put her glass down. Her eyes met Marijke's. "That
was a lie."

"What do you mean?"

"The baby," Nora whispered, as Rose's blue eyes and soft
red curls filled her mind's eye.

"*Kom nou,*" said Marijke. "What is it?"

Nora felt as if the world had dropped out beneath her feet. She took a long, ragged breath.

"Rose." Her breath was a whisper on the wind. "She is Nico's daughter."

13

Marijke looked stunned. "I can't believe you never told me this."

Nora felt miserable at Marijke's rebuke. "I'm sorry."

"Then why?"

"Because it was too painful," Nora blurted. "When Nico wouldn't come to Houston with me, it broke my heart. Then to discover that I was pregnant with his baby—it was too much. I couldn't bear to talk about it. Only my mother knew."

"That's crazy! How could you have his baby and not even tell him?" Marijke stood up and paced. Finally she stopped. "*Ach,* Nora, he had the right to know. Then he could have made his own decision."

Nora felt the same torment she always had when she reflected upon that fateful decision. "I thought about it, really I did. In fact, I thought of little else during those nine long months." She turned her palms up. "Do you think it was an easy decision? But I finally came to the conclusion that it was better. To make a fresh start. To raise Rose on my own."

"But Nora, I know him. He would have found a way for the two of you to be together."

"No. I refused to have him come to America simply because I was going to have a baby. He had made his position crystal clear. He had no intention of ever living here, even though I had been offered the opportunity of a lifetime, what I had always strived for." Just talking about it made her heart ache. "I had no other choice." The bitterness in her stomach felt like burnt sticks. "And he was willing to let us break up, refusing to even check out what he might be able to do here so we could stay together."

She gave Marijke a pleading look. "Please understand. I didn't want to trap him with Rose. If he had decided to come here for me, that would have been different." She stared across the room. "So when I left, I accepted that he was never going to be part of my life. I didn't want Rose to grow up confused, shuttling back and forth to Holland, never having a normal home."

Marijke sat back and crossed her arms. Nora saw the stubbornness in her eyes that she felt in herself. *The Dutch,* she thought, *we are a hopeless breed.*

"You were afraid. You wanted Rose all to yourself."

"I—I don't know." She was so exhausted she didn't know what to think.

Marijke slapped her hands on her thighs and then slid the phone across the coffee table to Nora. "Call him." Her voice was unyielding. "Now."

"I will."

"And tell him about Rose? That she is his daughter and in terrible danger?"

"No, just that my daughter has been kidnapped and that I

need his help to find her. I wouldn't even ask that of him if I didn't have to, but I have no choice." She sighed. "But I worry how bitter he may still be about the breakup."

"Nora, look at me."

"What?"

"I have also not been truthful with you. When you asked me never to speak of Nico again after you left, I honored that. Now I have to tell you something, as well."

Nora felt a sudden dread. "What?" she asked. "Is he sick?"

"No, nothing like that."

"Tell me!"

"He's married."

Pain slashed through Nora. "When?"

"Six months ago."

Nora was stunned. *Nico—married?* She had never expected that. At least not so soon. How could he—not even two years since he had told her he loved her more than anyone he had ever known? Obviously he hadn't. A metallic taste filled her mouth, as if she had bitten down on a piece of copper. She looked up at Marijke. "Is he...happy?"

"I don't know. I don't keep in touch with him. He avoids me since you left—probably too unpleasant for him. But I do know that he is now the Director of RIOD." She pointed at the phone. "So call him."

Nora opened a drawer in the coffee table. After digging around, she found her old address book and flipped through it. Her heart raced when she saw his home number. Probably wasn't the same now. Or a woman would answer. *Could she take that?*

No, she would call RIOD. She could reach him there. She prepared herself to be neutral, yet friendly. It didn't matter how she felt. She had to beg for his help. She looked at her watch. Nine in the morning, 4:00 p.m. in Holland. She placed the call through the overseas operator. It rang twice before a male voice came through.

"*Met* Leo van Es—RIOD."

Nora cleared her throat and forced her voice to sound professional. "May I speak with Dr. Nico Meijer, *alstublieft?*"

She heard a hesitation and the sound of papers rustling. "I am very sorry, *Mevrouw,* but Dr. Meijer is currently on vacation."

Nora's heart leaped, relieved not to have to speak to him, but that feeling vanished as fear replaced it. "When will he be back?"

Another rustling of paper. "Not until next week at the earliest."

"Do you have a number where he can be reached? It is very important that I speak with him."

"No, *Mevrouw.* Dr. Meijer did not leave a contact number."

She should have known. Nico never left a number when on vacation. Time away was sacrosanct. Besides, the history of Holland during the Second World War could hardly be perceived by anyone as an emergency. Except now, she thought. A vision leaped into her mind—Nico with his new wife in Italy or Greece, laughing, probably staying at the same hotels they had stayed in, making love…

"*Mevrouw?*"

"I'm sorry," she said quickly. "I have a very urgent research matter I wonder if you could help me with." She explained that she needed to obtain information about an Abram Rosen, killed near the end of the war, as well as the identities and activities of a few persons living in Amsterdam at the same time. She gave the clerk both names used by her parents.

"And how quickly do you require this information?" Nora heard surprise in his voice. *Why is this so urgent?* he must be thinking.

"Immediately."

"I'm afraid not," he said, finality clear in his voice. "We have only a very small staff here. Are you familiar with how we work?"

"Yes, I know all about that." She had, after all, lived with Nico for two years. He so often had complained about the problems at the *Instituut,* from the bickering of the historians who formed the board to the antiquated manner in which the documents had been cataloged.

The clerk's voice broke through her thoughts. "Of course, if your research is so important, you are always welcome to come here yourself."

Nora stifled a groan. She had hoped to persuade Nico to order that the research be done quickly so when she arrived in Amsterdam, she could follow up on any leads. "I live in the U.S.," she said. "Traveling is difficult for me at the moment. Isn't there any way you can help me?"

"I'm afraid not. Perhaps you could let us know when you can come and I will be happy to set up an appointment for you."

"If I did come, could I at least depend upon some assistance from your staff?"

"Of course," he said. "One of our *medewerkers* would be pleased to help you."

"Very well. I'll make my travel plans."

Marijke shook Nora's arm. "What are you doing!" she hissed.

Nora held a hand over the mouthpiece. "Not now."

The clerk was still talking. "So let us know when we can expect you. There is one proviso. Dr. Meijer recently made a new policy for access to the *Instituut*. You must present proper credentials."

"What kind of credentials?"

"Graduate students and professors of universities, noted historians and others we approve on a case-by-case basis."

"My understanding is that the public has open access to RIOD. It is supposed to be an educational tool for those interested in the time period."

"Yes, it has always been so," he said, "but now we must carefully monitor those who enter due to the alarming increase by certain factions who are attempting to establish a new Dutch Nazi party." He cleared his throat. "We have had disturbances, thefts of historical documents, particularly those pertaining to the NSB." He paused. "Do you know about the NSB?"

"Yes," said Nora, trying to fight off the image of her mother in her drab NSB uniform cheering at Hitler rallies.

"May I ask if you fall into one of the categories to whom we offer access?" asked the clerk.

"Yes, I do. I am a professor of European Studies from Stanford University, specializing in the Netherlands during the Second World War." She gave Marijke a sidelong glance and saw shock on her face. She pressed the receiver against her chest. "Marijke—not now," she whispered. She spoke again into the receiver. "I can be there day after tomorrow. I will most likely arrive at the *Instituut* before noon."

"Perfect." Nora could hear the relief in his voice. He was ready to get rid of her. "Your name, please?"

"Professor Aantje van Doren."

"*Tot gauw,* Dr. van Doren."

"Yes." She heard flatness in her voice. "Until then."

14

"You're going where?"

"Amsterdam."

"Why?"

Nora explained her plan.

"That's crazy!" Richards's voice blasted through the receiver. "You're chasing ghosts!"

"No, I'm not. There has to be a connection and I'm going to find it."

"Nora, the investigation is here, not in Holland. You have to be patient, not run off halfway around the world. I know you're afraid—"

"You're damned right I'm afraid. I'm not going to sit here doing nothing while the only lead we've got is to find Abram Rosen and why this madness happened!"

"At best all you'll learn is if your parents were Nazis. It won't get us any closer to finding Rose!"

"But you haven't come up with anything."

"You have to give me time," he said. "I've put the investigation at the top of my list. The goddamned FBI is coordinating with the Dutch. What can you possibly find that they can't?"

"I have to do this," she said softly. "What if it were your daughter?"

He didn't miss a beat. "Then I would do exactly what I'm telling you now. And what if the kidnapper calls? Are you at least leaving your friend here to handle that?"

"No, she has to go back to work. One of your female officers can respond to the tapped line."

"And if something happens here?"

"I can be home in ten hours."

"Damn it, at least leave me a number where I can reach you."

"I will. Please don't be angry." All she heard was a dial tone.

She hung up and turned to Marijke. "Let's go."

15

When Ariel finally emerged from Customs, juggling his carry-on and Rose, he saw Leah and smiled. Leah waved and rushed toward him. Then she saw the baby and stood rooted, a hand clapped to her mouth. Ariel walked over and placed Rose in her arms.

"Ariel!" she gasped. "Whose baby is this?"

Ariel put his arm around her, kissed her and then Rose. "She's ours."

Holding the baby awkwardly but tightly, Leah collapsed onto a chair. She pushed the yellow blanket back and stared at Rose, then Ariel, then Rose again. The baby began to cry. Leah cooed and kissed her until Rose nestled into her arms. When Leah looked up, tears fell like prisms from her eyes. Ariel sat next to her and told the bizarre story, the brutal murder, Isaac's death and his last wish.

When he finished, Leah shook her head. "Ariel, we have

to give her back! We can't steal another woman's child!" She kissed Rose on the forehead. "Oh, God, I wish we could."

Ariel cringed at the naked longing in her voice. She shook her head. "We have to go to the police."

"We can't, sweetheart. Do you want them to arrest and deport me? Throw me in jail for the rest of my life?"

"Of course not!" she cried. "But you have to find a way to give her back to her mother. It isn't right."

"Okay, we'll talk about it later. All I want now is to go home. I can barely stand up." He grasped Leah's elbow as they walked outside to the taxis.

"But what about Amarisa?" asked Leah. "She's waiting at the apartment. What will you tell her?"

"I'll worry about that when we get there." Ariel hailed a cab and they got in. He roused himself a bit as the taxi whizzed through the narrow cobblestone streets. When they approached their apartment, a different dread filled him. *Oh, God. Amarisa. How do I tell her?*

He paid the taxi, got his luggage and looked at Leah. Rose was sleeping. "I want you to take the baby and leave for half an hour."

"But why? I need to take care of her."

"Because of Amarisa. When I tell her that Papa is dead, she'll go berserk."

Leah jiggled Rose and shook her head. "But where will I go?"

"To the *Bijenkorf*. Buy her what she needs—clothes, blankets, anything I've forgotten."

"All right," she said uncertainly.

Ariel kissed her and touched Rose lightly on her cheek. "Don't worry, I'll take care of everything." He watched Leah amble down the street like any mother out with her baby for a morning walk, except she had no stroller. He took a deep breath, unlocked the door and went inside.

"Isaac?" His aunt ran into the foyer, pushed Ariel aside, flung open the door and looked frantically down the street. "Isaac! Where are you?" She whirled back to Ariel, her dyed black hair wild around her face. "Where is he? Where's your father!"

"Please, Amarisa, come and sit in the living room. We have to talk."

"Talk to me here!"

Ariel hung his head. "Papa is…dead."

"Dead!" She clutched her throat and staggered. "That's impossible!"

"Oh, God, Amarisa, I'm so sorry to have to tell you this way."

She backed up against the wall, her face ground chalk. Even her grotesque scar seemed whitewashed. "No, no, *no*—"

He gently grasped her arm. She twisted away. "Don't touch me!" Suddenly her legs buckled and she sank to the floor, wailing. Ariel knelt next to her and put his arms around her. She kicked him away and then struggled to her feet, shaking. Ariel couldn't tell if she was driven by grief or rage.

Although petite, she grabbed his arm with her talons, shoved him into the living room and pushed him onto the sofa. "Tell me—tell me what happened!"

Ariel felt the terror she always incited in him, like a small child who knew he was to be beaten just for being alive. "He tortured that Brouwer woman and then killed her!"

Her eyes were cruel slits, her voice hissing coal. "I knew he would kill her."

"But then he had a heart attack…" He choked up.

She slapped him—hard. "You little son of a bitch! How could you let this happen?"

Ariel rubbed his stinging cheek. "Please, Amarisa, listen to me. There's more."

She sat down, took a cigarette out of a silver case studded with diamonds, lit it and inhaled deeply. "Speak."

He saw Amarisa staring at him like a judge at Nuremberg. The tears on her face had dried, the ropy scar back to its hideous purple. While he talked, she stubbed out her cigarette and paced from one end of the sofa to the other.

When he finished, he stood and tried to put his arms around her again. But she came at him with her fists, punching his chest, his face. "You should have done something! Given him his nitro—it's always in his pocket—taken him to the hospital!"

He pulled back. "Stop! It won't help. He's dead and there's no way we can bring him back."

Amarisa collapsed on the nearest chair, her head in her hands, and wailed. Ariel had never heard such sounds, as if she were being eviscerated before his very eyes. He did not try to approach her again. After what seemed like hours, her sobs subsided. Her dark eyes smoldered. "But he killed that bitch?" Ariel nodded. "Well, I'm glad for that. I only wish I'd done it myself!"

Ariel sat on the couch. "There's more."

"More!"

"Yes. There's the baby—Anneke's grandchild."

A harsh laugh. "Why would I give a damn about the spawn of that traitorous bitch?"

"Because." His voice was a hoarse croak. "She is Abram's granddaughter."

Amarisa was speechless. Her dark eyes widened and her jaw dropped. Red rage flooded her face. "That lying whore! She ran off with that sniveling Nazi boyfriend of hers." She stood and grabbed her purse. "Whoever the father was, it wasn't Abram."

"Isaac thought it was," he whispered.

She stomped over to him. "What do you mean?"

He screwed up the courage to stare into the molten hatred of her eyes. "Papa made me promise to take the baby with me, to raise her as a Jew. It was his final wish."

She turned away, her body sagging. "This is too much... too much."

Ariel cringed at her grief and the frailty of her thin shoulders as she sobbed. He waited for her to stop. "Amarisa."

When she finally turned, she seemed to have aged twenty years. Her eyes were flat, her spine stooped. Ariel thought of an old, sick lion, abandoned by its pride to perish alone. "So what more do you want from me?"

"I have the child," he whispered.

"What?"

"Leah is bringing her home soon. I wanted to talk to you first."

"But how did you—"

"Never mind."

Something like hope flickered now in her eyes. "What is her name?"

"Jacoba."

16

―――

"Wilt U iets drinken of eten, mevrouw?"

"Nee, dank U wel." There was no way she could eat a bite. Groggy from the ten-hour plane ride amid intermittent and frightening dreams, Nora managed a smile for the engaging blonde stewardess offering orange juice and coffee, a good Dutch *broodje* and a cold slab of Dutch butter. She glanced at the headlines of the paper the stewardess had handed her. *Americans Taken Hostage in Tehran! Carter Holds First Press Conference. Vows To Bring Them Home.* She couldn't read any further. It should be Rose's disappearance that was sprawled across every headline! She lifted the window shade and stared down at the gray dawn breaking over the land. She felt her gloom lift.

It was how she always felt during the approach to Schiphol. Holland, even from the air, felt like home. Small squares of land, each centimeter of fertile polder put to purpose. Fields of green, flowers ripening under the rich earth and white-and-black cows lying together in the deep, green grass—looking like a swirl of chocolate-and-vanilla ice cream from the sky.

They dropped toward the runway at Schiphol Airport. She heard the wheels descend and then felt the satisfying bump as they landed. It was dark and rainy. Nora thought that the most boring job in the Netherlands was to be a weatherman. The forecast always the same. Rain, rain and more rain.

She turned to Marijke, who was still sleeping in the seat across from her, and tapped her shoulder. "Wake up, we're here," she whispered.

Marijke, her blond hair tousled, opened one eye and looked at her. "You know I always wanted you to come back and visit, but this isn't what I had in mind."

"Not my plan, either." Nora smiled. "But we're here now and I have the feeling we're going to find something. You think so, too, don't you?"

Marijke did not respond, suddenly busy putting her books and papers into her carry-on. Nora felt a sudden keening. *Where was Rose? Why wasn't she in her arms so she could wrap her more tightly in her blanket when she cried or plant soft kisses on her velvet cheeks?* No, *no.* She had to avoid such forays into her hyperactive imagination. They paralyzed her ability to think keenly, and that she couldn't afford. Most important, her fantasies didn't help Rose and Nora's instinct told her that only she could help her baby now.

She had called Bates from the Houston airport. He had reluctantly extended her leave for another week. The intimation was that she better be back by then or he would have to let her go.

She and Marijke stood in line for Immigration. The wait was maddening. It was never quick, but today it seemed as if flights from every country in the world had arrived at the same time. Nora finally reached the red line painted on the floor that meant she was next. After a few moments, the *douane* motioned her forward. Nora paid no attention to him other than to hand over her passport. She saw Marijke in line a few rows over and smiled at her. Marijke rolled her eyes.

"Are you in Amsterdam for business or pleasure?"

"Pleasure." If she had said business, she'd have had to explain what kind and answer other annoying questions she had no time for. She reached to take back her passport, but the *douane* shook his head and then looked up at her.

"Is there a problem?"

He stared at her, then looked down at her passport, turning its pages.

"I'm sure everything is in order and I'm in a hurry."

"Just one moment, please." He spoke with the stiff, authoritative voice of all petty officials. "Where will you be staying?"

Nora was surprised. She'd never been asked that. "With a friend," she said curtly.

"Address?"

"Is that necessary?" He just gave her a look that said he held all the cards. She shrugged. "Prinsengracht 353." He gave her another piercing look, copied the photograph page of her passport and then waved her through.

Nora hurried to meet Marijke at the exit. After a short tram ride, Nora stepped out onto the wet cobblestones and lugged her suitcase up the steep stairs to Marijke's flat, with Marijke huffing behind her. Fortunately, Marijke lived on the first floor, which in Holland meant the second. When Nora was last here, Marijke had lived in a four-story walkup. *"Godverdomme,"* Marijke cursed as she struggled with the lock. "Why do I live in an old canal house? I could be in the country with a rich husband and two children."

Nora put her bags down and walked to the large bay window in the living room. Outside people passed by with shoulders hunched against the wind, their feet sometimes slipping on the wet cobblestones. Looking past them, Nora saw the canal, its brown water flowing quietly by, interrupted by a guide blaring out the history of Amsterdam on yet another endless city boat tour. Nora smiled and pointed. "If you moved away, you wouldn't have this."

"Ja, ja." Marijke stood next to her. "You're right. I'm too set in my ways to change now."

After Nora unpacked in the small guest bedroom, Marijke insisted that she have a cup of tea and a *broodje* before she rushed off to the *Instituut*. Nora knew it would be useless to refuse. The Dutch believed that unless one fortified oneself constantly with coffee, tea or a heavy meal, one ran a risk of starvation, even if walking only from the Prinsengracht to the nearby Herengracht, where the *Instituut* was located.

"Why don't we call some of your friends?"

Nora thought of Fina, Gertrude, Liesbet. Fina laughing at parties, walking with Gertrude in the Vondelpark, the pleasant hours spent with Liesbet sifting through the flea markets. And there was Jan Brugger, her old boss. She shook her head. "What could they do?"

"They could give you moral support. Who knows how else they could help?"

"Fina is a lawyer, Gertrude is an insurance agent and Liesbet runs an employment agency."

"Don't you want to see them?"

"Not now. I can't spare time away from the *Instituut*."

"I could invite them to dinner."

"Marijke, it would seem like a homecoming party. While Rose is lost out there, I just can't deal with it."

"Perhaps later."

"Maybe." She smiled. "Besides, you're all the moral support I need."

"Tell me if you change your mind."

"I will." Nora finished the *broodje ham* quickly and stood. "It's time."

Marijke nodded. "I'm staying here. At least I still have a job."

"You're not serious?"

"You didn't hear me on the phone with the university president?"

"No."

Marijke winked. "I told him that I had contracted a terrible case of rare American flu that was highly contagious."

Nora laughed. "Let me guess. He begged you to stay away."

"Alders, in his heart of hearts, believes that all air travel is life threatening."

"And your mother?"

"I'll check in with her now that I have the plague."

Nora gave Marijke a quick hug. "Time to go."

"Good luck."

Tension snaked through Nora's body. Marijke must have seen it. She gave Nora another hug. *"Hou je sterk,"* she whispered.

Nora tried to reply, but the words stuck in her throat. *Whatever she found, would she be strong enough to face it?*

17

Shortly after his return to Amsterdam, Ariel sat at his station in the Immigration area behind a high white desk surrounded on three sides by glass. He faced a flood of passengers who had to be cleared before they could leave Schiphol and walk into Amsterdam. He had been an agent for so long that his mind today, as on most days, was on autopilot.

He thought about his life. He had always wanted to become a musician. His lifelong hobby had been playing the saxophone in jazz bands around Amsterdam. He had desperately wanted to study at the music conservatory and had asked Isaac to contribute part of the tuition. All he got was the skeptical, stubborn look Isaac had given him when he spoke of his future. *No*, Isaac had said. *I've been an immigration officer all my life. Isn't that good enough for you? Haven't I always provided for my family?* In the end, Ariel followed in his father's footsteps but castigated himself for his weakness. He had tried to keep playing with the band, but it meant late nights and lousy pay, and when he married Leah, he gave it up. Last year he had given his saxophone to a friend. It felt as if he had cut off his arm.

At least he had kept up his martial arts. It gave him a physical outlet and the grueling bouts reassured him that he was strong, that he did have some control, that he could use it if he needed it. It also gave him respite from mourning Isaac and the awful fear he felt about being found out and losing Rose. The only other thing he still did outside work was coach a Little League soccer team with Peter, his best friend and brother-in-law. He wanted so badly to confide in someone, to tell him about Rose, Isaac's murder, the whole mess. The pressure he felt was maddening. Maybe Peter could just listen. He had discussed it with Leah, but they had agreed not to tell anyone.

How could Ariel risk it? No, they first had to settle into their new life with Rose and let some time pass until he felt that he would not be found, arrested, jailed. *God, he couldn't think about it anymore!* Instead, he remembered the small trips he and Leah had taken around Holland, walking and occasionally visiting the graveyards of important writers. Both were well-read and, odd as it seemed, they enjoyed looking at the tombstones, which often revealed personal tidbits about the authors. But now Leah was consumed with taking care of Rose and had little time for him.

So he had spent the days since his return in boredom, looking at passports, checking that the face matched the photo and ensuring that the passenger was not on the daily list of criminals or those trying to sneak into the Netherlands illegally. Over the years, he had caught a number of such types, smiling calmly at them while he pressed the security button under his desk. The reaction when the guard arrived was always the same. *Who? Me? There must be a mistake!*

Ariel would shake his head. Did they really believe that, in 1980, the international immigration systems were blind?

But there was always someone who thought he could beat the system.

As he went through the motions, beckoning passengers, checking and then waving them through, Ariel thought about Leah. His heart lifted. Every touch of Rose's skin, every burbly smile, brought a look of delight to Leah's face that he had never seen before. As the days passed, a silent agreement unfolded between them. She did not ask him what he had done to try to return Rose and he didn't raise the subject.

But Amarisa had increasingly taken over. She demanded that Rose spend every other day with her. She did not disclose what she did with the child, but every time they returned, Rose sported a new outfit. Amarisa always seemed to be on the hunt for some baby accessory, such as the speaker device that let Ariel or Leah hear her from the nursery. And now Amarisa gave them even more money each month and had bought them a used *Daf* so they wouldn't have to rely on public transportation if Rose got sick. Amarisa had given a large deposit to a prestigious preschool with a long waiting line. By the time Rose was old enough, she would have a place. Amarisa had also begun a college fund for her and intended to see that she was properly educated.

No matter how uncomfortable Ariel was with Amarisa's newfound generosity, he had to accept it. Leah had quit her job to care for Rose. Without Amarisa's bounty, they could never have stayed in Amsterdam, the most expensive city in Holland.

Amarisa had also insisted that she be responsible for drawing up legal documents that confirmed Rose was their legitimate daughter. She had made it clear that this was contingent upon their agreement that she be named as Rose's guardian with power of attorney over any decisions about Rose's future. Ariel had no idea how she did it, but within a week, Amarisa had handed him a passport in the name of "Jacoba Rachel Rosen," as well as a fake birth certificate. Ariel knew from Isaac that Amarisa dealt with shady characters in the diamond trade, but he had never asked for details and she never told.

Ariel had signed the papers. *What choice did he have?* She could blow the whistle on him any time she chose. Maybe if he curried her favor, she would let them have more say in Rose's life. *Would she try to take her from them?* Ariel couldn't bear to think about it.

When they first brought Rose home, Ariel had explained to their friends and neighbors that Jacoba had come to them by way of a private adoption. Everyone was thrilled for them. An impromptu baby shower had followed. Amarisa had insisted upon attending, grasping Rose tightly in her arms and glowering from the couch. For Ariel and Leah, the celebration made it real. They finally had a daughter.

He now brought his mind into the present. The next passenger walked from behind the red waiting line and handed him her passport. He looked at it briefly and raised his stamp. Then the name jumped out at him. *Nora de Jong.* His heart lurched as he looked up at the woman. *Could it be?*

He gripped the passport to keep his hands from shaking as he checked the date of birth. It fit. When he saw the Houston address, he felt sweat snake down the back of his neck. *The same fucking address! But Abram's daughter? What in hell was she doing here?*

He could barely breathe. *Had he made a mistake? Left a clue that led her to him? To Rose?* Now he stared at her. Tall and thin, her black hair thick and unruly—just like his. His cousin! Damn it, he thought he saw the resemblance—dark eyes, high cheekbones, the slight dimple of his father's chin. He looked down at the passport, but it swam before him. *God, what should he do?* When he looked up, he saw her eyes dart from him to the exit.

"Is there a problem, Officer?"

Ariel felt nauseous. He managed to clear his throat. "Are you here on business or pleasure?"

"Pleasure," she said.

He picked up a pen. "And where will you be staying?"

"In Amsterdam."

"Address, please?"

"Is that really necessary?"

He shrugged. "New security policy."

She shook her head. "Prinsengracht 353."

He nodded briskly, wrote down the address and made a copy of her passport photo. She seemed too distracted to notice that this was unusual. Finally he stamped her passport and watched her stride to collect her luggage. Another arriving passenger walked toward him. Ariel waved him over to an adjacent line and put the closed sign on his countertop. He signaled a colleague who was on break.

"Ron," he said hurriedly. "I just got a message that my father is ill. Could you take over for me?"

"Of course," he said. "I hope it's nothing serious."

Ariel hurriedly gathered his things, then looked at his colleague. "I'm afraid it's a matter of life and death."

He almost ran to the airport exit, breathing heavily, not from exertion but terror. *What could he do to keep her from finding him—and Rose? What if she already knew? He caught a tram and couldn't wait for the passengers to board.*

Was there a way he could frighten her enough to go home without revealing himself? And if that didn't work, what then?

18

Ariel slammed the door behind him. The apartment had never been such a welcome sight. The white couch against the window, the coffee table covered with magazines, the antique dining table. "Leah! Where are you?"

Leah came running from the nursery. "Shh! The baby is sleeping. What's wrong?"

Ariel tried to calm himself. "The baby's mother—she's here!"

Leah's eyes widened. "How do you know?"

"She came through Immigration. I saw her passport."

"But why—?"

"I don't know, but she must have found out something!"

"Oh, Ariel! Do you think she knows it was you? Will she be coming here? What do we do?"

Ariel pulled her down on the couch next to him. His hands were shaking. "I don't know. Maybe we should just take the baby and leave until we're sure she's gone."

"We have to give her back! The police could be on their way right now!

Ariel wanted to cry. "Is that what you want to do?"

"Of course not!" Tears slid down Leah's cheeks. "But we have to—I told you that."

"We don't know what she knows. Maybe I can find out, follow her, see what she's up to."

"What good will that do?"

Ariel vigorously shook his head, jumped up and paced the room. "I don't know. I have to come up with a plan. We can't just give her up. You love her, too, don't you?"

"Oh, God, of course I do."

"Then let's not panic. I'll get a leave from work and follow her. I have the address where she's staying. Maybe I can scare her off."

Leah glanced at her watch. "Amarisa! She'll be here any minute to pick up Rose. What do we tell her?"

"Nothing. Not until we know more."

"She'll be furious if she finds out we've kept this from her."

"God only knows what she'll do if she thinks the baby may be taken away. I can't deal with her right now. We'll act as if everything is fine."

Ariel heard Rose cry. Leah stood and wiped away her tears. "I don't know how you think you can scare her off. It's crazy." She hurried to the nursery.

Ariel collapsed on the couch, his head in his hands. *Now what? How in hell can I make this go away? I can't take Rose from Leah. It'll kill her. And where could we go? What would we live on?*

The doorbell rang. *"Shit."* When he opened the door, Amarisa pushed a new stroller into the foyer. It was sleek, navy blue, state-of-the-art.

"Look! I just bought this for my sweet little girl." Ariel would never get used to seeing Amarisa smile. She looked up at him when he did not reply. "Why are you here? Shouldn't you be working?"

"I…took a day off."

Her dark eyes narrowed as she studied him. "Something is wrong. What is it?"

"Nothing."

Leah walked into the room carrying Rose. Her eyes were red and tears rolled down her cheeks. "*Dag,* Amarisa."

Amarisa pushed the stroller against the wall, took Rose from Leah's arms and laid her gently down. The stroller was so deep Ariel couldn't even see Rose burrowed somewhere beneath the covers. Then Amarisa faced them both with her bony arms crossed. "*Vooruit.* I want to know what's going on. Is someone sick?"

"Everything is fine, Amarisa," said Ariel.

The old woman stared at Leah. "Talk."

A sob broke from Leah. "It's the baby—her mother—" She ran from the room.

Ariel started after her, but Amarisa grabbed his arm. "Don't make me get it out of her. You know I will."

He shook her off. "Damn it, it's none of your business."

"What is it about the mother?"

Ariel felt his shoulders sag. She would find out, anyway. "She's here. In Amsterdam."

She looked aghast, then turned hard. "Does she know you have Jacoba?"

"I don't know." He felt so fucking miserable. "Leah wants to give the baby back—"

"Absolutely not." Her words were whips. "She is our legacy, Abram's and Isaac's."

"But Amarisa, what can we do?" He hated his whining. *Why couldn't he stand up to her?*

Amarisa walked over to the stroller, leaned down and gave

Rose a soft kiss. When she straightened, she glared at Ariel. "*We* aren't going to do anything."

"What do you mean?"

"I'm taking Rose with me—permanently. I'll protect her, give her a wonderful home, nannies, private schools, a proper place in society. And I'll never let her forget her ancestry."

"You can't take her—she's ours!"

"Yours?" A harsh laugh. "The *kidnapper?* The accomplice to *murder?* Don't fuck with me, Ariel. If you so much as come near Jacoba, I'll call the police and tell them that you confessed to murdering that bitch and stealing her grandchild."

"You wouldn't! *Please, Amarisa—*"

"You pathetic coward," she sneered. "Where is the bitch staying?"

What would she do if he told her? "I don't know."

"You're lying! I can always tell. Your upper lip twitches."

Ariel pressed his lips together. "That's ridiculous."

Amarisa pointed a bony finger at him. "The address, you moron!"

"Go to hell, Amarisa! Why do you want it?"

"None of your business." She waved her arm around the room. "You want to keep this lovely apartment, don't you? The car? What a shame if it all suddenly disappeared."

Ariel felt the humiliation she always brought out in him. "Why do you want to know?"

"None of your business."

"No."

"Ariel, we're in this together. Just give me the address."

He sighed. "Prinsengracht 353."

"What is her name?"

"Nora de Jong," he said. "But what will you do? She may already know I took her. And if the police find me, I'll tell them where Rose is, where you are!"

"Surely you haven't forgotten how very rich I am," she hissed. "I have more than enough money to protect Jacoba from you and that woman. If necessary, I will take her out of the country. You'll never see her again."

"Please, Amarisa—"

"Shut up. Do you have a photo of her?"

Ariel turned away. "No."

"Idiot. Just give it to me."

"No, I won't!" He turned to Amarisa. "If you don't tell me what you're planning, I won't help you."

"What if she finds out where Rose is? Without a photo, how will I know what she looks like?"

Ariel hesitated and then walked to his desk and removed the copy of Nora's passport photo from the bottom drawer. He thrust it at her.

She snatched it, stuck it into a fold of Rose's blanket and then fixed him with a searing look. "Is there anything else you're lying about?"

"Leave me alone."

"What are you going to do, just sit here and wait to be arrested?"

"And what is your grand plan?"

She shook a bony finger at him. "Don't forget I know important people in this city. Judges, Cabinet ministers—they've all bought diamonds from me. All it would take is one phone call and you'd go to jail. And never see Rose again."

Ariel knew all she said was true. Amsterdam was the largest diamond center in the world. She had been in the trade for almost forty years and had forged relationships with people in high places. "Stop threatening me, Amarisa. I'm not your puppet."

"Just get rid of this woman!" she snapped.

"But how?"

"Use your brain. It's in there somewhere." She grabbed the stroller bar and flung open the door. Rose was sleeping, her little face barely peeping out of the soft pink blanket.

Ariel rushed toward them. "Give her to me!"

When he reached for the baby, Amarisa kicked him, whirled the stroller around and stormed out of the house.

Ariel stood there, cursing under his breath. *She had him. Like a fly snared in a black widow's web.* He grabbed his coat and ran out. He would follow Rose's mother and find out what she was up to. *And then, God help him, he'd find a way to get rid of her.*

19

Trams screeched by Nora, running so shockingly close to one another that she was amazed they didn't crash. The one she had been waiting for finally careened to a stop. Nora boarded with the rest of the commuters en route to the *Centrum*.

Her thoughts turned to the research she wanted to do at the *Instituut*. Nico had given her a number of books to read about Amsterdam during the war. She learned that by the end of 1941, Jews from the coastal regions of the Netherlands were forced to move to Amsterdam. By April 1943, Amsterdam was the only city Jews were permitted to live in.

She thought of Leo, a friend of Nico's, who had lived near the *Hollandsche Schouwburg*. As they had walked to his house for dinner one evening, Nico had pointed out the white stately building and told her that it had been an actor's playhouse used as the central roundup point for Amsterdam Jews during the war. Nora imagined entire families huddled and petrified as they lined up to register their names, addresses and businesses.

Little did they know that everything would be taken from them, including their lives.

Had her mother handed out yellow stars to terrified Jews as they were herded into the majestic building? Did she join her friends— Nazis and NSB-ers—who sat in full evening dress enjoying that night's play?

Nora had viewed old photographs depicting the *Schouwburg's* lovely cream edifice, where she read that the Jews were torn from their families, thrown in trucks like trash and hauled to *Centraal Station*. From there, they were herded onto freight trains, screaming promises to their families, who stood crying at the station, arms outstretched for one last touch, one last look. "Don't worry! We will write! We are only going to the work camps!" *Like Mauthausen. Like Auschwitz.*

But now Nora could not contain her excitement. *She finally was doing something for Rose. So what if she was deluding herself? It was better than sitting in Houston, terrified and frantic.*

So, deep in her thoughts, she missed the stop for the *Instituut* and wound up stepping out at the *Dam* in the *Centrum*. She fell in with the people who thronged the streets, giving the impression that no one worked. A warm feeling of belonging grew with each step.

She walked by *bruin* cafés, the dark, wonderfully narrow bars with sand thrown on the wooden floors. She caught a glimpse of weathered tables and old men, already cupping their small glasses of *genever* at nine in the morning. They would drink, smoke and watch the world go by for the rest of the day. She walked by the *Begijnhof,* a tiny convent in the middle of the city, a jeweled garden of silence cut off from the noise and crowds. Inside, she knew, were tiny rooms where now only the oldest nuns lived. Their walled enclave was suspended in time, a quiet patch of flowers, statues and grass in a city that kept changing around them. She walked into the *Spui,* a pleasant square not far from the *Dam* and passed the *Hoppe,* a café good for people-watching. Nico considered it too posh for the intellectuals with whom he surrounded himself. She continued past the *Singel* to the *Herengracht.*

Finally she stood in front of the *Instituut,* her heart gripped with excitement, fear—and pain. Excitement that there might be a real chance that she would uncover information that would lead her to Rose, pain because of Nico.

She looked up at the stone facade. Two enormous columns, complete with grimacing gargoyles, framed the entrance to the forbidding building. The broad entryway spanned twenty feet, enclosed by thick borders of intricate stone carvings arched over modern glass doors.

Nausea roiled in her stomach. *Was she crazy? What could she possibly find on this wild-goose chase?* She closed her eyes a moment and focused on Rose's blue, laughing eyes and her soft fingers curled around Nora's own. When she opened her eyes, she took a deep breath, gripped her purse and rang the bell. She heard a buzz and a click and stepped inside.

The male receptionist gave her a baleful glance from his desk behind a glass wall. They must have taken the neo-Nazi threats seriously. Was the glass bulletproof? She stepped up and spoke into the speaker. *"Goedemorgen,"* she said briskly. "Dr. Aantje van Doren."

"Goedemorgen, Doktor. Kan ik U helpen?" The uniformed man seemed to be at least six foot three, with broad shoulders and a completely bald head. The voice from the speaker was gruff and unfriendly.

Nora reached into her purse, pulled out a white envelope and held it up. The man pointed down at a small metal drawer. When it opened on her side, she placed the envelope into it and pressed the button. He took the envelope and studied it. This time he looked at her with what appeared to be respect.

Amazing what a piece of paper will get you, she thought, *even a fake one.* Before she left Houston, she had dug up an old letter of Nico's written on the *Instituut's* stationery, and had lifted the heading of it to compose a letter of recommendation for one "Dr. Aantje van Doren," a professor at Stanford University.

The man frowned. "I am very sorry, Dr. Van Doren, but were you not aware the Dr. Meijer is out of the country?" He slipped the letter back into its envelope and into the drawer.

"No, I was not," she lied. "But as the letter explains, I have important research I must accomplish in a very short period of time."

"Of course," he said briskly. He turned to a set of keys behind him, selected one and put it into the drawer. "You may put your things in a guest locker—to the left there." His voice assumed the tone of someone who repeated the same instructions day after day. "Guests are not permitted to bring anything into the main document room except a pencil and a notepad. Making copies of the documents is forbidden. If you go straight ahead you will come to the *medewerkers'* desk—our research assistants. I am certain that they will be able to help you."

"I have particular documents that I must have with me."

He frowned. "Put them into the drawer. I will have one of the *medewerkers* bring them to you."

Nora slid a sealed envelope into the drawer. "And the archives?"

"Yes," he said. "They are located in the basement. You will have to ask permission if you wish to see them." He gave her a deferential glance. "We are honored to have such an esteemed guest, Dr. van Doren."

"Thank you." Nora hoped that he did not see her hand shake as she slid the key from the metal drawer. Thankfully, not much about the *Instituut* other than the new security measures seemed to have changed, particularly the reflexive assumption that something like letterhead should be taken at face value.

She passed a wide staircase on the way to the document room. Everything was the same: the dark, intricately carved balustrade that led upstairs to the offices of the war experts; the thick red carpet on the stairs—as if for royalty. The faded antique rugs she remembered were gone. Harsh gray linoleum had replaced the rutilant hardwoods she had so admired. The high ceilings with their carved crown moldings seemed incongruous with the cold white walls and modern furnishings. Nora found it unsettling. It drove home how long it had been since her life with Nico.

She looked up the stairs and glimpsed the long hallway. Nora knew where Nico's office used to be. She wondered if he had taken over the former director's or kept his own. A pain sliced through her. *Why did he have to be gone the one time she needed him most? Well, she'd do it alone. Where Rose was concerned, hadn't she always been on her own?*

She took a pencil and pad out of her purse, put her purse in the locker and then slid the key into her pocket. She entered the research room, glanced around and chose a carrel tucked away under a stairwell. Before she could pull the small wooden chair out from under the desk, a young man—no more than twenty-five—appeared at her shoulder. She looked up, startled.

"Dr. van Doren? Mijn naam is Koos Dijkstra. Mag ik U helpen?" The receptionist must have told him her name. They shook hands. He held the envelope containing her documents and then studied her pencil and pad as if he suspected her of bringing contraband into the holy hall. *Maybe he'll frisk me, too.*

His eyes widened when he unfurled and read the judgment against her father. He shook his head, as if pitying her.

She opened the envelope and handed him her parents' passports and the rest of the documentation from the attic. He leafed through them. "What precisely are you researching, Dr. van Doren?"

Nora forced calm into her voice. "As my letter explained, as a professor, I make myself available to researchers in the academic world who are interested in my specialty, the Netherlands during the Second World War." She paused. He nodded. She took a breath and went on. "In this case, I received a strange request. A week ago, I was contacted by the police in Houston, Texas, where a Dutch woman was murdered and her granddaughter kidnapped."

Dijkstra's pimpled skin grew taut as his jaw dropped. *"Echt waar?"*

She removed the documents from the envelope and handed him her mother's passport. The young man glanced at it and nodded. Nora then passed him Anneke's NSB identification card and Hans's passport with their real surnames, *Brouwer* and *Moerveld.* "They were married in Holland shortly after the war, immigrated to the States and changed their names." He nodded. She saw a glint of excitement light his pale eyes as he grasped the import of the document.

"Has it been determined that this—Anneke Brouwer—was indeed an NSB-er?"

Nora cringed. *Her mother. A Nazi.* "That is what we must find out. That and what connection there may have been between Hans Moerveld and this Abram Rosen that might provide a motive for murder."

Nora placed her reading glasses on her nose and nodded. "Yes, it is strange, but the police seem to believe that there is a connection between the Abram Rosen mentioned in that document—" she pointed at the judgment "—and the murder and kidnapping."

The *medewerker* looked confused. Surely no one at the *Insti-*

tuut had ever asked him to work on a present–day kidnapping or murder. "But what possible connection could there be?"

Nora peered at him over her glasses in what she hoped was an academic way. "I am not privy to the evidence, of course, but apparently the most credible theory is that someone related to this Abram Rosen may have engaged in a revenge killing."

The *medewerker* studied the judgment again. "Thirty years later? That's crazy!"

Nora felt angry. Even if "crazy" was everyone's favorite word for her theory, she was *not* crazy. "That is not for us to determine, young man. Dr. Meijer and I have been colleagues for many years. He agrees with me that this matter is of the utmost priority."

The *medewerker* lowered his eyes respectfully, but shook his head. "I am sorry. I do not mean to be uncooperative, but I am not certain that we can be of much service in a police in-vestigation."

Nora felt struck. "What do you mean? That you are not allowed to assist me because the events involve a case in the United States?"

"No, that is not what I meant. Please." He held out his hand for the documents. She bundled them up and gave them to him.

"I only meant that our system is…less than efficient. We have a unique cataloging system here." He waved his hand around the room. "During the war, a very important Cabi-net minister, David Prager, established this foundation with support from the government—"

"Yes, yes." Nora tried not to let her voice reflect the im-patience she felt. Every minute waiting around was another minute her chance of finding Rose became more remote. She might already be too late.

Dijkstra droned on. "—and we have therefore amassed a

most extensive collection of *dagboeken*—diaries—and every imaginable kind of original wartime documentation. It is all housed in this one building," he said proudly.

Nora looked at the clock and saw that fifteen minutes had already gone by. She could almost feel her blood pressure rise. "Yes, yes, I know all of this. As I told you, Dr. Meijer and I are close colleagues."

The *medewerker* looked stricken. Nora felt as if she had kicked a puppy. She could tell that this young man was rarely given an opportunity to express his enthusiasm or impart his knowledge of the history of the *Instituut*. He stiffened and assumed a businesslike air. "Please wait here while I conduct my research." He turned.

Nora put her hand on his arm. "Tell me what I can do to help."

The *medewerker* shook his head and stepped back, as if her hand on his arm was inappropriate. "No, no. It will go faster if I do it myself." He must have seen her disappointed look because his expression softened. "Well, you could look through the general index for any mention of these names." He nodded in the direction of the document room. "Will you please come with me?"

She followed him into another large room, feeling unprepared with only her pencil and pad. Dark, oversize drawers lined the wall in a room that felt to Nora as if it were hermetically sealed. A very old man with a white shock of hair pored over a brown-edged Rotterdam newspaper, his elbow propped upon a stack of thick, leather-bound books.

The *medewerker* pointed to one of the old wooden cabinets and pulled out a long narrow drawer. "This is an example of how our information is categorized."

Inside, Nora saw rows and rows of yellowed index cards smudged with the ribbons of ancient typewriters. Many of the cards also had unreadable marginalia scribbled in ink. She gasped as she looked at the floor-to-ceiling cabinets with countless wooden drawers. She felt as if she were searching for a pearl in an endless bed of oysters.

She turned to the *medewerker*. "Please don't tell me I have to read each and every card to find the information I need."

He looked at the floor as if ashamed. "Yes, I am afraid so."

"Is there a cross-index?"

He colored a bit as he shook his head. "Mijnheer Prager created the system using his own criteria."

"Isn't there anything that might shorten the process? This could mean life or death for a six-month-old baby!"

Dijkstra gave her a startled glance. "I am sorry. I wish I could give you a different answer." He drew himself up. "But I shall begin immediately and we shall do our best. Do not lose heart. If I find anything at all, I will inform you immediately."

"Thank you," said Nora, still feeling miserable. She sat down in the spare metal chair, feeling overwhelmed. She looked up at the *medewerker*. "Where are you going to do your research? Perhaps I could help you instead."

He shook his head, his eyes now hooded. "I will be working with materials that are prohibited from use by the general public."

"You mean because they involve the NSB."

"Yes, I suppose someone has explained to you that all documents and diaries relating to the NSB have been sequestered."

"Yes," said Nora. She felt the now-familiar tears form behind her eyes. She looked down so he wouldn't see.

"So," he said brightly. "Anneke Brouwer, Hans Moerveld, Abram Rosen. I shall get started with my task!" He almost ran from the room.

20

Ariel hunched his shoulders as he walked fast despite the rain. Yesterday, when Amarisa had taken Rose, he had rushed to the address the de Jong woman had given him, but he'd seen no one go in or out. This morning he meant to appear nonchalant as he strolled back and forth.

After a sleepless night comforting Leah and racking his brain, he had come up with a plan. That morning he had typed a letter and put it into a blank envelope, careful to wear gloves. Short, but to the point.

> *Your daughter is in Houston. Ransom is USD 50,000. Return there immediately and await further instructions.*

He would hand it to her in the street and then rush off. It was eight in the morning. Probably too early for her to come out. He walked past the house again, this time glancing surreptitiously into the lower windows. The Dutch never used curtains, thank God. Ariel wondered if this age-old custom arose to let in light on gloomy, rainy days, or if it simply permitted the inhabitants to sit and drink tea while pretending not to snoop on their neighbors.

He started to feel like a stupid chicken walking in circles. He decided to make one more pass in front of the flat. But this time as he reached the corner, he saw the American rush out and try to catch the *Spui* tram, only she missed it. He stood a good distance behind and followed her onto the next tram. When they got out, he would hand her the letter. He felt his palms sweat and his heart beat faster.

When the tram stopped, the woman stepped quickly onto the street. He was near the back, surrounded by a throng of commuters. He tried to elbow his way out, but the incoming passengers were just as eager to enter. *Damn! I'm going to lose her!* He finally exited, trying to catch sight of her through the pouring rain. *There she was, already a block away.* He almost reached her, but she stopped in front of an old building on the *Herengracht*. He watched her go through the doors.

He approached it, read the concrete inscription and his jaw dropped. *The War Institute?* Fear gripped him. *What in hell was she doing there? Had Isaac ever said anything about the* Instituut? *Records of some kind?* He could think of nothing.

He stood staring at the glass doors until he noticed the guard inside eyeing him suspiciously. If he went in there—and he had no idea if they would let him—he could pretend to be researching something and leave the note where she was sitting. No, that wouldn't work. The guard would have seen him and could describe him to the police.

He walked down the street to a pay phone, took out some change and girded himself. Amarisa was not going to be happy.

21

Nora stared at the *dagboeken* upon the desk in front of her and opened the first one. Each diary had a handwritten form pasted onto the inside of the cover. It seemed to Nora to be a pseudo-psychological summary of the *dagboek*'s author. Apparently Mijnheer Prager also fancied himself the Freudian arbiter of whether the subject matter and contents of a *dagboek* warranted reading.

She found handwritten comments in the marginalia, presumably written by Prager, regarding whether he judged the diary to be of historical or social import, and whether he believed the author to be reliable. As Nora skimmed a number of *dagboeken,* she learned that Prager had also deemed a number of the summaries not worth reading because they dealt only with the mundane daily lives of those who survived the occupation. And some were rejected because Prager found the writing style "too sentimental."

Nora felt annoyed. It was galling that a Cabinet minister

who had fled to England before the occupation had the arrogance to pass judgment on what was and was not worth reading and which diaries had sufficient historical importance.

Along with those remarks were snippets of advice to the reader typed on brittle paper by a typewriter whose ribbon must have expired during the First World War. So anyone seeking information had to first read through the summaries, which were not cross-indexed in any way, and then determine if the *dagboek* itself had something vaguely resembling what the researcher sought.

This is mad! Her heart clenched as an image of Rose—lost, trapped, hurt—bloomed in her mind's eye. *What am I doing here? I'll never find anything remotely related to my parents, Abram Rosen or Rose! I'm a complete fool.*

She put her head in her hands and sobbed. She allowed herself a few moments to cry, but then wiped her eyes when some of the *medewerkers* walking by gave her concerned looks. She couldn't stand the thought of anyone asking her if she was all right. *I'm not all right. I'll never be all right. Not until I know where Rose is.*

She girded herself to continue. It was the only thing she could think of to do. She had called Richards yesterday and had received the same response. "We're doing everything we can." If, after a few more days, it became clear that out of desperation she had idiotically jumped on an airplane, then she would go home. She refused to think about how she would feel or what she would do if she returned empty-handed, with nothing to do but wait. *And wait for what?* She banished the thought and turned to the stack that the *medewerker* had given her.

Dispirited, she opened the first binder. Her eyes caught the word "Index" and she felt a glimmer of hope. If the diaries were in alphabetical order, she might be able to shorten this impossible task. She glanced down the list. No such luck. She turned to the second page. *God! A second index—divided into cities.* Under "Amsterdam," she saw a list of hundreds of *dagboeken,* organized not by author but by numbers of particular index cards. She felt like crying. Maybe she could look at each summary sheet and try to discern which, if any, related to her parents or Abram Rosen. But she didn't trust Prager's biased assessment of what each *dagboek* contained. Or she could check each index card related to Amsterdam in the "Index."

She had no choice. She began.

28

Nora sat in the tram to the *Instituut* the next morning, trying to blot last night out of her mind, but she couldn't help reliving the panic and terror. Not to mention the throbbing pain she still felt in her neck and wrists. *Was he really some druggie looking for cash?*

She got off the tram and walked into the *Instituut,* where the guard waved her through. She pushed the glass door open, put her things in a locker and sat in her antiseptic carrel.

She looked at the stack of index cards and couldn't bear to begin. She set about trying to focus on an article the *medewerker* had given her about the NSB, a summary of its history. Most of it she already knew from her time with Nico. What she hadn't known was that during the occupation, the Dutch Nazi Party swelled from less than 20,000 to over 300,000. *Why had so many Dutchmen jumped to the Nazi call? Was it a question of survival or principle?* She hoped to God that it was survival in her mother's case, but still felt her cheeks flush in shame.

Ariel felt cold sweat under his armpits. He was again the little boy who had been whipped by her words, stung by her venom. "And if I can't?"

"Then I'm going to take matters into my own hands." Her voice was soft, deadly. "Now get off the phone and do something intelligent."

After Amarisa slammed down the receiver, she walked into the kitchen and sat at the table. She reached for her bag of *shag* and slowly rolled a cigarette, lightly running her tongue across the adhesive edge of the paper. She sat back and took a few deep drags.

Perhaps she had made a mistake. Ariel had always been a bumbling idiot and she had no reason to believe he would act with intelligence now. She flicked her ashes into a Delft Blue ashtray, weighing the pros and cons. If, by some miracle, Ariel was able to scare off the woman, it was the best solution. Now, thank God, she had complete control where Rose was concerned.

She thought of Isaac. He would have known what to do. God, she missed him. Now she had no one to talk to, no family who understood her, no one to fill her lonely days. And without Isaac, her night terrors had returned. Last night she awoke screaming, her nightgown dripping with sweat. Always the snarling faces of those bastards, the stink of them as they raped her, one after another. Then when she managed to calm down, she had slipped into Rose's nursery and touched the sleeping angel. As she stroked her soft cheeks her fingers shook. She had curled up on a blanket next to the crib, falling asleep to Rose's soft breathing.

Amarisa walked into her living room with renewed con-

viction. She had been reluctant to bring in a third party, as it meant someone else could inform on her. So she would give Ariel one more day. Even blind pigs got lucky.

23

It was late afternoon. After grabbing a quick *broodje kaas,* Nora had walked back to the *Instituut* under the leaden clouds and light rain that defined Dutch weather. The Dutch had almost as many words for rain as Eskimos had for snow. She would have labeled today as *motregen*—moth rain—that lightly fluttered against her eyelashes.

She barely noticed the shops and streets that were decorated for Christmas. Twinkling lights glittered up and down the canals. All Nora could think of was that this would have been Rose's first Christmas. Nora had already bought her a special red bonnet with mistletoe stitched along the border to match the bright green elf costume she was to have dressed her in for Christmas morning. What came to mind instead was the soft yellow headband lying pathetically on the living room floor, next to her dead mother. *No, she would not go there. Back to work.* She walked into the building. Before returning

to her toil, she swilled a cup of the *Instituut's* bitter black coffee that cost her two dollars.

She sighed. Each passing hour felt more depressing than the last. She had plowed through hundreds of note cards, quickly discarding those that had no relevance to the names she sought. Ultimately, she had found only eight *dagboeken* that seemed to hold even a vague promise of useful information. She hunched forward over the wooden desk and made her way slowly through the first five.

Each *dagboek* consisted of loose pages bound into an ancient, thick cardboard cover and tied by a dark, twisted ribbon. A few contained typed copies, but most had the original scrawl of the author, written in fountain pen on pages of dried onionskin, so delicate that Nora feared they would tear in her hands.

Many of the *diaries* were truncated, as if Prager had decided to omit certain paragraphs and, in certain circumstances, entire pages, based upon his subjective selection process. Others contained actual photographs of the original pages, which were blurred and almost impossible to read.

Perhaps the authors had insisted on keeping the originals, she thought, *especially if they knew what that idiot's criteria were for chopping a diary up or rejecting it outright. I know I would have.*

Some pages were pasted to a piece of cardboard with some kind of industrial glue. Those were the most difficult to read because the handwriting was crabbed and microscopic. She had gone to a shop in the *Spui* during her lunch break and bought a small silver magnifying glass. It helped, but it was an enormous strain to read that way for hours on end.

Nora rubbed her eyes and stretched her arms over her head. She pulled out one of the index cards and read it. She already knew that by 1944, there was no more meat; milk powder was scarce; and people started smuggling in potatoes and other staples from the north of Holland. Over 20,000 men, women and

children starved to death in what was called the *Hongerwinter*. This card, written by a housewife, told her something new.

We have no milk, no bread, no potatoes—just rotten peels. The boys now have to go far into the fields to pull frozen tulip bulbs from the ground. We grind the pulp and make thin soup and watery porridges from them. They are bitter, practically inedible, but we choke them down because otherwise we will starve.

Nora felt miserable. To her this represented the nadir of the war—starving Dutchmen forced to forage and choke down their national flower.

She imagined a young Anneke, dressed in her brown NSB uniform, sitting warm before a hearth, well fed and clothed as she watched her starving neighbors shiver in the bitter cold, standing in endless food lines for a scrap of rotten potato peel. *Had Anneke's family been NSB proponents before the war? Or had they joined after the occupation? Had any of them refused to join?* Her heart clenched. *If so, why didn't Anneke have the same fortitude?*

Nora could not reconcile that bitter image with her memories of Anneke, dropping off food at a homeless shelter and donating money and clothes to abused women with children. Nora felt her heart harden. *If I were an NSB-er during the war and had an ounce of remorse for what I had done—and God knows what horrible things Anneke did—I guess it would be easy to be generous after it was all over. Especially if I got off scot-free, as she did.* Now every time Nora thought of Anneke's generosity, it would be bathed in a shadow of shame. But there were many NSB-ers. *What could Anneke have done to single herself out for murder?*

She looked at the back flap of a book the *medewerker* had suggested she read. Seyss-Inquart, the *Rijkscommissaris* in charge of the Netherlands, had sent five million Dutchmen

to German labor camps. He deported 120,000 of the 140,000 Dutch Jews to three concentration camps in Holland: Vught, Amersfoort and Westerbork.

He personally plundered the Dutch economy so that barely a cent was left. Nora had not known that the Netherlands was the only country in Europe that not only had paid the Germans for its own occupation, but also for "administration costs" of eight and one-half billion guilders. The total damage was twenty-five billion guilders. Nora felt her jaw drop. *He was one of the greatest looters of all time.*

She glanced at the photo on the back cover. Seyss-Inquart was a slight, pale man with a receding hairline and round, thick spectacles. The eyes that stared back were black and intense. Nora felt a grim satisfaction. He was convicted and sent to Nuremberg to be executed with the others. Goebbels had already swallowed his cyanide capsule and lay dead. Seyss-Inquart had been the last to walk the thirteen steps up to the gallows. As they put the black hood on his head, he had spoken for the last time.

I hope that my execution will be the last act of tragedy of the Second World War and that the lessons will be that there must be peace and understanding between people.

I believe in Germany.

Nora flipped to the final photograph of him. He lay on top of his coffin, the thick black rope used to hang him noosed tightly around his neck, his tongue protruding.

She slammed the book closed. She wished she could have pulled the trapdoor herself.

24

Ariel stumbled away from the pay phone after Amarisa had hung up on him. *That bitch! She'd have no qualms about disappearing with Rose. And she'd be happy to turn him in if it suited her plans.*

Well, he wouldn't fucking let her. He'd plan something better, more forceful, and he'd do it today. As he walked back and forth in front of the *Instituut,* a plan bloomed in his mind. It was dangerous, but he had no choice. The clock was ticking.

With his martial arts expertise, he could disable Nora, rough her up and then tell her that Rose was in Houston. That if she didn't return on the next flight, Rose would be killed.

Ariel sat wearily on his bench outside the *Instituut,* but hours passed and not a glimpse of Nora. But the longer she stayed inside, the longer he had to refine his new plan. He visualized the sequence. First a leg sweep. Then he'd move in close, grab her across the body with his arm, place his leg behind hers and push. She'd fall flat. After that, he would twist her arms behind her. If she tried to scream, he would thrust

one arm higher toward her shoulder blades. She would shut up then—at least long enough to hear what he had to say. He looked up at the dull afternoon sky. Yes, he would have to strike at night, in a secluded place. He'd follow her from the minute she stepped out of the *Instituut*. And then wait until the moment presented itself.

25

Nora walked dispiritedly down the *Herengracht* in the dark, exhausted by her day's fruitless efforts, feeling the rain now fall harder onto her face. Not only was she making no progress linking her mother's past to Rose's kidnapping, but during her lunch break she had called Bates. She was fired. Though he spoke the words kindly, she had felt panic course through her. Her mother's estate was still in probate and the lawyer had told her that the amount she would net would be seriously diminished by estate taxes and the large amount left on her mother's mortgage. Now that she had been fired, it would probably take her a long time to find another job. And without a paycheck, how could she support Rose? She was so preoccupied that she almost ran into a black bicycle charging down the street. Only the harsh ringing of the man's bell and his shouts kept them from colliding.

Soaked, she now walked along in the darkness until she reached *Sampurna,* an Indonesian restaurant. She walked in,

took a quick look at the menu and waited until the waitress came over. Marijke had begged her to come home so they could talk and Nora could get some rest. Nora had refused, in no mood for conversation.

After dinner, Nora wandered aimlessly around the *Centrum* for half an hour, maybe more, staring dully into the cheerfully lit shop windows, looking at the Christmas lights up and down the canals, catching the laughter and constant motion of the city as they flowed around her. She had never been surrounded by so much life and felt so alone.

She could only think of her baby, of the first moment she had held the tiny, warm bundle in her arms. She could also not help but wonder when Nico would return and how, after all this time, she would tell him that Rose was his daughter. She pulled her jacket tighter around her. *What kind of life might she have had with Nico? Would they have been happy? Would the deep love they had shared be sustained over time?* At least Rose would not have been kidnapped. Her thoughts spun round and round, becoming tangled and more hopeless.

Weariness then hit her so hard that she could no longer think straight about Rose, Nico or her pathetic research at the *Instituut*. She turned down a narrow dark alley that would take her to the *Spui* and the tram to Marijke's. Then there were footsteps behind. When she stopped, they stopped. She walked faster and cast a glance behind her. She saw a large man dressed in a hooded sweatshirt and black pants, his face hidden in the pitch of the alley. Panicked, she began to run, but heard him closing in on her.

Then she felt a vicious kick to her legs and fell hard to the cobblestones. He towered above, then swiftly yanked her to her feet, twisted her arms behind her and grabbed her wrists with one hand. She started to cry out, but he clamped his other hand over her mouth and thrust her wrists upward. She felt

pain rip through her. He shoved her to the ground, grasped her by the neck and started to drag her across the street.

Finally she was able to scream. "Help me! Someone help me!"

He jerked her violently, dragging her quickly into an alley. Out of the corner of her eye, she saw a man run out of a nearby café. "Stop! Let her go!" Next thing she knew, the agonizing grip was released and she saw the dark figure run away down a black alley.

Gasping, Nora felt arms lift her to her feet. "There—down the alley!" she cried. The man released her and ran off. Sobbing, Nora limped into the café and collapsed onto one of the bar stools. She felt something trickling down her cheek and wiped it off with her fingers. *Blood. Must have cut herself when she fell.* She felt dizzy.

A moment later the man returned. "I saw no one—the alley is empty."

She must have looked as if she were about to faint, because he poured the remainder of a bottle of dark liquor into a large glass. "Drink," he commanded.

She obeyed, but it did nothing to slow the adrenaline that coursed through her body. She could hear the terror in her voice. "Did you see his face?"

He shook his head. "Probably a drug addict or a kid looking for cash." He gave her an annoyed look. "You have no business being out alone at night. Don't you know better?"

Nora stood and pointed at the telephone. "We should call the police," she said shakily.

The man shrugged. "I've been a bartender for fifteen years. They get these calls forty times a night. Whoever he was, he's gone now. You're just lucky you weren't hurt."

Nora sat, frightened to leave alone. "May I use the telephone?"

He nodded and turned to the few old men who held up their glasses for a refill, all the while staring at Nora. She felt stung by their bold curiosity. Nora walked to the counter and, with trembling fingers, dialed Marijke's number. When she heard her voice, she broke down. "Please, please, come and get me!"

"What happened?"

"Never mind—I'll tell you later."

Marijke appeared in fifteen minutes and took Nora home by taxi. When she explained what had happened, Marijke scolded her and made her promise never again to wander the streets alone.

Exhausted, Nora promised and then went straight to bed. *What hell would tomorrow bring?*

26

He had her, he had her! But then she had jerked free, some bastard came from nowhere and Ariel's fingers grasped only cold air. Then he ran, his lungs on fire, until finally he came to a café kilometers away. Now he sat gasping, peering fearfully up and down the street.

When the waitress came, she looked at his attire and smiled. Probably thought he had been jogging instead of running for his life. He ordered two Scotches, belting down one after the other.

He stumbled to the pay phone in the back of the café. He could barely dial, his hands were shaking so. "Peter!"

"Ariel?"

Ariel's words tumbled over one another. "Peter, for God's sake, come now! I need you!"

"Where are you? What's happened?"

Ariel gave him directions, hung up and collapsed onto a bar stool. By the time Peter rushed in Ariel had calmed somewhat.

Peter yanked out a seat next to Ariel. "What the fuck is going on? You look like hell! And why are you so far from home?"

Ariel hung his head, then spoke. "Oh, Peter. You won't believe what I've been through! I told you Isaac was dead, but I didn't tell you that he murdered someone. And then there's Jacoba—I mean Rose. I kidnapped her—Amarisa took her—the real mother is—"

Peter moved his chair closer and shook Ariel's shoulders. Ariel raised his head and looked into his brother-in-law's shocked eyes. Just knowing he could tell someone made him sob.

"What in hell are you talking about? *Kidnapping? Murder?*"

Ariel saw the waitress looking at them curiously. He stood and paid. "Let's get out of here."

They went into a dark park across the street. Ariel explained everything. When he finished, Peter just stared at him. "Why didn't you or Leah tell me about this!"

"I'm sorry, Peter." He felt guilty. "We should have, but we've been terrified about Rose, the police, everything."

"Ariel, this is outrageous! You've put everyone in jeopardy, but mostly yourself."

"I know, but you've got to help me. You're the only one I can trust!"

"Christ, Ariel—I'm a teacher, not a detective." He sat down hard, shaking his head. "I can't believe this! Give me a minute to take it all in."

Ariel felt sick. Telling the story again had made him realize how insane his life now was.

"And why in hell did you attack that woman in the alleyway?"

"To scare her off. I was going to tell her to go back to Houston or Rose would be killed."

"Have you gone *crazy?* Beating up women?"

"If I'd had *one* more minute, everything might have been fine." He heard the stubbornness in his voice. "And I'll try again. I'm not going to lose Rose."

Peter's eyes darted around. "The first thing you need to do is to go home and stay there. You're nuts chasing this woman around, exposing yourself in public. You'll get caught and then what will happen to Leah and the baby?"

"But Amarisa—"

"Fuck Amarisa. She's using you to protect herself."

"But Rose—we can't lose her, Peter. Leah will be devastated."

"Buddy, you've lost her already. That bitch has had her hooks into you for years and she won't be happy until she has your balls."

Ariel nodded. Peter was right, but all he saw in his mind's eye was Rose ripped from Leah's arms. *No! He couldn't bear it. He would handle Amarisa, outsmart her somehow. She took him for an idiot. He would prove her wrong.*

When they stood, Peter gave him a strong parting embrace. Ariel hung on longer than usual, so grateful for his friend, so relieved to have told someone. Now he didn't feel completely alone.

After he watched Peter walk away, Ariel stood a moment in the dark, wet night. He felt exhausted. He trudged slowly toward his flat. *But what about the money? Amarisa could ruin them.* He had asked his boss for a leave but had been given only a week.

Fuck them all. He would find another way.

27

Amarisa watched Rose sleep peacefully in the new crib she had bought. It was perfect, top-of-the-line. With its white gleaming wood and colorful mobile, Rose seemed happy nestled in the embroidered sheets, the thick comforter and her stuffed animals.

Amarisa had converted a guest room into an elaborate nursery with an antique rocking chair and a dresser full of diapers, blankets and crib sheets. The closet held neat rows of baby clothes made from soft flannel and fine linens. Amarisa surveyed the room and, satisfied, walked into her living room that overlooked the *Singel* canal, one of the stately neighborhoods in Amsterdam.

She sat on her couch and thought about Rose's mother, that Nora woman, now in Amsterdam. *What could she have discovered that had led her here?* Whatever the reason, Amarisa had to make sure Nora didn't find out that Rose was in the city.

The phone rang.

"Amarisa, it's Ariel."

She heard him take a deep breath. "Well, what is it?"

"I tried to scare her in an alleyway last night, but she got away—"

"You imbecile! Did anyone see you?"

"I don't think so, but she ran into a café and I took off down the street—"

"Shut up and let me think." Her mind whirred, clicking off possibilities. "Okay, here's what you're going to do. Stay home, don't go out and I'll get you out of town."

"No. I'm going to get this handled—"

"So you can screw it up again? Not on your life."

"What will you do?"

"None of your business!" she snapped. "Do what I tell you or the next thing you'll see is the police at your door. Do I make myself clear?"

"But I can do this. I need more time."

"No 'buts.' I'm hiring a professional."

"Amarisa, I *said* I'm going to handle it and I will!"

"You listen to me. Simple commands. *Home. Stay. Good boy.* Got it?"

She slammed down the receiver. *What a cretin.* Some part of her must have known this would happen. Yesterday she had bought two one-way tickets to Geneva, where she owned a second home Ariel knew nothing about. If that woman was close to finding Ariel—and who knew what clues that moron had left—then she'd take Rose and start a new life. Efram Hertz, her partner, could look after the routine aspects of the business and she could oversee anything important from Geneva.

But this was not what she wanted, to leave Amsterdam and her business and start over in a strange country. She was too damned old for a new life, especially with a baby. No, she'd

be damned if she'd let anyone shove her around. The Nazis had done it once. She had sworn it would never happen again.

But now Rose was all she had. She had to make sure no one separated them. And there was someone who could do the job. She stubbed out her cigarette and opened her address book.

22

Ariel dialed the number with dread. "Amarisa?"

"What?"

"I followed her."

"Brilliant. Where is she?"

"At the *Oorlogsinstituut*."

"What in hell is she doing there?"

"How would I know?"

"Well, keep following her. How are you going to get rid of her?"

Ariel told her of his plan, the contents of the letter. "It's too risky for me to go into the *Instituut*. I'll have to wait until she leaves."

"Well, it's your own damned fault we're in this mess," she snapped. "Give her the letter and beat it. James Bond you're not."

"Damn it, Amarisa, it's only ten. I'm doing my best."

"That's what I'm afraid of. I'll give you one more day."

Obviously it was not a topic bandied about by the Dutch after the war, nor was it what the world remembered. What flashed in the collective consciousness was Anne Frank, resistance fighters, heroes. But the dark underbelly, the truth, was that in many families, it was not unheard of for one brother to be a resistance fighter and another an NSB-er.

She felt sick. *What had her mother done?* For the first time since that hideous day, she felt anger toward Anneke. Whatever it was, Nora was now paying the goddamned price, just as Anneke had. Except Nora's price was Rose.

She put her head down on the desk, not caring if anyone saw her. *She had nothing!* Only a crazy puzzle that led nowhere. "I will never find Rose," she whispered. Hearing those words out loud made Nora feel they were true. Her anguish felt unbearable. *How much could her heart take?*

Nora spent the rest of the day plowing through the Amsterdam index cards. During her lunch break, she used the *Instituut*'s phone book to mark every "Rosen" in Amsterdam. There were so many she had no idea where to start. She went to the receptionist for change and simply began. After the fifteenth Rosen, she stopped to assess. None of the people who'd answered had had any idea who Abram Rosen was. The remaining five refused to speak to her. The Dutch valued their privacy. *Besides, she reasoned, wasn't she asking for the impossible? Who would know about this after thirty years? Maybe his family had been sent to the camps and were all dead.*

She returned to sifting through the interminable stack of cards. Hours later, she looked up. Five o'clock. The whole day had passed her by and she had nothing to show for it. She stared blankly at the stack of cards. She heard a rustling at her elbow.

"Dr. van Doren?" It was Dijkstra, the *medewerker*.

"Yes?"

"I believe I have finally found something about a member of Anneke Brouwer's family." He held a slim green volume.

"Who? Who is it?"

The *medewerker* shook his head. "I regret that I cannot disclose that. The information is classified."

Nora felt hot blood rise in her. "What do you mean, 'classified'?"

The *medewerker* shrugged. "This relative of Mevrouw Brouwer was a van Tonningen follower."

"A what?"

"Rost van Tonningen. Do you not know this name?"

Nora felt her face redden. She was supposed to be Aantje van Doren, the Dutch war history expert. "Well, of course, but…"

"Then you know what I mean." His eyes narrowed when she did not answer. "Dr. van Doren, you are aware of the movement of which I speak?"

"Yes."

He nodded but seemed unconvinced. "Then perhaps you are also aware that all documents and information relating to NSB-ers are now kept in a separate archive that is not open to the general public?"

Nora's heart sank, but she took an aggressive tone. "As my letter states, Dr. Meijer and I have been colleagues for many years. Surely that prohibition does not apply to me?" The *medewerker* stared at the floor. She went on. "Must I remind you that this may be critical information in a murder investigation?"

"I am truly sorry. But by order of the Dutch government, all NSB-related documents, *dagboeken,* uniforms, medals— everything has been sequestered and I cannot make an exception, even in your case."

"This is ridiculous." Now she wanted to smack him. To

have come halfway around the world to find nothing and now, when there *was* something, she would not be allowed to read it. "I am going to have to insist that you give me that book. If not, I will have to report your noncompliance to Dr. Meijer and he will not be pleased, as I am sure you know."

"*Doktor,* please—I am only doing my job. Dr. Meijer would fire me if I gave you this volume." Nora saw the pleading look in his eyes, but felt no sympathy. He went on. "This rule was put into effect not only to provide privacy and protection to the children and relatives of the NSB-ers, but to inhibit any re-birth or development of such a movement in the Netherlands."

Nora knew when she was losing. *Damn Nico—where was he? Surely he had to come back soon.* But as soon as she posed the question, she knew. He'd always taken long vacations with her, why not with his new wife? "Isn't there something I can do?"

The *medewerker* smiled for the first time. "Yes. You may make a formal application to the *Ministerie van Justitie.* If approved, we will be pleased to give you access to the NSB archives."

"Wonderful. Do you have the form?"

"Yes, I will get one for you." He started to turn away.

"Excuse me," she said. "How long will such an application take to be considered? I leave for America in a matter of days."

"That is impossible. Such an application would require a lengthy written essay and an interview—"

"I don't have time for all that!" Now she saw people were staring at her. The *medewerker* crossed his arms and gave her a studied look. She knew he must see the black circles under her eyes, the desperate look on her face. She was about to blow this completely. She took a deep breath. "Please accept my apology. I am very tired."

He nodded. "Perhaps I have a solution. I learned this morning that Dr. Meijer may be returning at the end of this week. I believe he might be willing to assist you. In the past, such requests have been known to be granted in twenty-four hours."

Nora sighed. "Is there nothing you can tell me about this *dagboek?*"

"No," he said, "although I am still searching for living relatives of Hans Moerveld."

She smiled tightly. "Thank you for all your help."

He gave her a slight bow. Before he left, she saw him give her that odd, confused look again.

She got up and took her key to her locker. Then she shoved some coins into the machine and watched as the thick, dark coffee filled a foam cup. Armed with her cigarettes and jacket, she walked out and sat on a bench overlooking the *Herengracht*. The canal's water seemed ugly today, a murky brown. She tried to think. *Who in the hell was Rost van Tonningen?* She thought she remembered vague references Nico had made about certain NSB-ers, but for the life of her she could not recall anything specific. She had wanted to blot out everything to do with Nico.

She stood and ground the cigarette butt under her heel. She had to get that diary. The air was brisk as she looked out over the canal. Small waves pushed against the concrete sides as a few gray ducks swam downstream. The coffee warmed her hands and cleared her head. She had to approach this as she would one of her surgeries—with a clear mind and confidence. There had to be a solution, a way of getting what she needed.

She crumpled her empty coffee cup and threw it into a trash can. She walked back inside deep in thought. Another *medewerker* rushed by, a stack of books in his hands, almost knocking her down. He apologized as he struggled to balance the books while opening the half door of the *medewerkers'* station. He walked in and reached into a small wooden cube on the wall, muttering to himself. Soon he found what he was looking for. He opened the half door and let himself back out into the foyer, his face red from the weight of the books.

She saw a metal post that stood about three feet high against the wall that she had not noticed before. The *medewerker* held the tower of books under one arm and with his free hand inserted a plastic card into a small box on top of the post. To her surprise, a floor panel receded and, after a few moments, a large dumbwaiter rose and stopped just above the floor. Still struggling with the books, the *medewerker* stacked them in the dumbwaiter and pushed a red button on the box. Just before it descended, Nora caught a glimpse of the slim green journal Dijkstra had refused to give her.

She had her answer.

29

Amarisa heard the teakettle scream from the kitchen. As she let the tea steep, she smiled. Yes, she had an excellent solution. She would call Dirk, Efram's son, the little bastard. He'd grown up a petty thief until one evening she had caught him in her house trying to replace some of her diamonds with fakes. He didn't know she had an alarm at home that quietly alerted her to any intruders. In return for not turning him in or telling his father, she had used him whenever she was forced to deal with unsavory types—dealers who tried to swindle her, customers who refused to pay. She had never learned how he managed such swift results, nor did she care.

She dialed his number. After the tenth ring, she heard a confused mumbling. She obviously had woken him. She instructed him to show up in ten minutes and he did, looking as if he'd spent the night in an alley sleeping with mangy dogs. His long dirty hair and ratty clothes exuded an execrable odor.

They sat at the kitchen table and, without any small talk,

she gave him a Xerox copy of Nora's passport photo and his marching orders. "Find this woman and convince her it is not in her best interest to stay in Amsterdam. That if she persists, she will never see her daughter again."

He raised an eyebrow, but Amarisa waited until he recovered from her odd request, which he soon did. "Is the child in Amsterdam?"

"That is none of your business."

He shrugged. "Fine. Where is this woman staying?"

Amarisa handed him the address. "But yesterday she spent the entire day at the *Oorlogsinstituut*."

"Why?"

"If I knew that, why would I need you? My stupid nephew, Ariel, tried to run her out of town and botched it. I need a professional."

He shifted in his chair. Amarisa could smell last night's alcohol on his breath. "So, your nephew won't get in my way?"

Amarisa shrugged. "I gave him orders to go home and stay there. If he doesn't, the police will be most interested in certain illicit acts of his that I happen to know about."

He shoved a greasy lock of hair from his right eye and stared at her. "You'd turn in your own *nephew?*"

"I prefer that you not harm him, but if he interferes, do what you have to do. Just be very, very sure none of this can be traced back to me."

The young thug picked at the dirt under his fingernails with a switchblade. "What about the woman? How far do you want me to go?"

"I told you. Scare her off. Convince her to go back to Houston."

"What's it worth to you?"

"Two thousand now, five after it's done."

"Not good enough. Four now, four after."

"Take what I offer or forget it."

He shrugged. "All right. But how am I supposed to do it?"

Amarisa slammed down her teacup. "If one more idiot asks me that, I'm going to go nuts. You're a professional. Do what it takes."

"And if I can't?"

"Then get rid of her."

Both his bleary eyes were open now. "Hang on, Amarisa. That's not in my line."

"Well, it isn't exactly a great leap, either."

He shook his head. "I'll do what I can. If I can't run her off, I've got guys in mind who could handle the other."

"No! Just you. No one else must know about it."

His eyes glittered. "That'll cost more."

"Just do as you're told."

He snapped his knife shut and stood. "I'll keep you in the loop."

"See that you do."

Once he was gone, Amarisa sipped her tea, feeling pleased. The only person who could cause her problems now was Ariel and she had him on a tight leash. She smiled. Now she would pull the noose tighter. She would let them have the baby for the afternoon. To remind Ariel of what he didn't want to lose—contact with Jacoba. And to make sure he didn't stick his nose into her plans and screw up again.

She went into the kitchen and prepared Jacoba's formula. She would no longer call her Rose. This child was hers now. She could hardly believe how fiercely she already loved her. Holding Jacoba in her arms, feeding her in the rocking chair as the sunlight played on her red curls, giving her a bath as she chortled and splashed.

How had this wondrous creature wiped clean the slate of Nazi hatred that had consumed her for thirty years? In its place now was joy. She still missed Isaac terribly, but every time she touched Jacoba, she felt as if she had vindicated him and Abram. Jacoba was the future, the proud inheritor of the past. She would have every advantage life had to offer. Amarisa would see to that.

30

The document room was now empty except for a woman poring over a large, wrinkled map and the old man who was there every day with his leather binder and bifocals, reading yellowed newspapers. She looked at her watch. *Five-forty.* She knew that the *Instituut* would close in twenty minutes. The *medewerkers* had all gone home. She saw only the reception-ist, and he was due to begin locking up in a few minutes. *God bless the Dutch,* she thought. They kept strictly to their sched-ules. Like their trains that were never late.

She picked up her notepad and pencil and went to her locker. The receptionist walked by her into the document room, recognizing her with a brief nod and tapping his watch. Nora nodded. She knew that he would clear the room and wait until everyone had left through the main entryway.

Now. She snuck behind the locker area, past reception and hid behind a row of bookcases next to the staircase. She peeked around its corner. The receptionist was talking to the old man with the newspapers, his back to her. She took off her shoes and walked quickly to the ornate wooden balustrade that led upstairs, her footfalls silent on the deep carpet. She felt as if she had stopped breathing.

Nineteen steps up, she reached the landing, turned right and ran down the red hallway to the last door on the right. Nico's office, or at least it had been. She tried the knob. Locked. *Damn.* She ran back to the landing, crouched down and peered through the balustrade. The beating of her heart blotted out any hearing. *Where was the receptionist?* She had no clue what he did after he ushered them all out. Hopefully he just locked up, went to a café and drank beer.

The lights went off downstairs, save for the chandelier over the entrance to the main doorway. In the dark, it felt to her like the setting for a horror movie—the ruby carpet, dim light, the gargoyles she glimpsed through the windows on the second floor. She still wasn't sure if the receptionist had left. *This is crazy.* She closed her eyes and listened.

She saw him before she heard him. A white hand on the banister, a black shoe on the first step on the plush carpet. Instinctively, she crouched lower and glanced right and left. *Where could she hide?* She tiptoed down the hallway, frantically yanking on the knobs of four offices. *Locked, all locked!* She heard the receptionist near the landing. *Oh, God, what could she do!* Desperate, she scanned both sides of the hallway.

She heard him spin a knob on a door somewhere, but not open it. Probably checking to make sure they were locked. Only minutes until he found her. *What then? Would he call the police? How would she explain herself?*

Then she spotted it—a door without a handle. She pushed on it and burst into a small space, the door whooshing closed behind her. It was so dark that she was blinded. She almost cried out when she stubbed her toe on something. She blinked as her eyes finally adjusted. It was a tiny WC. The toilet and a miniature sink were all it held.

She heard his footsteps nearby as her fingers groped for a lock on the door, but her fingers made no purchase. She clambered onto the toilet, perched with one socked foot on the lid and the other pressed against the middle of the door. As if that would keep him out. *Was she out of her mind?*

Nora kept her eyes closed and tried to calm her breathing. Her foot slipped off the toilet lid—*damned socks!* She tensed her leg muscles, spread her hands out against the narrow walls and steadied herself, straining to listen. The footsteps seemed to go to the end of the hall and pause. She heard him try the knob to what she thought was Nico's office. She opened her eyes and heard his footsteps passing by her. She tried not breathe. Finally the footsteps receded. Minutes later, just as she feared she would fall from her precarious position, the sliver of light under the door went out.

Drawing ragged breaths, she climbed down and sat on the lid. She waited forever until the phosphorescent hands on her watch told her it had been thirty minutes since the lights went out. She put her shoes back on, picked up her purse and jacket and cracked the doorway. *Nothing.* She opened the door and peered down the hall. Black as coal.

Time to get down to business. She crept down the stairs to the lobby, peering around corners. Satisfied that she was now alone, she let the dim light of a chandelier guide her to the elevator. She would get what she needed quietly and simply and then somehow get the hell out of there.

She pressed the button for the elevator. *Nothing.* She pressed again. This time she groaned. Locked or turned off. *What now?* She ran down the stairs to the basement in the pitch-dark, feeling her way by clutching the handrail. She tried what she believed were the doors to the archived documents, but they were also locked. She banged on the glass, furious.

She ran back up to the main floor. She spied the half door of the *medewerkers'* station. She opened it and turned on a small desk lamp on the counter. Pulling the cord as far from the wall as it would go, she shone the narrow light into the cubes affixed to the wall—the ones she had seen the *medewerker* scan that afternoon. She checked the one she thought he had focused on and then she spotted it. A white plastic card. Hands shaking, she grasped it and held it under the light. Its edges were furled and worn. She snatched it up, walked through the half door and inserted it into the box as the *medewerker* had done. A green light flashed and then she heard a whirring from below. A floor panel receded and the dumbwaiter ground its way up to the surface. Nora smiled.

She folded herself into the dumbwaiter, pressed the red button on the metal post and climbed in. She had to hug her knees to her chest and curl up tightly. *Thank God the thing was slow to close*. It had to be ancient. When the door finally closed over her, she was thrown into darkness. As she felt it descend, she tried to breathe normally in the claustrophobic space. Gears grated against one another until it jolted to a stop. The metal doors opened and she crept out.

She found herself in a dank room, so dark that Nora felt she was trying to see through India ink. She made her way past tables and chairs, groping along a wall until she felt a switch. She turned on the light. What she saw made her gasp.

A man decorated in a studded uniform pointed a black gun directly at her. She leaped back until she realized it was a mannequin. The shirt sported a black-and-red triangular patch with an N at the top, an S in the left corner and a B in the right corner. She recognized it from a photograph she'd seen in one of the books the *medewerker* had given her. The Dutch symbol of a lion roaring on its hind legs was in its center, but this lion held a golden sword and arrows against the backdrop of an orange, white and blue shield. Nora had read that the red and black stood for blood and soil, the shield represented the Netherland's heroic past on the world seas, the lion the power of the Dutch people. The ominous black stripe had but one meaning. Nazism.

Nora took a slow look around the enormous room. The walls were lined with glass shadow boxes of what seemed to be war medals and weapons. She then walked to a smaller adjacent room and flicked on the light.

"Oh, my God." All she saw were bookshelves, floor to ceiling, crammed with books of all sizes. Nora pulled one down. It appeared to be a *dagboek* similar to the ones upstairs. She stepped back and took in the enormity of the task of looking through these countless diaries. "Damn!" She studied a few more closely. At least they were arranged alphabetically. Someone sane had actually attempted to create order.

She put her hand to her forehead. She didn't even know the name of the person who wrote the *dagboek* she sought. If it was a married relative of her mother's, she would never find it. Nora went to the B's and flipped through the dusty bindings until she got past the Br's. *Nothing.* "Think!" she said aloud. "You have to think!"

Then she remembered that the *medewerker* had shown her the mysterious *dagboek* late in the day. Perhaps it had not been reshelved yet. She walked about, looking for a book cart or an in-box. Nothing. *I don't care. I'm not leaving without that damned book.* She walked into a smaller room, avoiding the NSB memorabilia on the walls, searching every inch. *Still nothing.* She began to panic. *She couldn't stay there all night. She had to find it!*

She studied three of the four walls carefully and then she spied it. A slim green volume. It stood alone on a narrow shelf near the door. "Hold," read the handwritten card clipped to the front cover. *And hold it she would!* She snatched it from the shelf and sat at a smooth, polished table, florescent lights glaring overhead.

She took a deep breath and carefully turned to the first page. In flowery script was written: *Het Dagboek van Miep Elizabeth Brouwer.*

Nora stared at the page. *Who in hell was she?*

31

Hunched under his raincoat, Dirk stood across the canal from the address Amarisa had given him. *Shit, he was so sick of rain.* Maybe when he got the dough, he'd head off to Greece or Spain. Somewhere warm, sunny.

He looked up. There she was, the woman. He shadowed her to the tram, got off when she did and tracked her to the *Instituut*. Amarisa had told him she was doing some kind of loony research. *Christ, would he have to hang around there all day?*

Then he noticed something. One of the passengers he'd seen on the tram was loitering around the entrance to the building and then sat on a nearby bench. Dirk wandered a bit, watching him. The man never left the bench, huddled in the pouring rain, his eyes fixed on the glass entryway. He seemed nervous. And then it hit him. Amarisa's nephew. Apparently he wasn't the obedient hound she thought he was.

Dirk strolled around the neighborhood, dark thoughts crowding his mind. *God, how he hated that bitch, being her slave.*

He thought for the thousandth time how to get out from under her. Every goddamned dirty thing she wanted done, old Dirk was her guy. He felt furious every time he thought about the noose she had around his neck. Paying his gambling debts, then threatening to cut off the money. He pushed up the sleeve of his raincoat and rubbed the sore place inside his elbow, feeling the tracks there. Damn, Amarisa somehow knew about that, too, keeping him strung out until she threw him a wad of dough to get high. She'd probably had him followed just like he was now dogging the American nutcase.

Whenever Amarisa slipped him extra money, they both knew what it was for. *And if she stopped—no, he couldn't go there.* He needed the stuff more now than ever just to maintain. And she'd given him the two grand up front, so she had to be serious about him getting this job done. *God, what he wouldn't do for a fix!*

He lit a cigarette. Calmed the jitters. *Maybe he could just give the old bat false information about the woman.* Amarisa would still have to pay him. That would get the bookies off his back and buy him some smack. One thing about Amarisa, for such a tight bitch, she paid good bucks when the job got done.

He dropped his cigarette in a puddle and pulled a bottle from his jacket. He upended it and took a long gulp. Crap, but it was better than nothing. He wandered up and down the canal for another hour. *Nothing.* Just that idiot Ariel glued to his bench. Probably going to pee in a cup so he wouldn't miss her.

Dirk looked at his watch. Almost noon. He smiled when he thought of Greta. She'd be home for lunch right about now. He glanced once more at Ariel. *Let the moron do the grunt work. He'd hit the Prinsengracht house tonight. Right now he was going to get himself a truly great piece of ass.*

32

For a long moment Nora just sat, staring. Hands trembling, she began to read.

May 17, 1942
Oh, what exciting times! The war has been dragging on for two years, but I feel it my duty to keep a record of each day, however insignificant, until our glorious return to the Fatherland has been accomplished. I am certain when Hitler wins the war, my diary will be an important chronicle to be read by future generations.

For those who read this, I am the sister of a very important man: Dr. Joop Willem Brouwer. Not only is he a respected physician, but next week he will be named by Mussert to a high position in the NSB. Just today the Fuhrer named Mussert as the leader of the Dutch people and it has been decided that even after the war, he shall be the spokesperson for the land. Quite a feather

*in his cap! He also mentioned that Joop may be asked to become
a member of the SS—a very rare invitation for a non-German!*

*To celebrate, we built a big fire in the hearth and I made Joop
a wonderful dinner of potatoes, meat and vegetables. I don't
know where Joop gets the food or how we always manage to
have so much coal, but our German friends never let us want
for anything.*

*The evening was perfect in every respect. Anneke, who is al-
ways running around somewhere, surprised us all by bringing a
stunning young SS officer with her. Joop was thrilled. She even
lifted a glass of wine to congratulate her father. It is the first time
in ages I have seen Joop beam at her, congratulating her in turn
for her choice of dinner companion. For once we didn't have arguing at the table—over politics, the war, anything.*

*I know Joop is not happy that Anneke stopped going to the
university, but he knows that she is dedicated to the Fuhrer's
cause and that is all that is important. She really is a good girl
at heart—an excellent example of what a young NSB-er should
be, even at twenty-two.*

*After dinner, she excused herself to attend a great athletic com-
petition between two of the German teams. I am certain Anneke will be cheering from the sidelines. With that handsome
SS officer, she will be the envy of her friends.*

*I look forward to tomorrow night, as well. Joop and I are to
be the guests of the well-known writer, Dirk van Roessel—a
Dutchman who wrote the book* The Devil's Trinity. *He is
an SS-er now and, with the support of our German friends,*

*has made a name for himself. Maybe it is a sign that Joop will
be admitted to the SS soon.*

Nora closed the book, desolate. Despite what she had found
in the attic, she had so hoped that Anneke was not a Nazi.
Feeling fresh grief, she opened the book again. She had to
know the whole truth, especially if it led to Rose.

The next entry so transfixed her that the events it described
came to her mind's eye like a grainy black-and-white film.

May 29, 1944
*This morning, I hurried to make breakfast for Joop. Last night
he brought home two precious eggs and a few slices of ham!*

*Oh, Anneke! Joop was so displeased when he found out she
would not join us for breakfast. She flew out of the house with
just a stack of NSB flyers. He should be happy she is so committed, but my brother is a very strict, principled man. He has
always had a temper, but never without provocation.*

*I was so proud when he asked me to move into his house and
take care of Anneke when Antonia left. I still wonder what happened to her. Joop forbade us to mention her name. I wonder if
I'll ever see her again.*

*I have to write this quickly as Joop wants us to accompany him
to the installation of the Kultuurraad in Pulchri at the invitation
of the Rijkscommissaris. Apparently Rost van Tonningen will
be there—I'm so excited! I know Joop doesn't care for him, but
Mussert had better be careful. He still believes that the Netherlands and Germany have one ideology, but should remain two
separate countries. Not a popular view these days.*

Now the worst part of the day. Joop fired Margriet, our maid. It was awful. She showed up for work today and Joop wouldn't let her in. He demanded her house key and told her never to return! I tried to speak, but he silenced me with one of his looks. Margriet begged and pleaded—this is the only money she makes for her four little children—but Joop grabbed the key and gave it to me. "Wash it," he said. Then he turned and slammed the door in her face. His cheeks were purple, he was so angry. "Vermengde gehuwd. Married to a Jew and failed to report it." "What about Margriet?" I asked. "She isn't Jewish." He was so cold. "It is too late. A pure Dutch woman has lain with a subhuman. She will go with him to the camp, along with their half-Jew mongrels."

I'm exhausted. I have just enough time to lie down for a short rest before this evening. And maybe Anneke will meet someone tonight!

Nora shut the diary and threw it on the floor. She clasped her hands together, but they were ice. These entries made it all so *real*. In her mind's eye, she saw Anneke as she must have been, one of the NSB-ers in the crowd, screaming her fanatic allegiance to Hitler. Nora imagined her mother's young face, eyes bright, an evangelist for the New Order.

Nora closed her eyes. If she kept her body still, she might not throw up.

33

Amarisa sat in Jacoba's room, sun streaming in despite the earlier rain clouds. The sweet weight of the tiny body against Amarisa's breast and the rocking left Amarisa almost breathless. She closed her eyes, inhaling the scent of Jacoba's skin after her bath. Now, this moment, Amarisa felt whole, as she once had before the war. She felt tears roll down her cheeks. She marveled at the miracle. *How had this baby repaired her heart, her soul?*

She laid Jacoba gently into her crib, tucking the pink blanket around her. Jacoba slept so well after her bath. Amarisa straightened and caught a glimpse of herself in the mirror. *A smile. On her face. Was it her imagination, or did the purple scar that slashed from lip to ear seem a little lighter?* She glanced at her black blouse. She would buy something lighter, more colorful, to match the new woman she had become.

She walked into her bedroom and sat. Time to think. Ariel was a waste. Dirk, although useful in the past, was a drug addict and a bum. Not as stupid as Ariel, but she couldn't help worrying that he, too, could botch everything. Jacoba had a new mother now and she was not going to be raised by the daughter of a whore, not if Amarisa had anything to do with it.

No, just to frighten that woman would not be enough. She stood and walked to her medicine cabinet. She saw her answer.

34

Nora opened her eyes and stared at the gray walls of the basement. She clutched the green-covered diary and stood, her movements mechanical and awkward. She flipped off the lights and climbed into the dumbwaiter, the diary clutched to her chest.

She rose slowly, the mechanism groaning as before. When she stepped out, all was dark and eerily quiet. She made her way to a lumpy couch at the back of the research room and switched on a small lamp on a side table. She looked at her watch. *Midnight*.

She flipped through the *dagboek* again, her eyes taking in line after line of cramped, scrawled words. So many, many pages to read! She lay down on the couch. If she had just a few more hours she would be able to finish it, maybe take some notes and leave it here. She wanted to take it with her, but the receptionist had Marijke's address. If they discovered it was missing, they would find her and make trouble.

She walked out to the lobby and pushed against the glass doors. That was futile and she knew it. *Wasn't there some way she could get out of here?* She felt panic rise as she scanned the walls on either side of the doors, hoping for an emergency exit button. *Nothing.* She walked over to the *medewerkers'* workstation. Locked, of course.

She groaned and walked back to her sofa at the back of the research room. She read a few more pages of Miep's diary and then felt herself get drowsy. She stood up and stretched, not bothering with the coffee machine. She knew it had been emptied at five. She lay back down and decided to close her weary eyes for just a few minutes.

When the *dagboek* fell from her chest onto the marble floor, she awoke. She started and looked at her watch. *Three in the morning!* She stood and walked around, her body stiff and achy from her nap, her mind racing with thoughts and memories.

Anneke, laughing in her beloved garden as she held up a handful of weeds and shook the dirt free from her precious roses. Nora as a young girl, her head in her mother's lap as she felt the delicate, loving stroke of Anneke's cool hands through her hair and the soft kiss on her cheek before she fell asleep.

Then, staring into the darkness, another scene played in her mind—black and terrifying. Fourteen, yes, she was fourteen, had just started menstruating. It played before her eyes as if it were happening all over again.

Midnight. Nora slept that narcotic sleep of a teenager, deep and full, after a day in the surf in Galveston, her parents sleeping in their bedroom down the long hallway.

Suddenly her overhead light flashed on. She raised her hands to cover her eyes, blinded. *Something must be wrong,* she thought, *if Mama and Papa were waking her in the middle of the night.*

Soon her eyes adjusted to the glare and she saw him stand-ing there. A lean young man in a ripped T-shirt and frayed jeans. His eyes seemed crazed—what was it? She felt a slic-ing terror. As he leaned over her, his sweat smelled foul and sour like an animal cornered, yet attacking, holding a hand-gun inches from her face. She in her flimsy pajamas, feeling naked. Her eyes fixed desperately on the door.

He shook his head. *Don't scream,* he whispered. *You scream and I'll kill you.*

Nora felt vomit come up. She forced it back.

Tell me where the money is, he hissed.

Nora shook her head. All she had were a few dollars from babysitting. But looking into his wild eyes, she could tell he thought she was refusing him. His eyes bulged as if bursting. He brought the gun closer, almost touching her forehead, but something inside made her stay perfectly still.

She was transfixed by his eyes. Especially the whites. The whites were what she would always remember—stretched, red lined, crazed. She remembered thinking: *These are the last eyes I will ever see.*

Suddenly his eyes narrowed and the whites retracted, as if some thought caused him to lower the gun a fraction. She felt him take in her long tanned legs, her powder-blue pajamas, her small breasts. He laid the gun on the floor next to the bed, unzipped his pants and dropped them. She could not move her eyes from his and saw him do those things with only her peripheral vision. His stink and animal intent made her choke. She couldn't breathe.

Hardly thinking, she raised her leg, bent her knee and kicked him in the groin with all her force. When he fell back-ward, howling, she struggled to get up. *Run! Run! Just make it to the door!*

But he had the lightning instincts of all evil men. He kicked

free of his pants and grabbed her leg before she could get a
foot on the floor. And then Nora found her voice. Her scream
pierced the silence.

Suddenly, Anneke was at the door, silent, eyes hard, black
stones. Her right foot was planted apart and forward of her
left, her right arm straight out, her wrist supported by her left
hand. She held a black gun with something red on the handle.
Nora took all this in while seconds crawled like days.

The man grabbed his gun from the floor, yanked Nora
up and out of the bed and held her in front of him, a human
shield. Again there was this rank odor, her skin scraped by his
stubble. His fist clutched around her throat, the gun shoved
against her temple. His hiss slit the air. *Drop it or she's dead.*

Anneke's face was flint. She did not speak, nor look at Nora.
Only the flicker of her eyes on his, a quick half step to the
right and the deafening, sickening sound in Nora's ear as the
bullet slammed into him. It was as if his entire head exploded,
covering Nora with hot blood, shards of bone, scraps of flesh.

The last thing she remembered was her mother's black eyes.
They hadn't moved.

When she awakened, she was in her mother's bed. Anneke
was by her side, calmly stroking Nora's hand. Sounds filtered
up from the living room. She heard her father's voice and then
a deep, strange one. The police, she thought.

"What happened?" asked the deep voice.

"I told you." Hans's accent sounded more pronounced by
the terseness of his tone. "This man tried to rape my daughter. I shot him. He's dead."

"What about the gun?" he asked. What is this, anyway—a
Luger? And this swastika, what are you—German?"

"Absolutely not." Nora heard the anger in his voice. "I am
an American."

"But where are you from? That accent, I mean."

"From the Netherlands."

"Weren't you afraid you would hit your daughter—kill her instead?"

He paused and then answered. "No. I was in the war."

Nora looked up at Anneke. She sat perfectly still on the side of the bed, her hands folded in her lap.

"How did you know he wouldn't...kill me first?" Nora's words were a throttled whisper.

Anneke looked at her. Her face was still hard. "His gun wasn't cocked. Mine was."

After the police left, Hans explained to Nora that the rapist's gun was a single-action weapon. In other words, it had to be cocked before it would fire. Anneke's Luger was a double-action semiautomatic. Anneke could either cock it or simply squeeze the trigger. After this brief explanation, her parents told her that they should never speak of this again.

Now in the darkness that enveloped her in the *Instituut,* Nora had her mind on another track. Anneke obviously knew guns. She must have had extensive training to do what she did without a moment's pause. *Had she killed before? She thought of her mother's stone expression when she killed the man and her impassivity afterward.*

And how did she happen to have a Luger with a swastika on the handle, a gun she knew how to shoot as easily as she would flick a fly from her hand? *And why had Hans taken responsibility?* Another thought gripped her. *Could her mother have shot Abram? And had Hans taken responsibility for that, hoping to protect her?*

She thought of her gentle father, a mild-mannered, quiet intellectual, taking Anneke and fleeing the Netherlands. Changing their names and making certain that he led a carefully orchestrated, low-profile life as a classics professor at St. Thomas University. Nora wondered if that was why they had

had so few friends and cut off all contact with their families. It must have been always in the back of Hans's mind, that he might be discovered, deported and stand trial for war crimes.

And be hanged by the neck until dead.

35

Amarisa drew out a brown vial from her medicine chest and examined the label. *Levorphanol Tartrat, ten milligrams.* Van Brunt had prescribed it for her ten years ago to allay the awful pain she still suffered from the steel bar that Nazi bastard had cracked against her leg. For taking too long in the soup line.

It was a dangerous opioid, he had warned her, eight times as strong as morphine and highly addictive. She was to use it only when the pain was unbearable. He had given her the option to take it in pill form, although the injection would bring her speedier relief. Amarisa had chosen the injections. Even now when the agony hit, it brought her to her knees, screaming. But she had not abused the drug. And after so many years, he was convinced that she was trustworthy in its use.

The vial glinted in the sunlight. Amarisa drew a syringe from the package in the medicine cabinet, inserted the needle into the rubber top and drew all of its contents into the needle. A vial lasted her almost a year, if she used it a few times a month. She then set aside the syringe and withdrew another prescription bottle. *Vicodin.* Prescribed for lesser pain.

She went into the kitchen and removed the porcelain mortar and pestle she used to grind herbs. Its heft felt cool, purposeful. She examined the Vicodin bottle. She then ground a full bottle of pills into dust. To that she added grain alcohol, making it a deadly mixture. By the time she had drawn the rest of her potion into the syringe, she knew there was no way that woman could survive.

Ha! *Overkill.* She laughed at her own joke. Just what the doctor ordered.

36

Nora put her head in her hands. How could she have so repressed that terrible event? She must have been traumatized. And they never did speak of it again, as if it never happened.

One thing now seemed certain. Anneke must somehow have managed to grab her Luger from wherever she had it hidden. *And Rose, had the killer hurt her in front of Anneke?* Nora's heart slammed. She knew if Anneke was in a situation in which Rose's safety was threatened Anneke would have offered herself up. Just the sight of those men closing in on her granddaughter— No, Nora could not go there. All she could do now was keep trying to find Rose and bring an end to this hideous nightmare. She willed herself to breathe.

The next thing she heard was the sloshing of a mop and clanking of a pail. She looked at her watch. *Eight-thirty! The cleaning staff was here before the* Instituut *opened.* She grabbed the *dagboek* and crept behind the *medewerkers'* station, praying that the cleaning person wouldn't start there. Her breath quickened. *Shit, the receptionist. Surely he was there already, preparing to open the doors. How in hell could she escape?*

Then she heard the clanking move upstairs, thank God. *Now!* She tiptoed to the wall and peeked around. The receptionist was leaning down, putting his belongings underneath the kiosk. She clutched the *dagboek* and her purse in one hand and darted toward the front door. At that moment, he straightened and his shocked eyes met hers.

"Dr. van Doren!" he demanded. "What are you doing here?" Nora ran for the door as he darted to intercept her. "Stop!" he shouted. "Right now!"

Breathless, Nora grabbed the icy metal handle of the glass door, pushed against it with all her strength, burst through the entrance and slammed into a man's chest. He reeled backward. For an instant their eyes locked. Then she pushed past him and ran.

All she could feel was her heart clawing at her throat, a desperate bird whose wings beat against its prison. She ran through a gray side street into a wet and miserable alley. The cold now joined with a biting rain that pierced her face with what felt like shards of ice. The wet cobblestones seemed to shudder up her body with each step. In a cramped side street, she collapsed against a rough wall and gasped for breath, eyes shut, the diary clutched in her hands. Slowly, her shaking became a mild trembling and her lungs stopped searing. And then it hit her.

The man she'd run into as she dashed from the *Instituut*—his eyes! In her panic, she'd fled before they could register. The last thing she'd heard as she bolted in the freezing rain was a single word. "Nora!"

That voice was unmistakable—a scar in her heart. The same voice she'd heard the last time she'd fled Amsterdam.

It was Nico.

37

Nora felt the wind along the canal lash one final time as she reached the massive stone entrance of the *Instituut*. It had taken her half an hour to walk back. She saw her blurred reflection in the glass front doors. Her hair was plastered to her head, her leather jacket black from the rain. The gargoyles above the doors seemed to look down upon her with wrathful eyes.

She took a breath and pressed the buzzer. She saw the receptionist's eyes widen. He picked up a phone and spoke to someone, never taking his eyes off her. Nora shivered. The temperature had dropped during her trudge back. She steeled herself as the guard got out of his chair and strode toward the entrance. He opened the door.

"*Dr. van Doren,*" he said tersely. "*Kom binnen.*"

As she walked in, she tried to put confidence into her words. "*Ik zou graag Dr. Meijer zien.*"

The guard looked as if he wanted to put her in shackles there and then. "*Blijf U daar staan.*"

She obeyed his order for her to stay put. Rain dripped from her and pooled on the floor. She rubbed her eyes. When she looked up, she saw Nico walking down the red-carpeted stairs. Her heart lurched—with hope for Rose, she told herself.

He seemed taller and thinner, but his long, thoughtful face was the same. His dark hair made his green eyes stand out. It was those eyes that had captivated her and did not leave hers now. She felt something electric and unbidden go through her.

She saw yesterday's *medewerker* appear and move toward her. Without shifting his gaze from her, Nico held up a hand and Dijkstra stopped. The guard stood, glaring at her as if she were planning a terrorist attack on the *Instituut*.

Nora stepped closer to Nico. In so doing, the green *dagboek* slipped from her jacket onto the slick floor and skittered a few feet away. She froze. Nico walked slowly across the room and picked up the diary. He scanned the first few pages and stared at her.

"That's it!" cried the young *medewerker*. "The NSB diary I told her she couldn't have. She broke in and stole it!"

Nico waved the *medewerker* away and walked the few steps to Nora. She could smell a faint trace of his spicy aftershave mixed with a scent distinctly his and then saw the small patch of stubble he always missed when he shaved. Now they were alone in the lobby. It felt to Nora as if they were the last two people in the universe, frozen in unbearable tension.

His voice was low and harsh. *"Kom."* He turned. Nora followed him up the stairs, down the hall and into an office different from his old one. He held the door open as she walked past him and then closed it. *"Ga zitten."*

There were two plain chairs in front of the desk. She chose one, sat and looked around. She saw the dark wooden desk he had used at home when they lived together. It felt so familiar— covered with books and papers opened to passages he had marked in the blue ink he used to buy at his favorite pen shop around the corner from his house. Two large windows offered a splendid view of the *Herengracht*. A silver frame faced away from her. She felt a stab knowing that the face must be his wife's, not hers. She turned the small ring she always wore on her left hand so that the design of silver tulips was hidden. She did not want him to know she still wore it.

Nico walked slowly to his desk. His face seemed shut down—tight. She had seen him like that only a few times. Times she had willed herself to forget. Nico placed the diary carefully on his desk, sat behind his desk and crossed his arms over his chest. "What in the hell are *you* doing here?"

Nora pressed her palms together to keep them from shaking. *"Waarom spreek je geen Nederlands met mij?"*

He glowered at her. "Why should I speak Dutch with you? You left Holland, if you will recall. You're an American."

Nora started to speak, but he held up his hand. "Just answer my questions," he said. "Why are you here? Why did you fake a letter of introduction to get into the *Instituut?* Did you really steal a diary from the archives?" His voice rose. "Have you lost your goddamned *mind?*"

Nora stared back at him, stung. She would gladly take whatever he dished out, as long as he helped her find Rose. "Please stop yelling at me," she said quietly. "I have excellent reasons for everything I've done."

"Wait a minute," he said icily. "I'm calling the shots here. Let's summarize, shall we? The guard tells me that someone I've never heard of shows up when I just happen to be on vacation and hands over a letter of introduction *from me.* Not only does she waltz into the research room, asking questions about people whose names are unfamiliar to me, but what am I greeted with the day I return?"

Nora almost interrupted but decided against it. When Nico

was angry, it was pointless to reason with him until he had gotten it all out. She focused on staying calm.

"The day I get back, I try to open the door to my place of business and some crazed woman bolts out of the door and almost knocks me down. As if that isn't astonishing enough, I look down and see you. The woman who swore to me that she would never set foot in Amsterdam again. Does she stay and tell me what the hell she's doing here? No, she runs off like a criminal." His face tightened. "Just like she did almost two years ago."

He took a deep breath. Nora saw the pain on his face. "Then I'm greeted by a *medewerker* who is about to fall on his sword because during his shift, a *dagboek* of some NSB woman has disappeared. Apparently not only is the *dagboek* missing, but so is the mystery woman. This esteemed professor of Netherlands Studies, from Stanford no less." Nico pushed back his chair. His eyes were fierce.

Nora felt a flush of anger. "Are you finished?"

Nico sat back. "For the present."

"Good. Then if you'll listen for just five minutes, I'll tell you everything you want to know."

"Wouldn't that be amazing?"

The sarcasm brought tears to her eyes. She felt so damned tired. And the horrible, horrible things she had read about her mother. She pointed at a small table in the corner. "Could I have a cup of coffee before you have me arrested?"

Grim faced, Nico walked to the coffeepot, poured a cup, added two sugars and brought it to her. He hadn't forgotten. His fingers touched hers as she took the cup. She tried to ignore the sudden spark she felt. She took a sip. Her hands trembled. She knew he saw her pain, but his face remained unchanged. She took a deep breath. "First, you have every right to be annoyed with me."

"Annoyed?"

"I should never have fabricated that letter," she said quietly. "I tried to call you, but they told me you were on vacation."

"It must be something very important indeed for you to contact me." His voice was glacial. "I'm fascinated, particularly since you made it clear you never wanted to see me again."

"Please, Nico. I need to talk to you about something critical. I really *must* have your help."

"And why did you think I would help you?"

Nora felt like screaming. "Because even though you're still mad as hell at me for leaving, I knew I could count on you."

"The Nico you knew would have done anything for you," he said quietly, "but not the Nico I am today."

She stared at the thin gold band. "You're married."

"That, *Dr.* van Doren, is none of your business. Not anymore."

Nora looked away, trying not to break down, but tears now streamed down her face. Not only did Nico not care for her anymore, he despised her. He would not help her. She stood and Nico's face blurred, the furniture spun and the dark waves of the *Herengracht* disappeared as she looked through the window.

Suddenly everything tilted. She imagined Nico moving toward her in slow motion, just as he had in the dreams that never, ever went away. The arms that reached out for her seemed so strong, so safe—no, she wouldn't faint. Not here, not now. She had to tell him about Rose. He *had* to help her.

Nico put his arm firmly around her waist as he walked her back to her chair. She collapsed into it. He stood over her. She saw the concern on his face. "What is it? Are you ill?"

She took a breath and shook her head. "No, just a little dizzy."

"Not eating again?"

"It's not that." She grasped his arm. "Please sit down, Nico. I have to talk to you. So much has happened."

Nico took his seat, his face brooding, wary.

"I really need your help." She hated the desperation in her voice.

"So you said. Now what is this all about?"

"My mother is dead—murdered."

"What! Murdered by whom?"

Nora felt more tears start. Her voice shook. "That's the problem. I don't know who did it."

"Nora, this is crazy!" he said. "Who would want to kill your mother?"

"That's what I'm here to find out."

"What could possibly be here that would lead you to discover that?"

"It's a long story, Nico, and I will tell it to you." She paused. "But even more horrible is that someone with the murderer, kidnapped—" she paused for another breath "—my daughter." Nora felt a sharp pang seeing the shocked expression on his face.

"You have a *daughter?* When did all this happen?"

"After I moved back to the States."

"Obviously," he said coldly.

With shaking hands, Nora pulled her wallet from her purse and opened it. The photo of Rose she always carried smiled up at her. Silently, she handed it to Nico.

He took it, stared at it and then handed it back. He cleared his throat. "What is her name?"

"Rose," she whispered.

"But why do you need my help?" Now his voice was normal, even businesslike. "Surely the police are investigating?"

"The Houston police, the FBI, the Dutch authorities—they haven't found anything." She started crying. "Rose has been missing for over two weeks now. They tell me that she may never be found—that she may be *dead*."

Nico moved his chair closer to hers and took her cold hands into his. His warmth sparked hope into her.

"Nora, I am so sorry," he said softly. "But what does that have to do with your coming here and doing all these crazy things?"

"The killer had to be from Holland—someone from the war. He murdered my mother for revenge."

"What?"

"I'll tell you, but you have to *promise* to help me! It's as much for you as it is for me."

Confusion filled Nico's eyes. "What does *that* mean?"

"It's Rose."

"But Nora, where is the father?"

"I'm looking at him," she whispered. "Rose is your daughter."

38

Nora sat with Marijke in her living room after a simple dinner. As Nora related her confrontation with Nico, Marijke was rapt.

"What did he say when you told him Rose was his daughter?"

"He was shocked, as you might imagine. He must be sitting at a café having a few strong drinks before he has to go home and tell his wife."

"No question about that! But is he going to help you?"

"He said he would do everything he could. He has the *dagboek* and I explained about my mother—that she was an NSB-er, Abram Rosen's murder, the judgment and how I suspect that her murder was a revenge killing. He promised to stay at the *Instituut* until he had put all the wheels in motion with his staff and that he would let me know the minute he finds anything. God, I'm so relieved."

"That he is going to try to find something?"

"Definitely that. But also because he finally knows about Rose."

Marijke shook her head. "I wouldn't want to be his wife right now. Is he angry at you for not telling him?"

Nora felt again the fury Nico had unleashed upon her. *How could she not have told him,* he'd yelled. *She had no right!* "Angry is too mild a word. He couldn't believe that, despite what happened between us, I would deprive him of the chance to make a different choice because of the baby."

"He's right, you know."

"I know," she whispered. "I guess I didn't feel I had any other option."

Marijke put her wineglass on the coffee table and shrugged. "Well, at least it's all out in the open."

Nora nodded. But she did not tell Marijke that when she stood to leave, he had walked her to the door. Before she could open it, he'd grabbed her and given her a rough kiss. As she'd walked away, the joy of his lips on hers remained. She didn't know if he still had feelings for her or if knowing that they had a child together had prompted the kiss.

Marijke looked at her watch and stood. "I have to go. I'm meeting my boyfriend at his place."

"Quite a fiery romance you have going on there, judging by how many nights you spend with him."

Marijke laughed. "I do rather like the man."

When she left, Nora gave in to her exhaustion, put on her robe and drew a hot bath. Before she could step into it, the phone rang. *Shit.*

"Met Nora de Jong."

"Nora, it's Lieutenant Richards."

"I was just thinking of calling you! Have you gotten anywhere?"

"No, neither the P.I. nor I have found anything new."

"So what now?"

"We keep looking. Are you coming back soon?"

"Not yet. But I've found someone to help me and I think we'll move forward more quickly now."

"Who?"

"The head of the Dutch War Institute, Nico Meijer. He can research this far more quickly than I ever could."

"How do you know this guy? Is he legit?"

Nora was glad he couldn't see the flush she felt on her cheeks. "He's—well—he's Rose's father."

"What?"

"It's hard to explain." She felt flustered. "I lived with him in Amsterdam, but it didn't work out and I went back to the States."

There was a short silence. "Well, do what you need to do. Maybe you'll get somewhere. We certainly haven't. And don't worry, I'll keep you informed about the investigation here. You let me know if you find something."

"I will."

"Goodbye, Nora."

She stood wearily and went back upstairs, added more hot water and sank gratefully into the steaming tub. But even then she couldn't relax. In her mind's eye she saw Rose resting on her legs, wriggling in the soapy water and laughing as Nora planted kisses on her tummy. *Would she ever hold her again? Where was she now? Was she sick, dead?* She closed her eyes, sank down farther in the tub and willed herself to believe that Nico would solve this. *They would find Rose. God couldn't be so cruel, not before her baby had even begun her life.*

Just as the tenseness in her body began to melt, she heard steps on the creaky stairs. "Marijke?" She must have forgotten something. But she heard no answer, only footsteps creeping up the stairs. Nora felt the hair on her neck prickle. She jumped out of the tub, almost falling on the slick tiles, threw on her robe and locked the door. She tried to keep the terror out of her voice. "Who is it? What do you want?"

She heard heavy breathing and saw the knob spin, but not open. She looked around the tiny bathroom for something to use as a weapon. All she saw was a nail file, a plunger. *What could she do?*

She heard a hard bang against the door. It was a man, cursing under his breath. At that moment, the doorbell rang.

"Help!" she screamed. "Someone has broken in!"

She heard steps racing down the stairs and a shattering of glass. *Was it safe for her to dash downstairs and run to the door for help?*

A loud voice yelled through the front door. "Nora! It's Nico! Are you all right?"

She ran down and flung open the door. Nico grabbed her and held her close. "What's happened? Are you all right?"

"A man!" She gasped and pointed to the rear of the house. "I heard a window break."

"Wait here. I'll be right back."

Nora stood shivering in the doorway until he returned. "You're right. There's glass all over the floor." She buried her face in his neck. "It's all right, he's gone now."

He led her into the living room, sat her on the couch and poured her a Scotch. She gulped it down and spluttered. "Nico, I'm so scared."

He sat down beside her. When he put his warm, strong arms around her, she finally caught her breath.

"It was just a burglar," said Nico. "Happens all the time in Amsterdam. We should call the police, although I doubt it would do much good."

Her mind now flashed on the night at the café. "Someone attacked me in an alley a few days ago."

"God, did he hurt you?"

"No, but he ran off before anyone could catch him. The bartender in a café across the street looked for him. He said it must have been a drug addict or just someone looking for money."

Nico held her tightly. "That must be what it was. Poor sweetheart."

Nora drew back. "What if it wasn't a coincidence? What if someone is after me?"

"Why would that be?"

"Maybe I'm close to finding out something. Maybe someone wants to stop me."

Nico shook his head. "Seems unlikely. But it still might be dangerous for you to be alone."

"What can I do? Hire a bodyguard?"

"No, I'll make sure you're safe."

"What made you come here tonight?" She grasped his arm as fear and hope consumed her. "Did you find something? Tell me fast!"

"*Ja, ja, rustig maar.*" He pulled a small notebook out of the inner pocket of his jacket. "I was able to contact someone I know who specializes in wartime genealogy, one of those permanent graduate students with an obsession, in this case one that works in our favor."

"What did he find?"

Nico patted her hand and smiled. "Give me a moment to explain. René—the graduate student—has a particular interest in high-ranking NSB-ers."

"Why?"

"His father was shot down by an NSB-er for stealing food for his family. As you may know, we now have a growing problem with the resurgence of the national socialist movement. René decided that his thesis would focus on if—and how many—NSB children have become part of the new movement."

"But how does that help us?"

"That's the beauty of it. As it happens, your mother's father, Joop Brouwer, was a prominent NSB-er. He was also admitted to the SS, extremely rare for a Dutchman. He was notorious for his savage treatment of the Jews." He paused. "Apparently he was brilliant at locating Jews, whose names he then turned over to the Nazis."

Nora felt sick. "How did he do that?"

"He knew Amsterdam. He was adept at ferreting out hiding places because he was so familiar with the city's buildings. He also turned in many of his neighbors whom he felt were obstructing the unification of Holland with Germany."

"But what did your friend *find?*"

Nico handed her the small notepad. "He read it to me over the telephone."

She scanned the page, disappointment welling in her. "But I know this already. Joop, Miep—"

Nico shook his head, leaned in closer to her and pointed to a scrawled word. "Read this."

She looked again, this time more closely. She saw it—a chicken scratch of a line across from Miep's name. *Saartje Steen.* Stunned, Nora looked up. "Who is she?"

"I'm not sure. René thinks she may be their sister."

"Why wasn't she mentioned in Miep's diary?"

Nico shrugged. "Maybe they had a falling out.... Or she moved away during the war."

"Do you know if she's still alive?" Nora was so afraid. She didn't know if she could endure another dead end.

Nico pulled out another piece of paper and handed it to Nora. "She's alive—old, but alive."

Nora grabbed it and read it quickly. "Was she married?"

"Apparently," said Nico. "Which is why the *medewerker* didn't know to look for her."

Nora clutched the paper. "I have to see her. Right now."

"Not tonight."

"Why not?"

"Look at the address," he said. "She lives in Schiermonnikoog."

"Friesland? Why in God's name would she live there? It's up north in the middle of nowhere!"

"Who knows?" he said. "Anyway, I found her."

"And?"

"It's the address of a convent," he said. "Saartje is a nun."

39

Amarisa opened the door. Dirk stood there looking bedraggled and filthy, as usual. "Wonder of wonders." He grunted and then followed her silently to the kitchen. They sat on opposite sides of the table.

"Well, have you found anything? If you've screwed it up, I'm not paying you a cent—"

Dirk glared at her. "If you'd shut up for a minute, I'll tell you."

"Don't push me, Dirk. Let's not forget what side your bread is buttered on."

"How could I forget? You shove it up my ass every day."

"Get on with it."

"Okay, I broke into her house last night after I made sure she was alone. But as I was going up the stairs, she heard me and screamed. Then some asshole came to the door, so I had to beat it out of there."

"In other words, nothing."

"Hey, nobody saw me and now she knows someone is after her."

"A common burglar, nothing more."

"Christ, Amarisa, don't be such a bitch. I'll still get her. She's going to Schiermonnikoog. Train leaves at eleven."

"How do you know?"

"'Cause I hung around outside under the bitch's window and heard them talking. Some guy named Nico Meijer. Meeting her there tomorrow."

"What in hell is in Friesland?"

"If you knew, you wouldn't need me, now would you?"

"Don't fuck with me, Dirk."

"Okay, okay."

"I'm going to tell my worthless nephew that the woman is on her way to Friesland. I'll tell him to take the afternoon train. You may need a patsy to blame if it all goes wrong. And don't fuck up like last night or you won't see a single guilder."

"Will you listen! It wasn't my fault—"

"Save it."

Dirk started to rise.

"Wait," said Amarisa. "I have something to give you." She stood, opened her refrigerator and took out the capped syringe, admiring her handiwork. Then she handed it to Dirk.

"What's this?"

"What does it look like? Take it to Schiermonnikoog and inject it into her carotid artery. Do you even know where that is?" Then she demonstrated with her fingers.

His eyes widened. "What will it do to her?"

"Don't worry, it works quickly."

Dirk flung the syringe on the table as if it were a cobra ready to strike. "Look, Amarisa, whatever else I am, I'm not a murderer."

"No, but you're a thief, a heroin addict, a gambler and a

thug who hurts people when I tell you to. This is just one step further." Amarisa could see the hate in his eyes. "This isn't a request, Dirk. It's an order."

"Goddamn it, I'm out of this!" He slammed his fist on the table. "Now you want me to *kill* this woman. And who do you think the police will be after? *Me!* Then even if I finger you, who do you think they'll believe? Some street guy or a rich bitch with a diamond business? No, I won't do it!"

Amarisa looked at him coolly. "Fine." Suddenly she reached across the coffee table and yanked up his sleeve. "Look at those tracks. You think I don't know you're still dealing? I keep tabs on you, darling Dirk." She handed him back the syringe. "And don't forget. One tip from me to the police and you can kiss your life goodbye."

"Stop threatening me!"

"You have five minutes to make up your mind. So just sit here and think about what you have to lose." She strolled into the nursery to check on Jacoba. A few moments later, she came back.

Dirk hung his head in his hands. *Fucking bitch.* The thought of killing someone made him feel sick. He knew he was a bum, but a *murderer?* Then a thought struck him. *Wait! Maybe he could run his own show.*

"Sit down." His voice was harsh. Amarisa sank slowly into the soft armchair across from him. "Here's the deal—and it's not negotiable. If I do this for you, then it's over between us. You pay off my debts—all of them. Then ten thousand to do the job and a ticket to Greece with five thousand more to get the hell out of here and start over. That's it."

Amarisa stared at him, thinking. She lit a cigarette and inhaled deeply. "Deal."

"And I mean it." He glared at her. "You fuck me over, get

me arrested, do anything to lay all this on me and I'll turn you in so fast it'll make your head spin."

"Dirk, I hold the same cards against you. So it serves neither of us to be pitted against the other." She held out her hand. "Truce?"

Dirk looked at her warily. Finally he stuck out his hand. They shook. He stood and put the syringe inside his jacket pocket. "I'm out of here. I'll let you know."

"Good boy."

He glared at her and stomped out.

40

Nora was so excited about Nico's news that she threw her arms around him. "I can't thank you enough," she whispered. Sobs of relief racked her.

"Ach, lieveling," he murmured. He held her in a tight embrace until her crying subsided. She reveled in the safety of his arms. She buried her face in his neck, overwhelmed that this man she had loved would help her despite how she had left him, despite his marriage to another woman and despite the bitterness he must still have toward her.

She felt as if she were falling back into the past. There was no ending to their bodies when they were this close. It had always been that way. They just—fit. As her trembling subsided, she inhaled the soaped leather scent that was his alone. It affected her like opium. She felt herself give in, give way, give up as she lifted her lips to be kissed. His warm, kind hands held her face, his mouth so close to hers. At that moment, she opened her eyes. Nico gazed at her, his lips a moment from hers, his eyes searching hers. She drew a shaky breath as the moment hung between them, then pulled back.

"Nico," she whispered. "I don't want to hurt you like I did last time—or your wife."

Nico raised his hand and placed two gentle fingers on her lips. *"Nee,"* he said softly. Nora kissed them, not wanting the moment to end. "I want you to answer a question."

She nodded. "Anything."

"Other than the horrible things that have happened, are you happy with your life?"

How to answer? Words first caught in her throat. "With Rose," she murmured, "I am as happy as I can be."

Nico took her right hand and held it up. "You still wear my ring," he said. "May I ask why?"

Nora knew she should pull her hand away, but it lay in his, an egg in its nest. "I don't know."

He turned her hand over and kissed her palm. "Don't you?" he whispered.

"Nico, please don't," she said softly. "You're married. It isn't right."

"Since you came back, nothing is right."

"I don't want to interfere with your life."

"It's too late for that," he said quietly. "I have a daughter. That changes everything."

"Oh, Nico—"

"You are going to let me be involved in her life?"

"Of course, if that's what you want." Relief filled her until reality hit. "But what about your wife? Wouldn't she mind that you're kissing my hand?"

"I'm sure she would mind terribly."

"Then how can you be here with me?"

Nico eyes looked sad. "My wife and I lived together for a year after you left. I was in such terrible shape that I let myself begin a relationship when I shouldn't have. My wife had just divorced her husband, who cheated on her. Both of us were on the rebound. I did her a great disservice. She is a very good woman." He sighed. "She knew about you, but thought I'd get over it. We both did. Obviously I haven't. Then when we got married, everything went downhill fast. We've been separated for two months. She filed for divorce almost immediately."

"Have you told her about Rose?"

"Not yet. I don't think it would make a difference. The marriage is over."

Nora looked away as the old pain coursed through her. "We had our chance," she whispered. "And we ruined it. It's too late."

He clasped her to him. "It is never too late."

A long moment passed. Nora stood and motioned for him to do the same. She took his hand and led him upstairs to the bedroom.

41

Nora sat in the train on one of the red seats with a view out the window. Dark rain whipped against the glass. Wet, green blocks of land fled by, taking her farther and farther from Amsterdam. She looked around, saw a few older passengers eating sandwiches, their heavy luggage on the overhead racks. The morning crush of people going to work had emptied as the train chugged farther north to Friesland.

She looked at the slim diary she had finished during the train trip. It had been more of the same. Miep's sick adoration of her brother, concerts she had attended, a fur Joop had bought for her. Only snippets about Anneke. The NSB functions Anneke attended, their pride at Joop's induction as an SS officer, Miep's fervent hope that Anneke would marry the SS soldier she had continued to date. It made Nora feel sick.

She glanced at her watch. She had been to Schiermonnikoog with Nico one winter and the journey felt familiar. In an hour, the train would pull into Leeuwarden, where she would take a bus to Lauwersoog, then hop on the ferry to the island of Schiermonnikoog. The trip would be a long one—about five hours.

Nora nestled back into her seat and closed her eyes. She could still feel Nico's warm lips upon hers. They had not spoken as they held each other close, their bodies entwined. It was as if they had never been apart. The naturalness of their coming together felt to her as if the pain of the past had disappeared. They were one, murmuring as their bodies spoke to one another. It was as it always had been. Sitting in the train, she could still feel his body over hers. Their love was still there—always new, always old, always forever.

After their first time, Nora had sobbed quietly as Nico held her. Her tears were not from the pain that had gripped her during the past weeks, but tears of coming home to her place in his heart. Last night she had reclaimed it—and him. Whatever happened next, she could live knowing that she had loved and been loved.

Nico had awakened early that morning and gone to the office. He had an important conference with members of the Cabinet that afternoon regarding measures that were under consideration involving the neo-Nazi movement. It could not be rescheduled and he had no idea how long it would last. The trains to Schiermonnikoog were infrequent and he had wanted Nora to wait for him so they could go together. He had reminded her that she had been attacked twice now and that he couldn't let her risk it happening again. She needed protection.

But Nora had been too nervous to wait. She had finally convinced him that she would take the early train and that if all went well, Nico would join her that evening. If he couldn't get away, they would be apart for only one night. When she promised that she would alert the railway guards if she saw any strange characters and then go straight to the hotel, he had finally agreed.

When she told Marijke what had happened, her friend had offered to come, but Nora knew that she was scheduled to be in Germany for the next two days. Marijke had made her promise to call when she arrived and said that if Nora needed her, she would hop on the next train.

Nora was stirred from her reverie by the clacking of the coffee cart rolling down the aisle. She nodded at the sour-looking man, handed him five guilders for a cup of coffee and then waved him off when he tried to give her change. She clasped the cup as it warmed her cold hands and the hot liquid slithered deliciously down her throat. *Dutch coffee. The best.*

"Leeuwarden," the conductor announced in a gravelly voice. Nora picked up her purse and small overnight bag, stepped down and walked out of the station. She had a ten-minute wait for the bus to Lauwersoog. After she reached the ferry terminal and boarded, she felt her impatience grow, continuously checking her watch during the forty-five minute journey to Schiermonnikoog. She so wanted to be there, to talk to Saartje. *There has to be so much she can tell me!*

She imagined Richards's desk piled high with thick files, Rose's shoved underneath, where it would disappear, unsolved. *No!* Richards would not stop trying. Nora wiped tears from her cold cheeks. *So what if her parents were Nazis?* All she wanted was her darling back in her arms. Saartje had to be the link that would bring her to Rose. The alternative was unthinkable.

42

Amarisa slammed the door behind Dirk. *Friesland!* The whole thing was getting out of hand. She sat, looking out her window into the sunlight. Maybe he'd still pull it off and that woman would no longer be a threat.

Then a thought struck her. She grabbed the phone book from her desk, picked up the receiver and dialed.

"Rijksinstituut, central operator. May I help you?"

"Yes, this is Nora de Jong. I would like to leave a message for Nico Meijer."

"I believe he is in his office—"

"No, thank you," said Amarisa quickly. "I am in a terrible hurry. Please tell him I'm going back to the States today. That my daughter has been found. I'll call when I arrive."

"Then could you please give me the flight information and a number where he can reach you?"

"Just give him the message," she snapped, and hung up.

Ha! That should keep this Nico, whoever he was, out of the picture for a while.

43

Nico stared at the message his secretary handed him. He closed his eyes, feeling miserable. While he knew he should feel thrilled that Rose had been found, he felt scared. *Would Nora be out of his life now? He wondered what last night meant to her. Perhaps she would she go back to Houston and never return, and he would never get to know his daughter.*

He crumpled the message and threw it in the wastebasket. *Was he now supposed to wait until she called from Houston? He couldn't bear it.* He buzzed his secretary. "Book me on the next flight to Houston, Texas."

A few moments later, she buzzed back. "All of the flights to Houston are already booked. I can get you out early tomorrow morning."

Verdomme. "Keep trying. Maybe there will be a cancellation. I need to get there right away." He turned to stare at the muddy water of the *Herengracht.* This time he would not let her go. He would fight for her and for his daughter.

44

Ariel stood at the platform and glanced at his watch. He had ten minutes to make the six-o'clock train. He found a phone booth and called Leah. "Leah, Rose's mother is on her way to Schiermonnikoog."

"How do you know?"

"Amarisa called me. Told me to follow her."

"But why would she go to Friesland!"

"I don't know."

"What are you going to do?"

"I've got to warn her." *The murder, Rose, the hiding, the terror. He couldn't take it anymore.*

"What?"

"Remember when Amarisa told me she'd hired a 'professional'? I'm afraid Nora's going to get hurt—or even killed. Amarisa is crazy enough to do it."

"Have you lost your mind? Amarisa will turn you in. You'll be arrested! And we'll never see Rose again."

Ariel felt a sharp pang. "Sweetheart, you must know now that Amarisa will probably never give her back to us, don't you?"

He heard her choked sob. "Oh, Ariel. It's just so hard to let her go."

"We have to. It's the only way to set things right. My father killed her mother and I stole her daughter. I couldn't live with myself if anything happened to her, too." He heard her crying. "Listen, the train leaves in a minute. I'm going to find Nora and find a way to tell her where Rose is and warn her about Amarisa."

"But how? Once you tell her, she'll scream for help and you'll be arrested!"

"No, I won't let anyone see me. I don't arrive until eleven tonight, assuming the train is on time. I'll wait until morning and then tell her when she's alone."

"Ariel, it's so dangerous!"

"I know. But I have to. She isn't just Rose's mother, she's my cousin."

"Please be careful!"

"Listen, ask Amarisa to let you keep Rose for the night. Then maybe we can tell Nora where she is without Amarisa knowing."

"She'll never do it."

"Just do your best." Exhausted now, he hung up and joined the queue for the train. He found a seat next to the window on the last row. He pulled his hat over his face and slumped down as if asleep. He felt like crying, but the relief was overwhelming. Finally he was doing the right thing.

45

Nora looked at the shuttered gift shops in front of the station as she waited for the shuttle that would take her to the *Hotel van der Werff*. When she and Nico had gone to Schiermonnikoog, it was in the dead of winter. It was hard to imagine that it was boiling in Houston. She pulled her jacket tighter to ward off the icy wind.

Schiermonnikoog, she knew, was one of a necklace of islands on the Netherlands's northern coast. When she and Nico had spent a weekend there, he had told her that it was only ten miles long and three miles wide, the smallest of the inhabited islands in the Wadden Sea. She had been amazed at low tide. In winter the shallow sea actually disappeared and one could walk all the way to the next island.

Nora shivered. Schiermonnikoog certainly was not a winter resort. In summer, tourists came to engage in *wadlopen*, mud hiking, where they plodded through soggy flats and observed wildlife—worms, shrimp, crabs and fish. It was a

dangerous sport and, under Dutch law, required accompani-
ment by trained guides. It wasn't just the precarious plodding
through the deep, slippery sludge, but also involved forging
through chest-deep water.

She and Nico had taken long walks on miles and miles of
sand, holding hands, sharing cold lips and warm embraces.
They had watched gulls, spoonbills and herons. Once they
even saw a seal sunning itself on a large rock.

A small van pulled up. She climbed aboard with two other
passengers, feeling excited. *She had made an appointment for ten
the next morning. Would Saartje have something important to tell
her? Tomorrow she would know something, she just felt it!*

After the short trip, she walked up to the old stone building. It loomed large and dark. Icy rain slammed her as she
hurried to the entryway, clutching her small bag and purse.

She walked into an enormous lobby, her footsteps muted
by thick carpet, twelve-foot ceilings and dark wood panel-
ing that shone from the floor up to an elaborate crown mold-
ing. A sense of déjà vu filled her. Everything was exactly the
same. The musty smell and deep burgundy of the chairs in
the lounge, the view of the misty beach from the window,
the fire roaring in the bar.

The desk clerk eyed her small bag when she told him that
she was there only for one night, two at the most. No one
came to Schiermonnikoog for just one night. The journey was
considered to be an intercontinental one for the Dutch, who
packed fruit and sandwiches for any train ride over an hour.

Nora checked in and went upstairs. It was the same room
she and Nico had shared. A good omen. She put her things
on the bed and walked to the window. Although it was only
three in the afternoon, the beating of the rain on the leaded
glass made it gloomy. She wished that Nico was with her,
but he had probably been unable to get away. Oh, well, she

thought, he will be here tomorrow. And she would rather see
Saartje alone. Perhaps she would open up to Nora more than
if Nico came along.

She looked at the beach but could barely make out the thin,
gray strip where sand met sea. It seemed as if the shoreline
went on forever, that the sea was simply a sailor's mirage, a
siren song.

Exhausted by the trip and the roller coaster of her reunion
with Nico, Nora lay down. She fell into a dreamless sleep.
When she awoke, the room was dark. She turned to the clock
on the night table. *Six thirty-five.* She groaned and sat up. Hunger pangs reminded her that she had not eaten since a roll at the
station in Amsterdam. She went to the washbasin and looked
into the mirror. Black smudges seemed embedded under her
eyes, her face sickly and pale, her hair tangled. She turned on
the tap and splashed icy water on her face. It left her breathless but woke her up.

Downstairs, Nora walked into the hotel restaurant, seeking
a modest meal. She couldn't handle more than that. She looked
around. A few tables were occupied, more than she would have
expected this time of year. She noticed the bartender polish-
ing a few glasses and chatting with a man at the bar.

A waiter appeared and led her to a table, where she sank
into a leather chair and asked for a Bordeaux. She ordered fish
and then sat back, taking a long sip of wine. She felt it flood
and rejuvenate her. This was the closest she had come to re-
laxing since Rose disappeared. She immediately felt guilty.
How could she relax even for a moment without Rose?

The waiter appeared with her meal. She took a few bites of
her grilled fish and put down her fork. She knew by the aroma
that the food had to be delicious, but somehow it tasted like
burned paper. She pushed away her plate and drank another
glass of wine. As exhausted now as she was before her nap, she

stood and walked up the one flight to her room. Once inside, she took a steamy, hot bath and crawled into bed. A sliver of hope glimmered in her before she fell asleep.

46

Dirk waited impatiently as the few passengers exited the bus for the ferry to Schiermonnikoog. He picked up his overnight bag and could hear his binoculars and camera jostle inside it. And his pistol. Never left home without it.

He had missed the earlier train. Amarisa had kept him too long with her bitching. No matter. He would be there around six. Before he left Amsterdam, he had called the *van der Werff*, the only decent hotel on the island, and had confirmed that Nora was a guest. He had asked for her room number, saying he was her brother and would be joining her, and was surprised when they gave it to him. *Small town. No crime.*

Once in Schiermonnikoog, he took a bus to the side of the island opposite from her hotel and rented a small cabin, making sure that the clerk was aware that he was an ornithologist, there to observe and photograph birds and wildlife for a few days. It was one of the island's main attractions, even in winter.

He would case Nora's hotel to see if he could slip in later

that night. If not, he would wait until he could find her alone. *Goddamned Amarisa.* He still didn't know if he had the guts to kill this Nora, but then he thought of the money. He knew Amarisa was good for it. And he'd be flush for the first time in years.

He'd make quick work of it before he lost his nerve. *But what if he failed? What if, at the last moment, he couldn't do it? What would Amarisa do to him then?* No, he had no choice. *He had to be rid of that bitch once and for all.*

47

Nora walked out very early the next morning and found a cab at the hotel entrance. She had slept fitfully, waking often during the night. She kept wishing Nico were here, but she would see him soon. Knowing that he was so busy yesterday, she had not called him.

She handed the address to the driver. When they reached the convent, Nora tried to peer out of the window, but the hard rain blurred everything. She paid and stepped into a bitter wind that lashed her hair into whips and stung her face.

She looked up at the massive edifice that seemed as if its stone had been hewn in medieval times. The rain made it appear black, foreboding. *Het Huis van Onze Heilige Moeder* was carved into a wooden plank above the narrow entryway. To her left, a small, sad statue of the Holy Mother held out delicate hands from a niche in the wall.

Nora pulled on the rope that hung in the doorway. A low, deep clang reverberated through the heavy door. Moments passed. She pulled her jacket tighter around her. The temperature had dropped and the clouds were low and full, promising no end to the foul weather. She reached again for the rope, but before she could grasp it, the door opened with a grating sound. An old nun appeared in the cramped doorway. A tiny woman, she wore somber, black robes, her wimple wrapped so tightly about her face that her plump cheeks seemed ready to burst. An enormous crucifix hung from a braided chain and bumped against her black belt.

"I am Sister Magdalena." Her voice was clear and strong. "May I help you?"

Nora had trouble understanding. Her Frisian dialect was strange to Nora's ear. She knew Frisian more closely resembled Old English than Dutch and when there were Frisian programs on television, they had Dutch subtitles.

The sister held out a cool hand. Nora took it. "I am Saartje Steen's great-niece," she said. "I called you yesterday?"

The old nun nodded. "Oh, yes. Please come in." She silently led Nora to a small office near the entrance and ushered her in. Nora sat and watched as the old woman took a seat behind a massive wooden desk. She cleared her throat as she fixed Nora with a calm gaze. "Saartje Steen has been with us many years. She is Sister Josephina now. After losing her husband in the war, she left her family and gave her life to the glory of service to the Lord." She shook her head. "Sadly, it appears that she is now near the end of her path."

"Is she dying?"

The sister smiled. "We are all dying, of course. But no, Sister Josephina's body is sound for someone her age. It is her mind, you see. It has begun to leave her. In that respect, I believe she is truly blessed."

"But...how can that be a blessing?"

There was a light knock. Sister Magdalena stood and walked

to the door. A sleeved hand passed something through the opening. When she returned, she handed Nora a clay cup of aromatic tea and returned to her chair. She peered at Nora. "You are very young, my dear. Let us just say that when God sees fit to heap intolerable tragedy upon one of His true believers, one is fortunate if, by whatever means, that pain is lifted."

Nora felt like crying. *Another dead end.* She looked up at the nun. "Is she insane?"

The nun smiled her quiet smile. "That depends upon whose definition you would employ."

Nora put down her cup, feeling so, so weary. "I would be happy to accept yours."

"I would say that Sister Josephina is caught in time and space—between heaven and earth."

Nora felt as if she would burst. She had had such high hopes. Now they were dashed like the waves on the rocks outside. "May I see her?"

The nun's blue eyes were a laser. "I will permit that, with one proviso. My concern is for Sister Josephina's soul. It has been entrusted to me and I must see it pass easily from this life to the next. You must promise not to disturb her. You must agree to enter her time and her mind." She paused. "If you cannot do this, I must ask you to finish your tea and leave us."

Nora felt as if she were a specimen under a microscope. "I have no wish to disturb her."

The nun studied her, stood silently and walked to the door, letting Nora pass before her.

Nora followed her through dark, winding hallways, their footsteps the only sounds on the cold stone floors. Sister Magdalena explained that there were only twenty elderly sisters left at the convent. Their order required that they spend their days in silence, prayer and meditation. She instructed Nora not to speak to any of the other sisters if she should see them. She was to avert her eyes so as not to distract them from their prayers.

They climbed a narrow, pitched staircase. Nora thought she could feel the wind blow right through her. She glanced behind them. There was no way she could ever find her way back to the entrance without a map—or a nun. The wind was howling outside, the rain pelting on the roof. She shivered.

After what felt like an hour, they came to the end of a long hallway. Another elderly nun sat upon a hard chair outside of an arched doorway, a black rosary in her hands. She stood and left them, never raising her eyes.

Sister Magdalena turned to Nora. "I shall leave you to enter and greet Sister Josephina. More than one person at a time is too much for her. It would be best if you enter silently and permit her first to acknowledge your presence." She gave Nora a flinty look. "I must remind you of our agreement."

Nora nodded. *What in hell was wrong with Saartje? Was she schizophrenic or just your garden-variety demented?* It didn't matter. Nora had to reach her.

As she began to enter, Sister Magdalena grasped Nora's arm. The old nun held out her white hand, palm up. "Please give me your watch."

"My watch?"

"Time disturbs Sister Josephina."

Nora unclasped her watch and handed it to her. The nun seemed satisfied, and yet she did not leave. "Is there something else?"

"One last thing." She pointed at the raging storm outside. "The lightening. It frightens Sister Josephina. Please try to comfort her."

Nora nodded and watched as the nun disappeared down the dark hallway. She braced herself and opened the door.

The room was larger than she had expected, all white, with

high ceilings and a black slate floor. It had a single bed, a small wooden desk, a sink and a toilet, dimly lit by a floor lamp in the corner. Three thick candles glowed as if to ward off evil spirits. An icon of the Virgin Mary hung above the bed, surprisingly rich in its reds, blues and shimmering gold. Her sad eyes seemed to follow Nora as she approached the bed.

It was perfectly made, white sheets pulled tight. A flat, white pillow lay uncreased at the head, a thick woolen blanket folded neatly at the foot. Nora spied a bell on the nightstand. *This is ridiculous. No one is here.* She stepped back toward the door. She'd find Sister Magdalena.

Then she heard a thready voice from under the bed. A tremulous Dutch voice reciting prayers. *"Beloved Virgin, protect your servant. Oh, Heavenly Mother, do not abandon me now! Keep me safe from harm."*

Nora crouched down, her knees on the icy floor. She peered under the bed. The dark was partially lit by the soft glow of the candles on the night table. From Nora's angle, they looked almost like stars. Gradually her eyes adjusted. Under the far side of the bed, Nora saw the slight, crooked form of an old woman who wore a thin white nightgown. Her eyes were closed as the words came softly from her lips. *"Mother full of tenderness…"*

Nora felt moved with pity. "Saartje," she whispered. The woman's eyes were sealed shut. Nora reached forward and took her arm. She pulled the small creature toward her. The old woman did not resist, but let herself be moved like a rag doll. When Nora had finally maneuvered her out, she saw a face as fine as porcelain and milky blue eyes that did not focus on hers.

Nora lifted the almost weightless form and placed her on the bed. Saartje's head lolled back on the pillow as Nora straightened her legs and tucked the rough woolen blanket around her chilled body. Still no response. Nora cupped the pale cheeks in her hands.

Suddenly, a blaze of lightning flashed in the window, followed by a clap of thunder. Saartje's eyes flew open. She screamed—a hawk's screech—and beat upon Nora with her small fists. She rose up to dive under the bed, but Nora held her tight. She kept her voice soft and soothing.

"Saartje, it's all right," crooned Nora. "You're safe. Its just a storm."

Saartje moaned, wrenched herself free and pulled the blanket over her head. "No! No!" she screamed. "It is the airplanes—the bombs! We have to hide!"

Nora gently pulled the blanket away from her face. The eyes that moments ago seemed lost to the world now locked on hers, clear and bright. Saartje began sobbing as she lunged forward and clasped Nora in a desperate embrace. Then the words poured forth. "Praise God!" She turned her gaze upward. "My prayers have finally been answered. You are here!"

Nora tried to soothe and quiet her, but the old woman was clutching her fiercely, her thin, cold face pressed into Nora's neck. "It's all right now, it's all right," whispered Nora, her own tears flowing.

After a time, the old woman stopped sobbing. The eyes that fixed upon Nora's were sharp and lucid. Nora smiled nervously. "You don't know me, *Tante* Saartje, but—"

The old woman sat bolt upright and clapped her hands like a little girl, her crooked smile wide as fresh tears streamed down her face. "What nonsense! Of course I know you!" She waggled her index finger at Nora. "Always playing games!" she chortled. "Come, after so long, you must not tease me." She began muttering again, mumbling disjointed prayers and unintelligible exclamations.

Nora could feel only dismay. The poor woman simply

wasn't there. She had so hoped to talk with someone who would have known who Abram was and why her mother was killed, and why—*oh, why?*—someone had taken her Rose?

She tried to pull away, but Saartje rose and clutched her again in a desperate embrace. Nora could smell her sweat. They sat that way for what seemed like forever, each in her own prison of pain.

Suddenly, Saartje released her grip. Nora felt the woman's body slump and then she sat up straight against the headboard, looking at her.

Nora sat there, staring, and then dropped her head, defeated. She could not stop her tears that fell onto the plain, cotton sheet. "I just wish you knew me—knew who I was!" she whispered fiercely.

Nora felt a cold, bony hand gently raise her face. "Of course I know who you are." The voice was firm and clear. "You are my Anneke."

48

Nora pulled back and stared at Saartje. *She thinks I am Anneke! What can she tell me? Can I believe anything she says?* Saartje gazed off into the distance, as if someone were calling her. Nora cupped Saartje's pale face in her hands and made Saartje look at her.

"Yes, *Tante,* it is Anneke," she said softly. "I have come back to get you. You are safe now."

Saartje smiled and then gave Nora a reproachful look. "Why did you leave us?" Her voice was stern. "You made us hide that boy. And now my Gert is dead!" She pulled away from Nora, sobbing.

"*Tante,* who is Gert?"

Saartje looked at her with amazement. "Your uncle! Don't you even remember your *Oom* Gert? He was so good to you!"

"Of course I remember him."

"It was that Jewish boy." Saartje sounded irritated. "It is all your fault."

"What Jewish boy, *Tante?* What was his name?"

Saartje shook her head. "I don't remember. It is all in the box—you know that. You gave it to me."

"What box?"

Saartje smiled. "The box with the important things in it. Don't you remember?" Her eyes wavered, looking confused. "It was when you brought that boy to us."

"Was his name Abram? Abram Rosen?"

The old woman waved her away with a listless hand. "The one the Nazis were after." Her gaze returned and fixed on Nora's. "*Ach kind,* so many horrible things have happened since you went away."

"What things? Tell me."

Saartje sobbed quietly and stared at the flickering of the candles. "All you told us was that the Jewish boy would die unless we hid him." She burst into tears. "And then one night I heard him arguing with Hans outside in the street and a gun went off!" She raised her arms as if to ward off the sound. "Then Hans came inside and told us to hide in the cellar." She burst into tears. "That night the police came and took away my Gert. And I never saw him again!"

Nora sat, shocked. Then she leaned forward and gently put her hands on Saartje's wet cheeks. "*Tante,* please. This is important. Did Hans kill Abram?"

Saartje shook her head. "I don't know who killed him," she cried. "You are the one who knows! You sent him to us!"

Nora didn't know what to think. "Did Abram have any friends? Any family?" she asked. "Anyone who came to visit him while he was with you and Gert?"

Saartje pushed Nora away and stepped down onto the cold stone floor. She began to pace, wringing her hands. "Only the boy, the young one. He came a few times."

Nora's heart leaped. *This could be it! The connection!* She stepped over to Saartje, took her frail elbows in her hands and looked into those wandering eyes. *Not now! She has to stay with me long enough to tell me the truth!* "Saartje, what was the boy's name?"

Saartje dropped her head. It felt to Nora that if she loosened her grip, the old woman would fall down. "Anneke, I am too tired. I cannot think about these things anymore. Please leave me alone, *kindje*," she whispered. "We will talk later."

Nora panicked. She shook Saartje gently and spoke more loudly. "Please, *Tante*—I'm begging you. Just think. What was the name of the boy?"

Saartje raised her head and gave Nora a reproving look. "Do you not know your Bible, child?"

"What do you mean?"

The old woman gazed upward. "Abraham's promised son."

Nora could tell she was fading fast. She knelt in front of her and clasped both of Saartje's thin hands in her own. She looked up. *She was so close!* Saartje's blue eyes grew dim. She placed her hand on Nora's head and gently stroked her hair. "You must study your Bible," she whispered.

"Please, *Tante*," whispered Nora fiercely. "Do you mean than Abram had a son? Is that who visited him?"

"No, no!" said Saartje irritably. "That's not it at all."

"What was his name?"

Saartje pulled away, crawled back into bed and assumed the fetal position. Nora rushed over to her, but the old woman's eyelids had drooped. Nora heard the last faded words fall from her lips. "Abraham's promised son."

49

The next morning, Dirk set out, nervous as hell. *Who wouldn't be if he was going to kill someone?* He wore the plaid birding hat, heavy jacket and thick pants. With binoculars and a camera around his neck, he pretended to observe the birds hopping on the beach a short distance away from the *van der Werff*. Every now and then he snapped a few shots, like all the idiotic bird-watchers who, being Dutch, refused to be deterred by shitty weather. He stomped around in the goddamned cold for hours, icy rain trickling down his neck. When by midmorning he had not seen Nora leave, he worried that he had missed her.

He called the hotel from a restaurant close by. No, Mevrouw de Jong had left early. No idea when she would return. *Damn it.* He hated having to hang around all day, but he had no choice. Finally, around three, he saw her get out of a cab and go into the hotel, but there were too many people going in and out. While pretending to take a few shots of the beach from the back of the hotel, he noted a service entrance. He

ANTOINETTE VAN HEUGTEN

tried it. *Locked.* Looking both ways, he pulled a switchblade from his jacket and jimmied the door. Then he walked calmly back to the road, hopped on the bicycle he'd rented and rode to his cabin.

Once there, he poured himself a shot of dark rum. He had the shakes so bad that some of it sloshed onto the floor. *God, he needed a fix.* His skin crawled and stung. He felt as if he were being devoured by fire ants. But all he had left was one dose and he had to save that for tonight. He lay in his bed all afternoon and evening, visualizing step-by-step every move he would make, anticipating how she would resist him, how he would overpower her.

Around eleven, he took a hot shower and slugged more rum straight from the bottle. Then he cut and dyed his blond hair a nondescript brown from a bottle. *Nice touch.*

Dirk shook the syringe that Amarisa had given him, the ominous yellow liquid in it swirling silently. It scared the shit out of him. Suddenly he went from feeling frightened to furious.

Fucking bitch! How could he have let her talk him into murder? What if he fucked this up? He'd shot himself up a hundred times, but he'd never done it to someone else kicking and screaming. If he got caught he'd go down for attempted murder, not just assault. He'd be the one rotting in jail. No way. He wasn't going to jail again—not for Amarisa, not for anyone.

But he *needed* that goddamned money. So he'd do it his way—with his bare hands, the way he'd always worked. He picked up the syringe, walked to the sink, removed the tip and plunged her shit down the drain. Now he felt in control.

Then another idea. He took apart the syringe, scrubbed it with dish soap and hot water and then rinsed it. From his overnight bag, he took out a small bottle of alcohol he always kept to make sure his needles were clean. He poured it inside and outside the syringe, plunged it through, over and over, and then rinsed everything again with hot water.

As it dried, he pulled an envelope from his jacket. *Heaven's powder.* So it wasn't white, just a shitty brown like all street stuff, but it'd get him where he wanted to go. He went through the drill of mixing it with water, adding some lemon juice he had bought in a grocery in town, heating it in a spoon and then—poetic justice—filling Amarisa's syringe with *his* shit. *What a great fuck-you,* he thought.

He felt the fierce need to shoot up, but he'd force himself to wait until just before he went to the hotel. It might give him the balls to go through it. At one in the morning, he walked to the beach, sat inside a stone cabana protected from the wind and watched the black waves crash onto the shore.

After what seemed like forever, it was two o'clock. *Surely the hotel was deserted by now, except possibly for the desk clerk. And that bitch was certainly asleep.* He slipped the syringe from his pocket, shook it, tied off and shot up. As he walked to the dunes behind the *van der Werff,* the smack hit him—hard. By the time he reached the service entrance and slipped stealthily up the stairs, he felt as if he were flying.

Killing wouldn't be so bad.

50

Exhausted, Nora dragged herself up to her room. It was too much for her to bear. The poor woman was demented. And Nora had felt so positive, so *certain* she would be able to get answers from Saartje, Anneke's very own aunt, who could have given her the key to end this torture. She was desperate to try again the next day, but the Mother Superior had refused. Her responsibility was to shepherd Saartje's soul and she would not subject her sister to any more traumatic experiences. Nothing Nora said had changed her mind.

She unlocked her door and dropped onto the bed fully clothed and almost immediately fell into a deep sleep. When she awoke, she looked groggily at her watch. Six p.m. She struggled out of her clothes and crawled into bed. She heard the wind as it whipped around the building, rain slamming against her windows. She fought tears, the piercing disappointment. The ferocity of her wails and sobbing frightened her. *It was hopeless! She was no closer to finding Rose.*

There was no life left for her without her baby, the softness of her skin, the wonderful heaviness in her arms when
she held her. Nothing else mattered. She cried until she could
cry no more, rolled over and let the twilight of sleep lull her
again. Thankfully, she sank into it.

51

Ariel stood at Nora's door. He had checked in under a false name at 11:00 p.m. and gotten Nora's room number from the clerk, which was a surprise. For some reason, the man believed that Ariel was her brother. Now that he didn't have to wait until morning, he snuck from his room upstairs around two, found her room and raised his hand to knock. A noise caused him to turn around. He saw a large man, a pistol pointed at his head.

Ariel raised his hands and jumped back. "Oh, God! Don't shoot!"

"Get the fuck out of here—now!"

"Who—who are you?"

"None of your business. Get your ass down the stairs—fast."

Ariel felt as if his heart had stopped. His arms, still above his head, began shaking. "This is a terrible mistake! Please, listen to me—"

The man now took careful aim. Ariel barreled toward him,

gave him a karate chop to the neck and then a swift kick to his stomach. The man staggered and grunted, almost falling, but recovered quickly. He sidestepped Ariel's next attempt, steadied his grip on the pistol—and fired.

Ariel recoiled as the bullet hammered into his shoulder. Before he could cry out, the man wrenched his neck into a half nelson and hissed into his ear. "The back way. Down the stairs. Two seconds. Don't scream or you're dead." He released him and kicked him toward the stairs.

Ariel felt as if he would pass out, but his terror made him clutch his bloody shoulder and run. He took the stairs two at a time and blasted out of the service door into the night.

52

Nora awoke and the room was dark. She'd been awakened by a noise outside her room. At first she forgot where she was. She turned to the clock on the night table—2:15 a.m. She groaned. The stupor of her sleep had affected her like a narcotic.

Suddenly a form loomed over her. Strong hands clapped themselves over her mouth. Her eyes flew open, but she could not see the monster in the pitch dark. She screamed, but the savage hands pressing down on her mouth prevented any sound.

He yanked her out of bed, still holding one hand over her mouth. He turned her roughly, facing her away from him. A guttural Dutch voice breathed into her ear. "Don't scream."

She didn't move, petrified. Then she remembered. She had unlocked the door and, in her exhaustion, forgotten to lock it behind her. The hands now clutched her throat in an iron grip.

"Who are you?" she croaked, fearing that if she moved he would choke her. "What do you want?"

His mouth was even closer to her ear. "I work for someone who has your daughter," he whispered.

"Rose, you have *Rose?* Where is she? Is she all right?"

The man squeezed her throat, not cutting off her air completely, but enough to make her feel faint. "Quiet! She's alive," he hissed. "And she'll stay that way if you stop what you're doing."

Nora kicked feebly at his knees, tried to twist around to see him. "Please!" she whispered. "Give her back to me! I'll give you anything you want!" She could smell the man's foul sweat.

"Get out of this country and your daughter won't be hurt. If you don't, she's dead."

"Tell me where she is!" she cried. "I can't leave without her—please!"

Nora clutched his fingers, trying to pry them from her neck and claw at his face, but he was too strong. *Goddamn it!* She would will herself to force the bastard to tell her where Rose was, to find out if she was hurt—anything! But he pushed her face down on the bed, shoving her head into the mattress and pressing it there. When she felt herself losing consciousness, he loosened his hold. Then she felt something cold and hard pressed against her temple.

"You want me to kill you, too? What will happen to your sweet baby then?"

"No, no! Please!"

"I don't think you heard me."

Suddenly, with all her might, she twisted and escaped his grasp. "Help me!" she screamed. "Someone help me!"

She heard a bang on the door. "Shut up in there! We're trying to get some sleep!"

"Shit!"

Nora heard the alarm in his voice and then felt him smash her on the temple. The last thing she heard was him running from the room.

53

Ariel ran down the narrow highway to the ferry as fast as his legs would take him. The road was not lit and only white gravel showed him the way. He felt as if he were swimming through syrup, his shoulder on fire. He felt dizzy, as if he might pass out. As he ran, ragged thoughts sliced through his mind. *Don't let them catch me! How many miles to the ferry? Surely he could make it!*

The snow had a deep layer of ice underneath it and he slipped and fell, trying not to land on his injured shoulder. He screamed out of frustration and pain. *Get up! Keep going! Forget about your shoulder!* He struggled to his feet and wiped the sleet from his watch. The green, glowing numbers told him it was almost three. He had checked the ferry schedule when he arrived. The first one left at four-thirty. *He had to make it.* Terror propelled him as his lungs felt as if they would burst.

Wild thoughts hammered through his brain with each footfall. *Had that maniac shot her? Was Nora dead? Even with the si-*

lencer, the pistol's report still rang in Ariel's ears. Someone must have heard it.

But would the son of a bitch be caught? And how many officers could they have in such a tiny place? He knew that Schiermonnikoog was barely ten miles long, but even if no cars were allowed, the police must have a squad car.

If anyone had seen him, it wouldn't take long for the police to set out to search the island. He ran faster than he thought possible. He glanced at his shoulder, horrified at the blood that had seeped through his shirt.

Now as he pumped his arms and willed his weak legs forward, he was bombarded by jagged fragments of what had happened that day, playing like a surreal film in his mind. *How had it all gone so horribly wrong?*

A stitch pierced his side. He stopped running, bent over and gasped for breath. His shoulder throbbed. He was done in. They would find him. He stumbled a few more steps and then looked up. *There! He saw it!* Through the fog he made out the blurred outline of the ferry station. And yes, the ferry was still there, tied up to the dock!

He looked at his watch. Four twenty-seven. He sprinted the last fifty yards, adrenaline driving his exhausted legs even though he felt as if his chest would explode.

Breathing heavily, he walked into the small wharf house. Hands shaking, he kept his head down as he bought a ticket from a bored clerk who didn't even ask him why he was panting or why he awkwardly used only his left hand to extract guilders for the fare.

He stuffed the ticket into his pocket and hurried to the upper deck. His shoulder still throbbed, a steady hammering of pain, but he was afraid to go to the men's room and examine it. *Was the bullet still lodged in his body or had it pierced the skin and passed through?* If so, the bullet had to be somewhere in the hotel hallway. Maybe the police would match the bullet to that son of a bitch's gun when—if—they caught him. *No doubt Amarisa had sent that bastard. Maybe to kill him, too.* The cold wind whipped about him as he waited, terrified that at any moment the police would rush ahead and put him in shackles. If they did, it would only be a matter of time before they got to Leah…to Amarisa…to Rose. He groaned. *Had it all been for nothing?*

After an eternity, he watched as the gate onshore swung closed and, after much creaking and groaning, felt the rumble of the engines as they started up. Finally, the ferry pulled away.

I made it—I'm safe! As soon as he thought it, he knew that the police could still stop him when the ferry landed in Lauwersoog. His body trembled so that he collapsed onto one of the hard iron benches. The vicious pain in his shoulder had returned. Still, tears of relief filled his eyes. As the gray light rose and the miles between the ferry and the island grew, he calmed down enough to think of his next move. He would go back to Amsterdam on the first train and tomorrow he would stake out the flat of Nora's friend. If Nora were still alive, she had to come back.

He had an overwhelming urge to hold his wife and take Rose onto his lap—to be the threesome they had become.

But the awful question remained. *Had the bastard scared her off? If not, what had he done to her?*

54

Nora opened her eyes, the bright lights hurting them. Then she saw that the young clerk was at her side. Next to him stood a thin, disheveled man who appeared to have been roused from a deep sleep.

The clerk, looking terrified, helped her sit up. "Are you all right?"

Then she remembered and struggled to her feet. "The man who attacked me! Did you catch him?"

The thin man shook his head. She saw the concern in his eyes. "I'm the manager, *Mevrouw* de Jong. All we know is that another guest heard something, went to your door and someone pushed past him and ran out of the building." He helped her to her feet. "We've called the police and a doctor. They should be here any minute."

"No! No! You have to send someone out to look for him! He has my daughter and he tried to kill me!" She yanked her jeans on under her nightgown, ran out into the hallway, down the stairs and pulled open the side door. *Nothing!* She stumbled outside, but fog enveloped her. She couldn't see two feet in front of her.

She raced back to the lobby, where the manager was talking excitedly on the phone. "You've got to do something!"

The young clerk took her by the arm and led her, weeping, to a stuffed armchair in the great room. "Please try to calm down, *Mevrouw,*" he said softly. "We'll find him. The manager is calling in our staff members and they will search the grounds."

Nora sobbed, her entire body shaking. Her thoughts were rampant, disconnected. "There was blood—on the carpet! From my room down the hall. Was it his? Or did he shoot someone?"

"We don't know, but it does not appear that any of our other guests were harmed. They have been told no one is allowed to leave until they have been interviewed by the police. Their rooms will also be searched."

He strode over to the bar, scooped some ice into a cloth and hurried back to her. She held it against her temple and then put it down. Tenderly, she touched her bruised throat, unable to banish the thought of that bastard's hands choking her. Her head pounded so badly she couldn't think.

The manager appeared, a large snifter in his hand. "Cognac," he said gently. "Drink it."

Nora took the glass. She saw him watch her shaking hands. *He was right. She had to calm herself. If she didn't, she wouldn't be able to think clearly and she'd never find Rose.* Numbly, she grasped the glass. Even with two hands, she could barely hold it. She sipped the stuff and sputtered as the fiery liquid seared her raw throat.

"Better?"

Nora tried to speak, but winced. She coughed and handed him back the glass.

"Would you like another one?"

"I'll be all right," she croaked. *Rose was alive! Unless it wasn't true.* The clerk came back and put a rough blanket around her. "Our staff is searching, but the fog is terrible."

Two officers then arrived and fired questions at her. Nora's words tripped over one another as she tried to explain what had happened, the background of her mother's murder and Rose's kidnapping.

A thin, pimply-faced young officer wrote everything down. When he finished, he clapped his notepad shut and said that their small force would scour the island. Unfortunately, the ferry had just left. Nora groaned and let her head fall into her hands.

Had he gotten away? Just like that? "If he took the ferry, can't the police catch him on the other side?"

"We're still trying to contact the station in Lauwersoog." He gave her a sheepish look. "No one is answering this early. It's winter."

She felt furious. *Christ, where was she? The Third World?* "What about the blood?"

"We have to have a sample analyzed and we can't do that here. Has to be sent to a lab on the mainland."

"How long will *that* take?"

"No idea. We've never had anything like this before."

"Well, what *are* you doing?"

"We're checking every hotel and resident, including the passengers who arrived on the ferry yesterday. Even though there are few tourists this time of year, it will take some time. We only have—"

"I know, a small police force." She heard her irritation. "Is there any way to ascertain how many passengers there were?"

"It's not a sophisticated system. Since no cars are permitted here—only bicycles—the ferry operator just eyeballs the number of passengers and decides if he has too many. He's been doing this for forty years."

"Is there someone I can call for you?" asked the elderly manager.

Nico! She almost ran to the reception desk, startling the young clerk. "Please," she said. "The telephone—I have to make a call."

The young man placed the telephone on the counter. *"Alstublieft."*

Nora dialed. It rang three times before she heard the voice she loved. *"Met Nico Meijer."*

"Nico—oh, Nico!" She burst into tears.

"Nora, what is it? Where are you?"

"In Schiermonnikoog!"

"I thought you were in Houston! That Rose had been found."

"What? Who told you that?"

"I got a message—never mind. What's happened? Are you all right?"

After many attempts and broken sentences, she told him the story. "Nico, he said that Rose is alive!"

"God, Nora, I hope he's telling the truth."

"He has to be!" she cried. "Why else would he do this?"

"Did you get a good look at him?"

"No, damn it. The lights were off, and then he cracked me on the head with his pistol and I passed out."

"Oh, God, are you all right? Have you seen a doctor?"

"They've sent for one, but I'm fine."

"I'm coming right away. I can't get a train until the morning, but I'll be there by early afternoon."

Nora shook her head, as if he could see her, then said, "No, there's nothing you can do here. It would be better if you contact the Dutch police and the U.S. Embassy and alert them. They know all about the case. I made sure of that before I left the States." She paused. "And you should call Lieutenant Richards. He's the officer in charge in Houston. I've got his number upstairs somewhere. I'll get it."

"No, stay where you are until the doctor comes."

"Okay. Just call Marijke. She'll have it."

Nico told her about the message he had received. "Someone thinks you know more than you do. They must have been following you to do something like this to get me out of the picture."

"But how did they even know I was in Holland?" she cried. "What do they want? The bastard said he worked for someone who had Rose. Who could it be? And what possible motivation could he have to keep her?"

"I don't know, but whoever it is, he appears willing to kill you."

"God, I must be getting close to something or this never would have happened. And there's no doubt now that this is connected to my mother's murder. Nico, I'm coming back to Amsterdam. The answer has to be there."

"Nora—no! I will not let you travel alone when some madman is trying to kill you. It's out of the question."

She felt a surge of love for him. "Nico, please. I'm positive he caught the first ferry and escaped. He'd be stupid to try to get near me now. But I need you to make those calls. If the police find anything here, I'll call you right away."

"What happened with Saartje?"

Nora's head throbbed. "She's not in her right mind. It was very sad. I didn't learn anything."

"You don't think you should talk to her again?"

"The Mother Superior won't let me. I upset her too much."

"Well, I'm still not convinced I shouldn't catch the next train." She heard a rustling of papers. "I'm looking up the numbers right now. I'll stay and make the calls if you promise me one thing."

"What?"

"That you'll come home right away. That you'll have a police officer accompany you to the ferry. I know the Amsterdam Chief of Police—we were classmates. I'm going to call him the minute we hang up and make sure that someone is with you the entire way to Amsterdam. Until then, you are not to move from that hotel."

The warmth in his voice did more for her than twenty cognacs. "I promise."

"Nora," he said hoarsely. "I can't lose you now that I've found you again."

She felt tears well up. "I'll be careful," she whispered. "I don't want to be lost."

55

"Met Dirk."

"Well, were you successful?"

"Not sure."

Amarisa heard the slur in his voice. "Are you drunk? What in hell is going on?"

"Yeah, I've had a few. Close escape."

"What happened?"

"Well, last night I went up to her room, but that nephew of yours was there, just about to knock on her door. He came at me and I had to shoot him."

Ariel, that little son of a bitch. "Did you kill him?"

"Nah, just clipped his shoulder. He ran off."

"Did he get caught?"

"How the fuck do I know? Think I'd stick around after it all went south? All I know is he bled all over the carpet."

Amarisa snorted. "So if they analyze his blood and match

it to him, they'll think he's the bad guy. Maybe he'll prove useful, after all."

She could almost hear Dirk shrug. "I guess so."

God, he was stupid. "What about the woman?"

"Roughed her up, but maybe not enough to scare her off."

"What about the syringe?"

"Got interrupted." Amarisa thought she heard a bottle clanking against a glass. "Some other asshole banged on the door when she screamed. Had to beat it and dump the needle."

"Moron. You damn well should have stuck her or shot her when you had the chance."

"I've had to lay low today. The cops were questioning everyone. Said I was a bird-watcher and they bought it."

"Where is she now?"

"No idea. Probably headed back to Amsterdam."

"Brilliant." She thought a moment. "Find out what train she'll be on."

"How do I do that with all these cops crawling around?"

"Hang out by the ferry. The minute you find out when she leaves, call me."

"Okay, but I'm not sticking my neck out."

"You will if you know what's best for you. And then get back here fast."

"Why?"

"What do you mean 'why'? To finish the job, you fool."

"Amarisa, this is turning out to be more work than we talked about."

"If you think now you're getting any more money out of me, forget it. You better damn well finish what you started."

"You're not listening. The cops are on it now."

Amarisa felt consumed with anger. "You do what I say. Or you'll find your ass in worse trouble than you ever imagined."

"Try it. I'll just disappear."

"Then I'll have to alert the police to your prior indiscretions."

He paused, then spoke. "All right, all right. I'll come back, but we have more talking to do."

"Oh, we'll talk, all right. Just get here. And don't fuck around."

She hung up and went into the nursery. Rose was sleeping. Amarisa ran a hand down her soft pink cheek. *Oh, she'd take care of Ariel all right.* Now she had another card to play to keep him under her thumb. Actually, Ariel had done exactly what she had hoped in the event Dirk screwed up. Now he would be the suspect.

She stared out the window. *Now what?* She had to be damned careful with her next move. And if that woman wasn't going to be scared off, then she was going to die.

56

Ariel stumbled through his front door, almost collapsing into Leah's arms.

"Ariel, what is it!"

All he could do was groan and clutch his shoulder. She helped him to the couch, ripped off a piece of his bloody shirt and gasped. "You've been shot!"

"Leah, please, I'm all right."

"*All right?* Who did this to you?"

He felt as if he might pass out. Leah propped the sofa cushions under his head. At that moment he was so, so grateful that Leah had done a rotation in the E.R. during her nursing training. She ran for her first-aid kit, rushed back and tore off more of his shirt. "Oh, Ariel!"

"Is the bullet still in there?"

She examined the wound with probing fingers. "No, it must have gone straight through. I can't tell if it hit the bone or not, but you've lost a lot of blood. Ariel, we have to go to the hospital!"

"No! No, we can't!" He explained what had happened, how he had gone to Nora's door to warn her, how some bastard had shot him when they struggled.

"But who *was* he?"

"I don't know. It was dark, he was dressed in black. He shot me before I could get a look. Then I just ran as fast as I could."

"I still don't understand."

"Amarisa."

Leah's eyes widened. "Her 'professional'?"

"Who else?"

"That *bitch*. Ariel, he could have *killed* you!" Leah kept on with her deft cleaning of the wound. Ariel tried not to cry out. "Is that what she wants? Is she so crazy that she'll kill to keep Rose? And what did this thug do to Nora?"

"I don't know," he sobbed. "But this is all my fault. I started it the moment I took that baby into my arms. Now her mother may never see her again. I know Amarisa. She's probably left Holland by now—remember, she said she would!"

"Let's forget that for now. I'm still worried about that bullet. I'm going to take you to *Sint Lucas Andreas*."

"*No!* Leah, you can take care of me here." He was feeling so woozy. "Right now we need to talk this out."

Leah sobbed. "Oh, God, Ariel, did any of your blood fall onto the floor?"

"I don't know, but I think it had to. I didn't exactly stop to find out."

"But what if they analyze a sample and match it to you—or your fingerprints?

"I've never committed a crime—that anyone knows of. Besides, there won't be a match."

"But what about the screening test for your job?"

"Oh, shit!" Everyone in Immigration was fingerprinted and blood typed as a matter of course. To make sure they didn't hire criminals—like him.

Leah strode to the phone and picked up the receiver. "I'm calling Amarisa. This has to stop."

Ariel struggled to stand. "No, Leah, put that down! If you call Amarisa, you'll just warn her and she'll run off with Rose. If you call the police, I'll definitely go to jail. We'll never see one another again!"

Leah stared at the receiver and slowly put it down. "So what now? We can't just sit and do nothing!"

Ariel collapsed back onto the cushions. "I have no fucking idea. But I am going to find a way to tell Nora everything. As soon as this shoulder will let me." He felt as if his world had flattened into nothing. "I don't care what happens to me anymore. It's gone too far."

57

After Nora checked out, she had the cab take her to the convent. Sister Magdalena had called and left a message. She had asked *Mevrouw* de Jong to come by at her convenience. There was something she wanted to give her. Nora thought about her conversation that morning with the chief of police. He hadn't found anything even after claiming to have interviewed almost everyone on the island.

When Nora pulled the long rope, the old nun opened almost immediately. She saw the question in Nora's eyes. She handed her a weathered cardboard shoebox, tied up with a dark burgundy ribbon. "This contains Sister Josephina's only worldly possessions. I thought you should have it."

Nora's heart quickened as she took it. "Thank you," she said. The nun wished her a safe journey and Nora walked back to the taxi.

At the ferry station, the same pimply faced police officer met her. They exchanged pleasantries and he told her that a train guard would accompany her back to Amsterdam. Once she took a seat, she wondered if the ferry would make it to the other side. It was rusty and its engines seemed to groan as they left the dock. She was still so exhausted that she closed her eyes and listened as it churned its way to Lauwersoog.

After the bus ride, the train finally ground its way out of the Leeuwarden station. Nora nodded to an older train guard who looked like a heavy-jowled bulldog. He seemed irritated but nodded back. A real Dutchman, she thought. Not much for small talk. Probably thrilled to have drawn the lucky bean to babysit her during the five-hour trip to Amsterdam. She didn't know if he was armed or not, nor did she ask.

She felt haunted knowing that she was onto something important enough to be killed for. She stared at the box in her lap. Surely it could only hold a few family photos, perhaps one of her mother in her NSB costume. Could she bear seeing that?

Sighing, she untied the burgundy ribbon and lifted the lid. She sifted through the stuff, its contents unremarkable. A photograph of a young Saartje in a wedding gown, smiling up at a blond man who must have been Gert. Two photographs of Anneke, both as a child. Nora sighed. She had been right to try to keep her hopes in check. She didn't feel anything. *It must be how oncologists dealt with deaths of their patients, she reasoned. As a young doctor, each death destroyed you. When it happened time after time, you just became numb.*

She was about to put the cover back when she saw something stuck to the bottom. She pried it off. It was a sealed envelope, but the yellowed adhesive was so old it had cracked. Inside was a thick piece of paper embossed with the words *Juliana van Stolberg Ziekenhuis.*

She glanced at it. *Mother: Anneke Brouwer.*

What? Did Mama have a child before me? Her eyes raced down the page.

Child: Nora Brouwer! Stunned, she pored over the document. *Date: May 1, 1945.* That wasn't even her birthday. The birth certificate her parents had given her showed that she had been born on May 15, 1945—in Houston, not Amsterdam. *Why would they have falsified this?* Her eyes skipped down to the box underneath her name.

Father: Unknown.

Nora stared at it. *It made no sense. Why wasn't her father's name in the box?* Then the reason shot through her. *Because Hans must have murdered Abram Rosen. Anneke couldn't risk listing his name as the father.* It seemed to confirm what she had suspected. Anneke must have delivered her just before they fled to the States. *Which must mean that her father was, indeed, a murderer.*

She felt frozen as she put the paper back into the box and tied the ribbon around it. Her entire life had been a lie, all lies.

She stared out and listened to the clacking of the wheels. She was weary and bereft. And nothing had gotten her even a step closer to finding Rose.

So what now? Nothing came to mind. Whoever the madman was, he had escaped. Hired by someone who had Rose and threatened to kill her. The throbbing pain in her temple returned as she drifted off to sleep.

58

"Amsterdam CS!"

Nora woke with a start. She looked groggily out as the train slowly pulled into the station. She felt as if every bone in her body ached. The old guard who'd come to protect her stirred and nodded to her as Nora gathered her things. She was lucky no one had tried to harm her again. The old man would have slept straight through it. He stood and mumbled a question. Did she want him to walk her home? She shook her head. Nico knew what time her train was to arrive and was probably already outside the station. Besides, she felt safe surrounded by the throng of commuters.

She walked to the doors. When they opened, a gust of cold greeted her. Shivering, she stepped down onto the concrete platform and pulled her jacket tighter around her. The old man followed and then disappeared into the crowd. As she walked to the exit, she heard her name called out over the loudspeaker.

"Mevrouw de Jong. Calling *Mevrouw de Jong.* Report to the ticket office as soon as possible. You have an emergency message."

Her first thought was that it had to be Nico. She rushed to the ticket office and waited impatiently in line until a surly man handed her the message.

I have information about your daughter. Go outside the station and look for a young blonde woman in a red hat.

Nora dashed to the exit and stood outside amid the crowd on the plaza. *Where was Nico?* She looked wildly around. *No Nico and no woman in a red hat.* She walked quickly back and forth through the crowd, craning her neck.

As she made a third pass, someone bumped her from behind. An older woman carrying a large package seemed to have lost her balance as her box fell to the ground.

"Please help me!" she cried. "It's a birthday gift for my niece and I'm afraid it will be trampled."

As Nora bent down, the woman knelt next to her. Picking up the package, Nora felt the woman grab and yank down the collar of her coat. At the same moment, someone jostled the woman and she hit the ground, moaning. "My leg!" A young man helped her to her feet.

Nora rushed over. "Are you all right?" The woman gave her an odd look and rushed off.

Still holding the package, Nora cried out for her, but she had disappeared into the crowd. As Nora turned, something crushed under her heel. She bent down to pick it up. It was a syringe. A yellow liquid had splattered on the concrete. *What in hell was going on? Who was that woman?*

Confused, Nora realized that she still held the package. She undid the ribbons and opened the box. It was empty. She threw the syringe into it and kept searching the crowd as it flowed in and out of the station.

There was no one in a red hat.

59

"Nora!"

Still grasping the package, she whirled around. It was Nico running toward her. She fell into his arms, her heart racing wildly. "Nico!"

He held her tightly. "Everything is all right," he whispered. "It's just me."

Nora let him hold her until she felt her breath return. She raised her face as he released her, his piercing eyes searching hers. "What is it?" he asked. "Did someone try to attack you again?"

"I think so." Her hands shook as she told him about the emergency page, the woman in the red hat, the old woman and the syringe. She handed Nico the package with the damaged syringe. "It's empty. I think she was trying to stab me with that needle."

"Who could she be?"

"No idea."

"You've never seen her before?"

"No."

Nico stared at her. "I bet it was the same woman who called me at the *Instituut*. The one who left a message that Rose had been found and you had already gone to the States."

Nora suddenly felt dizzy and her knees buckled. Nico caught her. "Nora, what is it?"

"Please," she whispered. "I have to sit."

He led her into a small café a few steps from the station. She sat while Nico brought her a paper coffee cup and then wrapped her cold hands around it.

"Goddamn it, Nora, I'm calling the police! This has gone too far."

She grabbed his arm. "No! If you do, they'll get involved, tell me to go home, and those bastards will take Rose away forever! I'm so close—you know that! That's why whoever these maniacs are, they want me dead."

"But you need protection!"

Nora shook her head. "I have you now."

He took her hand. "Okay, let's change the subject. What did they find in Schiermonnikoog?"

"Another reason not to call the police," she muttered. "All they do is fuck things up."

"They have no idea who the man was?"

"He got away. On the ferry."

"Sweetheart, I'm so sorry."

She felt comforted by his tenderness. For the first time in days, she didn't feel so desperately alone.

"I did find something."

"What?" She saw his eagerness. She pulled Saartje's box out

of her overnight bag, opened it and handed the birth certificate to Nico. He read it quickly and looked at her.

"You know what this means," she said. "My father had to have killed Abram Rosen. He didn't even dare put his name on my birth certificate.

Nico shook his head. "You don't know that."

"Well, I'll never know now. They're all dead."

Nico clasped her hands and gave her an excited look. "But I found something, too."

"What?"

He reached into his jacket pocket and pulled out a document.

She read it quickly and gave it back to him. "It's the murder judgment against my father. So what?"

Nico unfolded it farther and pointed to the bottom of it. "Look!"

She saw a line with a scrawled signature above it and shrugged. "It's probably just the name of the court clerk who filed it."

"No, read the name!"

Nora squinted at it, a chicken scratch. All she could make out was a capital H. She shook her head. "I can't read it. It's too small."

Nico reached into his jacket. "Which is why I looked at it with this." He handed her a magnifying glass.

She placed it over the signature. Now she could make it out. Her hands began to tremble. She looked up at Nico. "I don't believe it," she whispered.

"It's the signature of the complainant."

"Henny Rosen." She turned to Nico. "Who is *she?* A relative of Abram's?"

"That's what we're going to find out tomorrow."

Nora felt confusion rise in her. "Do you have her number?"

"Unlisted."

"But you know where she lives?"

Nico nodded. "Den Haag. I have her address."

60

Nora tugged the hood of her raincoat over her head. It was not the light *motregen* that made her shiver. She and Nico had taken the next train from Amsterdam to Den Haag. They had decided that it would be best if she spoke to Henny alone. If they both showed up at her door, Nora worried that Henny would feel overwhelmed and less inclined to speak to her. *Who was she, anyway?* Nora wondered. *A cousin, aunt, wife?*

And another troubling question. Whoever Henny was, should Nora tell her that Hans was her father? As a complainant against Hans, she must have believed he had killed Abram. If Nora revealed who she was, would Henny slam the door in her face? Nico had advised her to play it by ear.

On the train, Nico told her that he had seen his wife the night before and had explained about Rose. Nora wanted to question him, but when she started to speak, he just shook his head. Nora felt it best not to press him.

As they left the Den Haag station, Nora felt his love again

as she walked with her hand in his. It made her feel secure. As they made their way down the *Laan van Meerdervoort,* the longest street in *The Hague,* all she saw was an endless row of identical apartment buildings, a conglomeration of colorless bricks five stories high. Finally they stood in front of number 354, which, thank God, was on the ground floor.

Nico gave her a quick kiss as he headed for a café near the corner. He would stay there in case she needed him and would be there when she came out.

Nora shivered before the door to Henny's flat, her finger raised to ring the doorbell. *This could be it. Where she learned who took Rose.* She had tried to keep her hopes in check. This could as easily be another dead end.

She took a deep breath and pressed the buzzer. No response. She cupped her hands against the cold glass of the plain white door and stepped back on the *stoep.* It had the obligatory decorative tiles of so many Dutch homes. She rang the buzzer again, this time holding it down longer than considered polite by the Dutch. Desperation made her tremble. *Someone had to be there.* But she heard no sound.

Nora stood. *What to do?* The rain was heavier now. She looked around. She could go back to find Nico—and then what? She checked her watch—8:50 a.m. Maybe Henny Rosen worked and had gone out long ago. But surely she was too old. Nora calculated. If she was twenty in 1940, she would be sixty now. Or older. Or younger. Maybe she should come back after five. No Dutchman or woman of that generation would fail to be home *aan tafel* by six o'clock sharp. Beef, potatoes and overcooked vegetables. De rigueur.

Crushed, she turned to go. A scratching sound made her stop. She held up a hand to shield her eyes from the rain. She heard a latch being pulled back and saw the door open a crack.

298 ANTOINETTE VAN HEUGTEN

Nora stepped closer. She could see a blur behind the glass. Blue and white. The blur spoke.

"Wie is er?" The Dutch was terse, clipped. Definitely the voice of an older woman.

Nora stepped up, still straining to see the person behind the voice. She put her hand tentatively on the door handle.

"Blijf af!" Go away!

Nora released her grasp. This was not someone who would open to strangers, not even if the stranger were a thin, wet woman with no obvious harmful intent. She spoke slowly in Dutch. "Please, *Mevrouw,* let me introduce myself. My name is Nora de Jong."

"De Jong?" Her voice was brusque. *"Ik ken niemand die de Jong heet."* I don't know anyone by that name.

"I have come here all the way from America on urgent business."

"America?" she said in broken English. "I don't know anyone in America. You are mistaken."

Nora's hand shot out and grabbed the knob. The blur moved as the door opened. An angry woman with a shock of white hair and intense brown eyes stood planted in the doorway, cheeks flushed. She wore an old-fashioned blue-and-white dress, black, sensible shoes and thick hose. She continued to stare at Nora, her mouth turned down. *"Stop!"*

Nora tried to smile. *"Mevrouw* Rosen, please just let me come in for a moment. I am here on a very important personal matter. I think it will be just as important to you as it is to me."

The woman tried to push the door shut, but Nora held it open. She spoke in stilted, staccato English, her voice raised a notch. "You have no business with me. I do not know you. Go away!"

Nora took her hand from the door. During the split second it remained open, she uttered these words. *"Het gaat om Abram."* *It is about Abram.*

The door stopped. A blue-veined hand clutched the wood and seemed suspended there. Nora waited. Slowly, the door opened. Nora let out her breath and then pulled back the hood of her raincoat, which had obscured her face. The old woman stepped back and clapped a hand over her mouth.

"Mijn God—Anneke?"

Nora walked slowly in. *Mevrouw* Rosen stepped back, her eyes wide in fear or shock, Nora couldn't tell which. Her blue-veined hands clutched her chest as she sagged against the wall. Nora quickly put her arms around her. She felt as light as a sparrow and smelled of 4711 *Eau de Cologne,* the same scent her mother always wore.

Nora spoke Dutch in low, crooning tones. "It's all right. Let's go inside. I know this must be a terrible shock for you."

"Ik snap er niks van… I don't understand—who are you?" Her voice was thready, but she let Nora help her to a couch in a tiny sitting room. The sofa was covered with lace doilies, the room surrounded by familiar Dutch accoutrement—a few pieces of fine Delft, a pair of wooden shoes by the hearth, a set of tarnished teaspoons. Then Nora saw a simple silver menorah on the dining room table.

Nora sat slowly next to the woman and held her hand. "I'm so sorry I didn't call first to introduce myself…and to make an appointment to see you," she said. "Unfortunately, I didn't have your telephone number and I have so little time."

The old woman pulled her hand back. Her brown eyes were clear now. "You must be Anneke's daughter. You look exactly like her. Even your voice is the same."

Nora nodded. "So I am told."

"How is this possible?"

"I know it is strange, but can you first tell me, are you related to Abram Rosen?"

The woman gave her a bitter smile. "I am his sister, Henny." Her eyes lit up. "But Anneke, how is she? Why hasn't she contacted me in all these years?"

"She's...dead."

Pained eyes looked up at Nora's. "When?"

"A few weeks ago."

Henny wiped tears from her crinkled eyes. "Cancer?"

Nora hated to tell this fragile creature the truth, but she had to. "She was murdered."

Henny gasped. "*Murdered?* Who would do such a thing!"

"I don't know. That's why I'm here."

Henny clutched at her throat, her face paper-white. "No," she moaned. "My poor Anneke. I can't believe it!"

Nora moved closer and took her hand. "I'm so sorry to have to tell you like this. But my baby, my Rose—" Her voice broke. "I have to get her back."

"Baby?" The woman's eyes clouded as she trembled. She squeezed Nora's hand. "You poor child. Where was this? Do the police have any idea who did it?"

"We live in Houston, Texas. All the police know is that my mother's killer was found at the scene, dead. And whoever was with him kidnapped my baby, Rose."

"Oh, God! I can't—" Suddenly she collapsed against the couch, her breathing gasping and labored. "My pills—there." She pointed a shaking finger to a bottle on the coffee table.

Nora grabbed it. Henny put two tablets under her tongue and closed her eyes.

"Will you be all right?"

She nodded. "Heart. Give me a moment." When some color returned to her cheeks, she looked straight at Nora. "Who was the dead man?"

"We don't know. We believe he was Dutch. He had guilders in his pocket and a fake passport." Nora could see her trying to process this.

"But what does this have to do with me?"

"Whoever the killer is shot my mother in the head and hacked off her hair, just like they did to NSB-ers after the war."

Henny shook her head. "But I still don't—" She froze. Then she stood, avoiding Nora's eyes. "I need to think. Perhaps you would like coffee or tea?" Dutch manners mandated that refreshments be offered within the first few moments of a visit. If a government official had appeared and told *Mevrouw* Rosen that she was being evicted, she would first offer him coffee or tea, and he would accept.

"Thee, graag." Nora followed her into a doll-size kitchen. In a few brisk motions, Henny had filled the kettle, put it on the stove, taken out a teapot with a worn blue cozy and put cookies and *gebak*—pastries—on a pewter tray. She flapped her hand impatiently at Nora. "Go on, now. I will be in with everything in a moment."

Shortly she appeared and handed Nora a cup of hot tea. Sugar cubes were offered and refused. Cream was offered and accepted. Each sipped silently. Nora could feel the woman's piercing gaze. She put her teacup on the table, careful not to spill on the lace tablecloth. It was now her move. "Please, *Mevrouw* Rosen…"

"Henny. As Anneke's daughter, you may call me by my given name."

Nora nodded. "Obviously you knew my mother well. I am very hopeful you can…tell me about her."

A white eyebrow raised. "You want me to tell you about your own mother?"

ANTOINETTE VAN HEUGTEN

"When she was young," Nora stammered. "When she lived in Amsterdam."

The woman's face hardened. "I do not speak of that time. It is why I live in Den Haag."

Nora nodded. "Of course, I understand. But can you tell me if Abram knew my mother?"

A pained look came into Henny's eyes. "Do you know nothing?"

"I beg your pardon?"

"Tell me what you know of my brother."

"I know that he...died...during the war. I know he was Jewish. I don't know anything more than that."

"Died? He was murdered!"

"By the Nazis?"

A harsh laugh erupted from her. "The Nazis our Abram could have escaped. It was a Dutchman who killed him."

Nora gasped. So this woman knew. Maybe everything. "What do you mean?"

"Did you never speak of this with Anneke?"

"She never talked about the war. I never even heard the name Abram Rosen until a few weeks ago."

Henny put down her teacup so hard it rattled in the saucer. "Impossible! Your mother never spoke of the days during the occupation?"

"No."

Henny's eyes widened. "Of Abram?"

"No."

"Nor of my family?"

"No."

"How did you learn of Abram if your mother never spoke of him? And how did you find me?"

"That isn't important now. Could you please tell me how he knew my mother?"

Henny sat back and regarded her. "You want me to answer your questions, but will not answer mine."

"That isn't true, I assure you. It's just that I know nothing of my mother's life during the war. But it has to be related to why my baby was kidnapped."

Henny stood and walked slowly to a small table against the wall. She looked at a photograph, picked it up and handed it to Nora. It was a faded image of a tall young man with black curly hair. Nora recognized him as the same man in the photo found on her mother's killer. Henny rested an index finger lightly on the scalloped edges of the frame, as if asking the boy in the photograph to tell her what to say. She looked at Nora. "It is a long tale."

"I have time."

Henny sat back on the couch. "It is only because you are Anneke's daughter that I will tell you. It takes too much out of me. I feel so old these days and speaking of this only makes me older." Nora poured her another tea. It stood untouched as Henny stared off, as if willing herself back to a time she had vowed to keep sacred between herself and those long gone. Minutes passed before she spoke.

"Your mother and I went to university together. We were inseparable. I loved Anneke. She was a passionate girl and a fierce, loyal friend." She tapped a finger against her nose and smiled. "She was never still—I remember that about her. When she walked into a room, the energy seemed—electrified." She gave Nora an unbearably sad look. "She was light and life. I have never known anyone else like her."

Nora felt confused. *Who was this woman she was describing?* Not her mother. Not the quiet, often depressed woman Nora had known. Not that Anneke ever complained, it was just that Nora had never felt she had understood her mother, as if her feelings were locked tightly inside. But as a child, Nora had

seen bursts of the Anneke that Henny described—an overwhelming sense of joy at simply being alive.

"Surely you know this without my telling you," said Henny.
"Your mother was a remarkable, compassionate and deeply
committed woman." Her glance sharpened. "You know of
Anneke's father? The NSB-er?"

"Yes, just recently."

"Not only a Nazi," spat Henny, "but a horrible, evil man."

"Did you know him?"

"Only through your mother. We were Jewish, remember?"
She gave a bitter laugh. "She was not allowed to have Jewish
friends, much less invite one into her home. But that did not
matter. Anneke was part of our family."

Nora was afraid to ask but had to. "And...Abram?"

The older woman's faded eyes welled with tears and traced
a path down her lined cheeks. Her voice was soft as feathers falling. "*Ja, ja.* My darling Abram. An idealist. A voice of
certainty, of strength, in a time of total madness. Also a light
in the world."

Nora held her breath.

"A light that was snuffed out in its most beautiful moment.
A life that was betrayed."

Nora's voice trembled. "But not by Anneke, not by my
mother..."

Henny's gnarled hand grasped hers. "No, *kindje,* never by
Anneke. It was that 'friend' of hers." Henny's eyes turned cold
and hateful. "That Hans Moerveld—that *murderer.* The bastard sent us all to the camps."

Nora's heart throbbed painfully. Then it was true, her father was a murderer. She was relieved she had not told Henny
that Hans was her father. "But why?"

"You don't know?"

Nora shook her head. This could be the one stone she wanted to leave unturned.

"Anneke and Abram were lovers."

Nora froze.

"Lovers such as the world has never seen—before or since."

61

Nora and Henny worked in silent tandem to clear the dining room of their simple lunch: two small *kabeljauw,* a tender white fish; mashed potatoes with butter, salt and pepper; and boiled green beans. Nora did her best to appear that she enjoyed the meal, but mostly she moved her food around the plate.

Nora was grateful for the few moments of quiet kitchen work. She was in shock still. *Abram and her mother—lovers!* What an enormous risk her mother had taken. Any Dutch non-Jew caught having relations with a Jew was treated as if he or she were a Jew—forced to wear the star, arrested along with their husband or lover, sent to the camps with their beloved to be gassed, shot or starved.

Her mind ran wild with possibilities. So according to Henny, Anneke was not an NSB-er. That relieved her so— her mother, whom she had always loved and admired. *But did Henny know for sure? Perhaps Anneke did betray them, but Henny simply chose not to believe it.* Nora desperately wanted to believe

in Anneke, but she couldn't get rid of an awful doubt that Anneke had betrayed Abram. Miep's diary, the tales of Anneke's
NSB activities, bringing Nazi boys home for her father's approval, marches with the Brown Shirts. *Shit, it was too much.*
Questions led only to more questions. And where did Hans
fit into all this? Did he betray Abram or kill him out of jeal-
ousy? And if he did kill Abram, why had her mother run off
with her father and married him? She wondered if her mother
had even loved Hans.

Nora started to dry the dishes. She thought of the terrible suffering Henny must have endured. Losing her husband, her brother, almost her life. No wonder she had sworn
out that complaint. She'd wanted Abram's murderer hunted
down and hung.

Nora glanced at Henny, who was wiping the sink with brisk
efficiency. Henny smiled at her and then made a pot of coffee. They walked into the living room and sat on the couch.
She could see the woman girding herself to tell the rest of
her story. All Nora had to do was sit and listen. And pray she
would not have to reveal the identity of her father.

Henny looked at Nora. "I see you wear your mother's necklace."

Nora's hand went to her neck. The silver felt almost alive,
warmed by her body. She felt a different warmth rise in her
cheeks, ashamed that she still doubted her mother. "I never
take it off."

"Abram gave that to her," she said. "Have you ever opened
it?"

"What do you mean?"

"It is a locket," she said simply.

Nora, her fingers fumbling, opened the catch, took the
necklace off and inspected the oval, silver orb. "I've never

looked at it closely." She searched for a button or a keyhole, but found nothing.

Henny gently took it, pressed her fingernail into a small indentation at the bottom, and it sprang open. Sepia-colored snippets of the faces of Abram and Anneke faced each other. Nora thought that they shone—with life, love, their future.

"Oh, my God," whispered Nora. But she felt so bereft as she fastened the locket back around her neck, feeling it swing gently into place as it had on that terrible day. *So much time already! Oh, Rose. Will I be too late?*

But then other thoughts came. *How had her mother survived after losing the man she loved? How could she have married Hans, carried his child?*

She looked at Henny. She seemed agitated, staring across the room as if communing with ghosts. More questions raced through Nora's mind. *If Anneke had married Hans out of guilt for her unwitting role in Abram's murder, had it been enough guilt to make her bear him a child?* Nora felt nauseous. She was that child—the result of a loveless union. Heartsick, she looked out. The afternoon was waning.

Henny caught her glance and patted her arm. "I will tell you the rest now, as much as I know." She took a sip of tea. "We were all students at the same level—Anneke, Abram and I. Anneke was determined to be a teacher, Abram a professor. I had no idea what I was going to be." She gave Nora a crooked smile. "But that question answered itself when Hitler invaded and Seyss-Inquart took over. Do you know who he was?" Nora nodded.

"Each student was required to swear allegiance to Hitler, to the Third Reich." She grunted. "All three of us stopped our studies that very day, but we still had our freedom. It was strange. In those first years the restrictions on us seemed marginal."

She shook her head. "But Seyss-Inquart was smart. He wanted to win over the Dutch. Not us—he cared nothing for us—but he did not want to begin by alienating Dutch citizens who worked with Jews and had Jewish friends. Gradually, gradually—that was his game.

"And we were gullible. We hoped that the war would be over before anything dreadful happened to us. We heard rumors from other occupied countries—terrible rumors—but we hid our heads like ostriches." Nora saw her hands tremble as she put down her teacup. "My father was a diamond merchant in Amsterdam. He had worked with many Germans. He refused to believe that real harm would come to us. Abram—oh, Abram was a different story entirely."

"How?"

Henny smiled sadly. "He knew what was coming. He knew we would be slaughtered like all the rest." She walked over to the small table and selected another photo and handed it to Nora. It was a faded portrait of a younger Henny, a handsome Abram. Nora took a close look at this man whom her mother was said to have loved. He smiled into the camera with fearless, dark eyes, his arm around Henny's shoulder. He had a long, handsome face and stood far taller than Henny. His curly hair looked as if it had fought the comb that had been run through it before the photo was taken, if indeed it had seen a comb at all. His expression crackled with energy. *It was a face that would be so easy to love,* thought Nora.

Henny held up another blurred photograph. Nora looked up. Henny nodded. "My mother, father, aunt, uncle, cousins. Dead, all dead." She pulled up the sleeve of her blouse and showed Nora the faint numbers on the inside of her arm. "*Westerbork,* the Dutch 'labor camp.' Then *Theresienstadt, Tsjecho-Slowakije.*" She pointed back at the portrait. "My mother, father and two of my cousins were in one of the hun-

dred and three trains that left *Westerbork* for Auschwitz. The
rest died in *Sobibor*."

"I'm...so very sorry."

Henny tugged her sleeve until it covered the ugly brand.
"There is nothing to say. It was evil, pure evil."

"And you?" asked Nora. "How did you survive?"

She shrugged, her brown eyes indifferent. "I was beautiful in those days. An SS guard took a liking to me. He left
food scraps under my mattress." A bitter sound came from
her throat. "He kept me alive so he could brutalize me daily."
Then her eyes dimmed. "How did I survive? I pretended I
was already dead."

Nora put her hand on Henny's arm. She pulled away.

"Enough of me. You came to hear of Abram and your
mother. I have something else to show you." She went to a
small cabinet and turned a tiny key that was already in the
lock. It seemed to be a practiced motion. She pulled out a large
leather box and put it on the coffee table. "Maybe God has
kept me alive long enough to give this to you. He certainly
has never shown me another reason why I am still here."

Nora looked at the box. It was covered with finely grained
leather and embossed with a large *A* in beautiful script. Nora
waited. She knew Henny would reveal all in her own time.

"First I must explain about Abram and Anneke. They were
not lovers until almost 1943. Children of our generation did
not jump from bed to bed as they do now. Sex was not what
we did until marriage. But then the war came and everything
changed, accelerated things somehow. We feared for our very
lives. Yes, the Jews were more afraid, but non-Jews were, as
well." She gave Nora a wry look. "The Dutch do not like to
be told what to do, much less when and how to do it."

"It must be genetic," Nora muttered.

"All of us then felt a desperate kind of wildness. We doubted we would survive the war. In the beginning, we could not comprehend that the Nazis would win, but there they were running our country after only five days! It was unthinkable."

She took a lace handkerchief from her bosom and twisted it. "But it was real. When the Nazis occupied Holland, Anneke felt a deep shame about her father. She hated his Nazi ideals, was embarrassed by his position with the NSB and argued with him constantly about his hatred of the Jews."

Nora felt confused. "But I read her aunt's diary. It said that my mother took part in NSB activities."

"Which aunt?"

"Miep."

Henny grunted. "She was an idiot, always toadying up to that brother of hers. Anneke did those things to cover up what she was doing behind Joop's back. She stole coal and food from his house, searched his office for information about upcoming *razzias* and warned those who were in imminent danger."

"But then how could my mother still see you and Abram?"

"At first it was not so difficult. When they made us wear the yellow star, many Dutchmen did the same in protest." She smiled at Nora. "Anneke sewed hers into the inside of her jacket. She said that way it was closer to her heart." Henny's eyes darkened. "But by 1942, the Nazis became more brutal and Anneke knew she was risking her life by being seen with us, by even knowing us." She looked off in the distance, beyond her windows, deep into the past.

"So my mother kept on being an NSB-er, but helped your family on the side?"

Henny fixed Nora with a piercing gaze. "She was a hero. That's what she was." She shook her head. "I cannot believe she never told you this! Why would a mother hide such a thing from her own child?"

Because of Hans. The question remained. *Why would her mother have left Holland and immigrated with Abram's killer?*

The woman patted her hand as if Nora's silence was acceptance of her praise of Anneke. "Well, I will tell you about your mother. She was a very clever girl. She knew that open defiance of her father would only make him order her to stay home.

"So Anneke did the public things Joop wanted her to do. She went to Seyss-Inquart's speeches with him, entertained NSB and Nazi guests when they came to Joop's home, wore her uniform around town. She hated every minute of it, but she endured it to work secretly the rest of the time. So the neighbors and Miep thought she was as rabid a Nazi as her father."

Nora now felt pain for her mother—and admiration. *How brave she had been!*

"Joop," said Henny, "was marched down the street in handcuffs on Liberation Day. The crowds filled the street, jeering and throwing rocks at him. He served a few months in prison, unlike most of the NSB-ers," she said bitterly. "In any event, I always suspected that all this hatred of Joop was one reason Anneke left so soon after the war. Besides, her neighbors believed she was a Nazi whore. She would have suffered terrible reprisals."

"Oh, God, I never really knew her at all."

Henny put her hand under Nora's chin and looked into her eyes. "You must believe it, child. It is the truth. I've wondered so often what happened to your mother after she left Holland. I never suspected the answer would come from her daughter." She lowered her hand and sighed.

"In any event, your mother was a hero, working with a small resistance cell in Amsterdam. She was a courier, hid microfilm, smuggled food to us and other Jews, helped Jews escape Holland and found them places to hide when they could no longer leave. Oh, Anneke was a wild one. Her father never knew what he had living right under his nose. She gave away so many food coupons, I sometimes wondered if she ever ate herself. She was terribly thin, but she had the biggest heart. She could never stand to see anyone in pain or go hungry, especially the little ones."

Nora had a sudden memory of driving with her mother through poor neighborhoods in Houston, like the Fourth Ward. Whether a child was black, brown or white, if Anneke thought he or she looked hungry, she would stop the car, find the mother and give her some money. *"For the children. Buy them some food."*

One of Nora's earliest childhood memories was her mother's work at a Jewish orphanage. Anneke helped children get adopted, found them clothes and tried to make sure they learned their lessons. It was one of the few times Nora had heard Anneke speak with real passion. *Until Rose.* She turned to Henny. "How could she do all that and not get caught?"

Henny shrugged. "Anneke was careful. She knew every back street in Amsterdam. She rode her bicycle until she was riding on wood instead of rubber. She rode that bike until the *Moffen*—the Germans—took it away from her. After that, she went on foot."

"And her father never found out?"

"Not that I know of."

"Didn't she have more family?"

"Two aunts." Her eyes flashed. "That ridiculous Miep you spoke of. And Saartje Steen. She and her husband hid Abram during the war, but I never met them."

"No one else?"

"Only Antonia, your grandmother, but she disappeared when Anneke was quite young."

"Why?"

"No one ever knew, but there was something very wrong in that home. I often think that is why Anneke was so close to my family. We were like sisters."

Nora chose her next words carefully. "Did she have any other—friends?"

Henny shook her head. "You make me jump ahead. You must let me tell it in my own way. There is so much, so much you must understand about the time in which we lived." She offered Nora a plate of windmill cookies, the kind her mother used to buy at a specialty store downtown and always had on hand for company. Their cinnamon scent stabbed her with regret. *Why had she known nothing about the woman her mother was?*

Henny took a sip of her coffee. "Anneke was always on the alert for any threatening information about our family, particularly Abram. She was constantly finding new hiding places for him."

"How did she find them?"

"There were brave people, many of them religious. They took in Jews when things got bad." She shook her head. "But there were just as many who turned a blind eye to us, as if they had never seen us before."

Nora was well versed in this. She and Nico had had long discussions about it. Sentiment after the war was critical of the Dutch. The "gray" people, they were called—neither heroes nor traitors. They had stood on the sidelines and done nothing.

Nico argued that no one, unless he was an overt traitor, could be blamed for trying to keep his job, putting food on the table and protecting his family. Refusing to put one's family at risk was not being a traitor.

Nora had disagreed. Anyone with even a hint of humanity could not sit idly by and watch Jews be corralled and sent to their deaths without doing *something*.

But it was the final question Nico posed that had made her doubt her premise. *If you had a child, could you watch it die for lack of food?* Nora remembered his flushed face. *If you knew that if you got involved fighting the Nazis you would be risking the very existence of that child? Of your entire family?* As Rose's mother, Nora knew she would now have to agree with him.

"It must have been horrible for you," said Nora. "To watch your friends and neighbors turn away when you needed them so desperately."

Henny gave a harsh laugh. "You Americans have never been occupied, have no idea what it was like under the Nazis. All of you believe that the story of Anne Frank is the only story of the Dutch Jews—that every Dutch family took us in, fed us, hid us from the Germans." Her voice caught. "Yes, that story ended in tragedy, but only after the failed efforts of good Dutch people. For Jews like us, it was a fairy tale."

Her eyes were bitter. "I can only tell you our story. By late 1942, Abram had to go underground. It was Anneke who found him a hiding place. My father's manufacturing business was closed down, taken over by the Nazis. They took all the money in our bank accounts. We had nothing to live on. My mother sold her jewelry and then her clothes for food. Our Dutch neighbors shunned us. Not one offered to help or hide Abram. They wouldn't even share their food with us. It was as if we were already an invisible people."

Nora tried to pour more coffee into Henny's cup, but she waved it away. "In 1943, our home was given to an NSB-er and we were thrown into the street. We had to move in with my mother's sister, her husband and four children. We lived in an attic with no toilet, easy to round up when the *razzias* came." Henny's rough laugh bruised Nora's ears. "We thought even then that we might make it until the end of the war. But then in April of 1945, a few days after Abram was killed, they took everyone in my family except me and tossed them like trash into the back of a truck in bitter cold—in their night-clothes."

Nora felt the sob that wrenched Henny's body. When she took one of her hands, it was ice. "That night I was sneaking home from a girlfriend's after curfew and saw the *Groene Politie* pull up in front of the house. I crouched behind the garbage cans in the alley. I heard my mother's cries and my father's shouts. They saw me and motioned to me not to move. It took everything I had not to run to them, even though I knew where they were going. To the *Hollandsche Schouwburg.* From there, by train to *Westerbork,* where they worked sending other Jews to their deaths until they themselves were shipped to Auschwitz."

Henny's voice lowered to a sick whisper. "The last thing I saw was my mother, with her long, beautiful gray hair around her shoulders, clinging to my father as they both shouted to me not to worry...that they would write."

"So Abram was betrayed."

Henny seemed to have reached an impasse. Nora squeezed her hand and she went on. "That goy I told you about—Hans Moerveld." She spit out the name. "He killed Abram and then betrayed my family to the *Groene Politie.*"

"Who was he?" whispered Nora.

The old woman raised red, tearful eyes to Nora. "A student. A *friend* of your mother's, so he always pretended. Everyone knew he was in love with her. He was in the same resistance cell as Anneke. Pretending again."

"To do what?"

"To fight the Nazis." Henny snorted. "He was a mole, a spy. He claimed that he printed false documents for the resistance, that he spied on ammunition depots for the British. Blew them up. Killed Germans. Lies—all lies!"

"But how do you know it was a lie?" The documents she had found in the attic showed that both her mother and father had served in the resistance, that her father had coordinated with the British Secret Service. *Could that be true, no matter what Henny said? Could her father have fought on the right side of the war?* "Maybe he was telling the truth."

"I believe none of it."

"What did Anneke believe?"

"That she had known the Moerveld boy since he was a child. She refused to believe he was a spy."

"Why do you believe it?"

"Because the neighbors who lived next to Abram's hiding place later told us that on that terrible night, they heard a loud argument and then a gunshot. By the time they ran into the street, Abram lay dead." She looked at Nora suspiciously. "Do you know something of this Moerveld? Is that why you have come here?"

Nora felt her cheeks burn. "No, of course not."

"Because if he is still alive—"

"Where was Anneke during this argument?"

"That night? The neighbors said she was there. The *Groene Politie,* too. That bastard Moerveld must have followed Anneke to Abram's hiding place and shot him. Then he alerted the *Politie* like the filthy coward he was." Her shouders slumped. "Afterward I never saw Anneke or heard anything from her again. There were rumors that she had gone to the States. Now you tell me they were true."

"And what happened to you?" asked Nora softly.

"They found me a few days after my parents were sent away and I was sent to the camps like everyone else. When I finally made my way back to Amsterdam from *Theresienstadt,* I went to my father's house and looked into the window. Our next-door neighbor was setting the table with my mother's silver.

All our furniture was still in the house. The woman saw me staring at her. She walked over and closed the curtains. I never went back." She waved a tired hand. "So I live here in my little flat in The Hague."

Henny now noticed the tears streaming down her face. Nora handed her the lace handkerchief. Henny wiped her face, giving Nora a hollow, haunted look. "This is too much for me. I must stop now."

"I'm so sorry," whispered Nora. "Could I ask you one more question?" When Henny didn't answer, she pressed on. "Do you know of anyone—anyone—who might have hated my mother so much that he would kill her?"

Henny stared at the ground and twisted her lace handkerchief. Finally she met Nora's eyes. "I cannot imagine anyone doing such a thing. Not after thirty years."

"No neighbors, family members, someone Anneke may have harmed—"

"No, it is preposterous." Henny shook her head wearily. "Come here a moment and then I think you must go."

Nora followed her to a long, plain table that stood against the wall. Henny pointed at more photographs, each in an identical silver frame, plainly members of her family, so many that Nora couldn't focus on all of them. In front of each lay a stone. Nora thought they looked like the smooth stones one would find in a riverbed.

"Do you know why I have these here?"

"I know that Jews place stones on the headstones of their dead."

"Yes, but do you know why?"

"No," she whispered.

Henny picked up the stone in front of Abram's photograph and rolled it gently, lovingly, in her palm. "There are different explanations. In ancient times, stones were used as markers. The superstitious believed that stones kept the soul in the earth. This was necessary because the *beit olam*—the grave— was thought to still have within it some part of the soul of the deceased. I believe that we place a stone on the grave or headstone to show that we have been there, that our loved ones have not been forgotten." She put her arm around Nora's shoulders.

The feeling reminded her so of her mother's embrace that tears came to her eyes. Henny held her tightly and then opened her palm and placed Abram's stone in Nora's hand. It was still warm from Henny's touch. It felt alive, like her mother's locket. Nora's fingers clenched around it.

"It is yours. Your mother would have wanted it that way." Nora fought back her tears. "Are you sure?"

Henny nodded and kissed her softly on both cheeks. Nora hugged her and put on her jacket, careful to slip the stone into the inside pocket. Like Anneke's yellow star, close to her heart. She followed Henny's slow steps to the door. "I have no way to thank you—no way at all."

"Ach, kind," she said softly. "For these hours, you have given me back my Anneke. It is as if she and Abram lived for one more day."

As Nora turned to go, Henny stopped her. "You have not asked me about the photograph."

"Which one?"

Henny pointed at the long table again. "Come here." She picked up a blurred photo of a black-haired infant with dark eyes. "One of Anneke's resistance friends gave it to me after the war."

"Oh, the baby picture of Abram. Yes, I saw it."

"That is not Abram, *kindje.*"

Nora felt faint as Henny placed the silver frame in her hands. "What do you mean?"

"That is the baby of Abram and Anneke."

"What baby?"

Henny's brown eyes grew full again. "That is you, my dear Nora. Abram was your father."

62

After Nora left, Henny paced up and down. What could it all mean? When she heard Nora describe how Anneke was killed, a sick fear had shot through her. It couldn't be...not after all these years. Even Isaac wasn't crazy enough to do such a thing, was he? But the hacked hair, just like the NSB-ers... and how had he found Anneke?

Even as her questions formed, Henny knew the answers. After the war, she and Amarisa had shared a small flat in Amsterdam. Every day they would visit Isaac and his wife. And every day it was the same thing, both of them consumed with getting revenge against Anneke. Henny had no idea how Isaac had done it, but she just knew that somehow he had found Anneke and killed her. *Oh, God, what do I do now?*

She sat at her desk. Only one way to find out. She rummaged through a drawer until she found her old address book. *Did Isaac still have the same number? Same address?* She hadn't spoken to him or Amarisa in years. When she first moved to

The Hague, they'd exchanged birthday cards, but they didn't even do that anymore. All they did was remind her of the war.

And Amarisa, the older dominating sister. When Henny had gotten a new puppy for her birthday, Amarisa had whispered to her that she didn't deserve it. The next day it was found in the road, poisoned. When they had played together, Amarisa always won. If she didn't, she twisted Henny's arm until she cried. Henny had learned to always let Amarisa win.

But after the war, when all Amarisa and Isaac did was sit day after day and rave about the injustices they had suffered, swearing revenge against Anneke and Hans and belittling Henny's unshakable defense of her, Henny knew they would never change. So she had moved on.

Finally she found Isaac's number. Taking a deep breath, she dialed. No answer. *Should she wait? Try again?* She thought of Nora's desperation. Even if it was crazy, this notion that Isaac was involved, she had to find out.

She ran her finger down to the number under Isaac's name. A sick feeling ran through her. But she had to do it.

A mechanical voice. "The number you dialed has been disconnected."

Henny grabbed her address book and called Amarisa. Another robotic voice informed her that the number had been changed. Henny scribbled it down. Of course Amarisa had moved. It had been a decade since Henny had spoken a word to her. When she dialed, it was answered on the first ring.

"*Mevrouw* Rosen's service."

"Service?"

"Yes, all of *Mevrouw* Rosen's calls are routed through us. Name, please?"

"Henny Rosen. I am *Mevrouw* Rosen's sister. Could you please give me her number?"

"I am afraid not. We will contact her and, if she accepts the call, then I will patch you through."

"This is ridiculous," muttered Henny as she listened to clicks, whirs and then a ring.

"Met Amarisa Rosen."

"Amarisa, met Henny."

"Henny who?"

"Don't play games, Amarisa. You know I wouldn't be calling unless it was urgent."

"Oh, forgive me." Amarisa's sarcasm snaked through the line. "I wasn't sure you were still alive."

"Where is Isaac?"

"What do you care? You haven't spoken to either of us in ten years."

"I've tried to call him, but there's no answer."

"So try again."

"Amarisa, tell me what is going on." She hated the nervousness in her voice, the young girl still petrified by her older sister. "I had a visitor today. Anneke's daughter."

There was a short silence. "Who?"

"Nora de Jong. She told me that Anneke had been murdered, her baby kidnapped!"

"So the bitch is dead. All the better."

Henny felt terrified. Amarisa had answered far too quickly. *She wasn't surprised—not at all!* Henny hardened her voice. "What do you know about this? Did Isaac kill her? Is he hiding somewhere?"

Amarisa snorted. "What makes you think such a crazy thing? It was over thirty years ago."

"Because Anneke's daughter said she'd been shot by a Dutchman and that her hair was hacked off, just like the NSB-ers."

"You're out of your mind."

"And Isaac hasn't said anything to you?"

"Isaac won't say anything ever again. He's dead. Not that you give a damn."

Henny's heart sank. He was her brother, after all. "When? How?"

"None of your goddamned business."

"Amarisa!" she cried. "You're lying to me! Anneke's daughter told me the murderer was a Dutchman, that he died at the scene after killing her. Isaac must have killed poor Anneke and someone stole the baby. And I think that person is you!"

"What an imagination you have!"

"Amarisa, you must know that Nora de Jong is Abram's child! You owe it—"

"Don't you tell me what I owe my dead brother! I've spent my life mourning Abram while you turned your back on his memory and ran away!"

"But you can't do this to his daughter—to Nora!"

"She isn't his daughter!" thundered Amarisa. "She was stolen and raised by the man who murdered her real father—a Nazi! She is her mother's child, the daughter of a whore. Nothing more."

"I'm coming there," said Henny. "We have to settle this."

"Ha! You don't even know where I live. I moved years ago. Besides, I'm on vacation in Italy. My service forwarded your call."

"Then I'm going to call Anneke's daughter and tell her what I suspect!"

"You aren't going to do a goddamned thing." Henny started at the deadly hiss of her words. "You're just an old, delusional woman making wild speculations. If you repeat your crazy ideas to anyone else, you'll regret it. You know me. And what I'm capable of."

"But Amarisa! Who took that child? And why?"

"I have no idea what you're babbling about. There is no child. I'm hanging up. Don't ever contact me again."

Henny heard one sound before Amarisa slammed down the receiver. The faint cry of a baby.

63

Nora sat numbly with Nico in the train to Amsterdam. They were due to arrive in ten minutes. She had told Nico everything.

"I still can't believe it!" she cried. "What about all those years Hans loved me, took care of me, made me believe he was my father?" She dropped her head in her hands. "That must be why my birth certificate says my father was 'unknown.' If my mother had revealed it was Abram, she would have been marked as a non-Jew having relations with a Jew." Her voice cracked. "And she would have been sent to a camp and killed."

"And if Hans murdered Abram," said Nico, "it wouldn't have been safe for him to claim to be the father. He would also have been arrested because of his relationship with a woman who slept with a Jew. And if he stayed in Holland after the war, he ran the risk that Abram's family would have had him tried for murder."

Nora blanched. "After talking to Henny, I now think my mother loved Abram, but did she also love my father?"

He took her into his arms. "It doesn't matter, *lieveling*. They both loved your mother."

"And how can Henny be sure that I was Abram's child? My mother could have been sleeping with both of them!"

Nico shrugged. "She's the only source we have."

Nora felt spent. "I wonder when my mother decided to leave with Hans? It had to be soon after I was born in Amsterdam."

"Look, all we know is that Abram was killed just before the occupation ended. Your mother must have been desperate. Her lover was dead. She was pregnant and then you were born. She trusted Hans. Everyone thought he was a murderer and she was a known NSB-er. Maybe he just took over at that point."

"But how did he get them out of Holland? It was almost impossible back then."

Nico shrugged. "Who knows?"

"And why would he do that if he knew my mother was pregnant with Abram's baby?"

"Depends on how much he loved her."

She sat, trying to absorb it all. A thought struck her. "I forgot to tell you about the boy."

"What boy?"

"Saartje said that a boy visited Abram while he was in hiding."

"Did she know his name?"

Nora shook her head. "It probably didn't mean anything. It was at the end of our visit and she was saying crazy things. I tried to press her, but she just crawled into bed and wouldn't talk anymore."

"But she used the word 'boy'? That means he wasn't a baby."

"I don't know. But she called him 'Abraham's promised

son'. Abraham means Abram, but what did she mean by his 'promised son'? I asked her if it meant that Abram had a son, but she said no. Who could it be?"

Nico stared at her. "Is that precisely what she said?"

"Yes, but it doesn't make any sense—"

Nico slammed his fist on the table. "That's it!"

"What are you *talking* about?"

He grinned. "You know I was raised by a Calvinist minister."

"What difference does that make?"

He laughed and shook his head. "In the Bible, Abraham's promised son is named Isaac."

"Isaac? But what does that mean?"

"I think it means that Abram, Nora's lover, probably had a father who was named Abraham."

"So that would make Isaac—"

Nico grasped her hand. "Abram's brother."

64

By the time the conductor announced their arrival in Amsterdam, Nora was frantic. They rushed from the train onto the platform. Nora rooted around in her purse for the scrap of paper Henny had given her. She ran to a pay phone. Her hands shook so she could barely dial.

"Henny? It's Nora."

Nora heard a choked sob. "Thank God you called, child! I didn't know how to reach you!"

"What is it?"

"After you left, I called Amarisa—my sister."

"You have a sister?"

"Yes, and a brother—"

"Isaac?"

"Yes, yes. When you left, I thought I was crazy. It was so long ago." Nora heard her cry louder.

"*Tante,* what is it? Tell me, please!"

"Amarisa—she said he didn't do it, but I don't believe her, I know when she's lying—"

"What do you mean?"

Nora heard a choking noise and then Henny's broken voice. "Nora, I don't know how to tell you this. It was Isaac who killed your mother. He's dead. Amarisa confirmed it."

"Oh, my God!" The image of the dead Dutchman lying on Anneke's floor flashed through her mind. "I saw him! But who took Rose then?"

"I don't know, really I don't. The only thing I can think of is that it was Amarisa. She hated your mother as much as Isaac did."

"Quick! Give me her number, her address!"

"*Ach, kind,* I only have the number of her service. She screens her calls. She wouldn't even tell me where she lives."

So close, so damned close! "Isn't there anyone who knows where this woman lives? I've got to go there right now!"

Nora heard rustling on the end of the line. "Isaac has a son—Ariel. I don't know where he lives, but I have a wedding announcement here somewhere. I've been looking for it since I spoke to Amarisa—"

"Please hurry!" Nora whirled around to Nico. "A pen!"

Nico fumbled in his jacket and produced one. Nora took it and clutched the receiver.

There was a maddening delay. "Here! I have it! Tweede Leliedwarsstraat 624. But I have no idea if he still lives there—"

"I've got it. He *has* to know his own aunt's address!"

"Go, child. Go now."

"What about my Rose?" Nora struggled to breathe. "Did she say anything about her?"

"Oh, Nora, she didn't, but—"

"What? What is it?"

"I think I heard a baby crying."

65

Two days after Ariel's return, he and Leah sat hunched next to each other on the couch after their morning coffee. Ariel was about to raise his shoulder but thought better of it. Even though Leah had meticulously tended his wound, it was still sore as hell.

They had spoken of nothing but their options. Last night, Ariel had made his final decision. He had the Amsterdam address where Nora was staying. He would tell her where Rose was. Because Leah had called Amarisa to ask that they keep Rose tonight, they knew that she had not yet fled. Of course, she had refused their request.

They both stared at the telephone on the coffee table. Ariel looked at Leah, she nodded. He breathed deeply, picked up the receiver and dialed. The service picked up and put him through.

"*Met Ariel.*"

"*Ach,* my long-lost nephew." Amarisa's words were nails

being clipped. "I haven't heard from you lately. How are you? And Leah?"

"Don't give me that shit, Amarisa. I'm sitting here with a bullet hole in my shoulder."

"Oh, my God!" she cried. "What happened?"

"You know goddamned well what happened. You sent that goon to kill Nora and he shot me!"

"Why, Ariel, how could you think such a thing?"

"Listen, you bitch, you've gone out of your mind. *Killing people? Having me shot?*"

"Don't talk to me that way, you little *pisher.* You better remember who puts bread on your plate."

Clenching the receiver, he focused on the white of his knuckles. Now he would drive spikes into his words. "We don't give a damn about your money. I'm calling the police, telling them where the baby is and turning myself in."

"Ha!" she chortled. "I can just see you rotting in jail with that whimpering wife of yours passing you a nail file in an *appelgebak* through the visitor slot! You don't have the balls for it, Ariel. Stop bluffing."

"Fuck you."

He heard only a silence, then a clipped voice. "In the time it takes you to hang up, Jacoba and I will disappear where *no one* will ever find her again—not her mother, not the police and not you, Sherlock Holmes."

"I've called the police already, Amarisa. I've told them I know where Rose is. And who murdered Anneke. They're conferring with the American Embassy and the FBI as we speak." He let that sink in. "In fact, I told them you confessed that you went with Isaac to Houston, murdered Anneke and stole Rose. And that now you've hired an assassin to kill her mother—and me."

"You *bastard!*" she screamed. "You've just sealed your own coffin!"

"Now you listen to me, and listen well." His voice crushed ice. "I called them, but I haven't given them your address—yet. I've made an appointment to be at the station in twenty minutes. Told them I'm afraid to reveal my identity over the phone. And that you're a flight risk."

A harsh laugh. "I knew you were bluffing, you little shit!"

"I don't think you understand, *Tante*. You bring the baby here this instant and maybe we can make a deal. You can have Rose, but Leah and I want to say goodbye to her and start a new life in another country. And that will be very expensive."

"Half-wit! You're setting a trap. You've probably got the cops sitting there with you right now."

"Look at this sensibly." He struggled to make himself speak calmly. "It is in my best interest to make an arrangement with you. As you say, without your money, I can't afford to live here. And I am in danger of going to jail for a very long time."

He heard nothing. Then the viper was back. "You go to hell. I'm taking my baby and leaving right now."

"Do that, Amarisa," he said evenly. "The police station I called is one block from your house. Even you can't fly to the airport."

"*Godverdomme!*"

"And don't bring that hit man of yours here with you. If I so much as see his face, I'll call the cops."

"*You son of a bitch!*"

"Clock is ticking. You've wasted five precious minutes."

"If you have the cops waiting for me, I'll tell them the real story and you'll be the one behind bars! That you forced me—an old woman—to hide her, take care of her—"

"Move your ass." He paused. "By the way, how's that for balls?"

66

Amarisa slammed down the receiver. *"Godverdomme!"* She felt trapped. *And by that imbecile!*

She rushed into the nursery, where Jacoba lay sleeping. *Surely the dolt was bluffing. Still, she'd never have dreamed he'd have the guts to try something like this!* But why should she be surprised? He was only threatening because he himself had given up. *Weak little shit.*

She looked at her watch. If he wasn't bluffing, she had to get the hell out of Amsterdam fast. *And if he had the police waiting for her?*

She took out a suitcase and hurriedly packed a few things for her and Rose. *Didn't matter. Money bought anything, anywhere. Switzerland was no exception.* She then whirled the dial on the safe hidden in her closet. It sprang open and she grabbed the cash, flipped through it. *More than enough.*

She dialed from the nursery phone, the receiver crammed

between her neck and shoulder, as she stuffed the money into her purse. *"Met Amarisa."*

A groan. "Christ, Amarisa, what the fuck do you want *now?*"

"Shut up and listen. Ariel's trying to set me up. Get over to his place—now. I'm on my way."

"Slow down. Set you up how?"

"It doesn't matter," she snapped. "But I may need to get out of there fast. Your job is to make sure I do."

"Does this involve the *cops?* If it does, count me out."

"Get your ass over there! If you're such a pussy, you can wait outside."

"Fuck you. I'm done."

Amarisa glanced again at her watch. She had no time for this crap. "Look, I'm leaving tonight—for good. You do this one last thing for me and I'll pay you so much money you can do whatever you want with your shitty life. You'll be rid of me forever." *The shit, he was making her wait.*

"All right, goddamn it. But this is *it*. I'm not killing anybody. And you bet your ass I'll wait outside. *And* you pay me up front before you go in there."

"Deal. And bring your gun."

"On my way."

Amarisa called a limo service she had never used. Told them to pick her up. If things went wrong, the car would be waiting around the corner. She'd pay the driver more than he'd ever seen and she and Rose would race to Belgium and fly out of Antwerp. She'd be an idiot to leave from Schiphol, which would be crawling with cops.

And she was no idiot.

67

Nora held Nico's hand tightly as the taxi crawled to the *Jordaan*. Her heart beat with a wild rhythm. *She's alive, oh, God—Rose is alive! The son, Ariel, must know where his aunt lives, where Rose was!* She leaned forward. "Can't you *hurry?* This is an emergency!"

The driver just shrugged and pointed at the traffic jammed in the narrow streets all around him. Nico's extravagant tip may as well have been pitched into the canal.

"Nora, I still think we should call the police."

"I know, but we don't have time! Remember when I got my passport stolen? First, I had to sit in line for an hour while the proper Dutch officer made me fill out a form a mile long just to establish who I was. Then I had to talk to everyone in the station and convince them I wasn't fencing passports on the black market. And then—the last straw—they took a two-hour lunch and told me to come back in a week!"

"Maybe you're right. Look." Nico pointed to crowds of

young picketers with dyed green hair carrying garish signs and chanting as they marched around the *Dam*. "Greenpeace. You couldn't find a cop if you wanted one. They're all out on horseback."

She grabbed his arm. "We should have taken the tram!"

"We'd just be standing in line. Trying to get out of the crowd like everyone else." He put his arm around her. "Hold on, *schat*."

She couldn't speak, couldn't breathe. They had to find Rose now! Her baby was with a madwoman. Crying, said Henny. Hurt? Sick? Oh, God, this Ariel—was he her darling's only hope?

As they made painstaking progress toward the *Jordaan*, Nora's eyes flitted upon scenery that did not seem so changed since the war. Buildings that had seen the terrors of the *razzias* now displayed shops brimming with Holland's finest flowers, excellent restaurants and posh art galleries. They were going back to the neighborhood where the Jews had been corralled, beaten and taken away. How ironic it would be if she found Rose's kidnapper in the very neighborhood where her grandfather had been killed.

Tweede Leliedwarsstraat 624. Nora looked at Nico, feeling overwhelmed with fear and hope. The flat looked just like the others lined up neatly in a row, a simple *stoep* that led up to a recessed wooden door. The typical bay window. She hoped to God that the nephew still lived there. *That he could lead them to Amarisa…to Rose!*

Nora again gripped Nico's hand as they walked up the few stone steps. She could barely control herself. She wanted to break in and tear the place apart. *Hold on Rose, hold on.*

With a trembling finger, Nora pressed the doorbell. No answer. She waited a few torturous moments and then turned to Nico. She rang it again, longer this time. *Nothing.*

"No!" cried Nora. She banged her fists on the door.

It opened.

68

A short, stocky man with black hair smiled at Nico until his eyes fell upon Nora. Shock swept his face.

"Are you Ariel Rosen?" asked Nora.

He tried to slam the door, but Nico thrust his foot forward and stopped him.

"You have to let us in," cried Nora. "Your aunt has my daughter! Where is she? What is her address?"

"Stop!" he cried through the slit of open door. "The baby's fine, she's safe, but my aunt—" He whipped his head around and then back to them. His voice dropped to a whisper. "You go, I'll bring the baby to you, I promise, but—"

"Nico!"

Nico flung open the door and he and Nora pushed their way inside. Nora barreled into the living room. The first thing she saw was a young woman on a couch, crying, holding *Rose!*

"Oh, my God!" Nora leaped forward, but just as her fingers almost touched Rose's skin, an old woman in black who

Nora hadn't noticed wrested the baby from the woman on the couch and bolted to the other side of the room, gasping and staring at Nora with venomous eyes and an ugly purple scar from mouth to ear.

It was the old woman from the train station. "You! You tried to kill me! Give me my baby, you bitch!"

The man who had been at the front door grabbed Nora's arm. "Nora, I'm Ariel! Please let me explain!"

"Get your hands off me, you bastard!" She twisted but couldn't break free.

"Let go of her!" Nico landed a powerhouse punch on Ariel's shoulder. He gave a howl of pain and fell back onto the couch. "Leah!" he gasped. The woman held him to her, wailing.

Nora saw the older woman dash to the open bay window near the front door, screaming "Dirk! Dirk!"

Before Nora and Nico could move, a brown-haired man burst in. Nora saw his bloodshot eyes dart from Amarisa— huddled in a far corner with Rose screeching in her arms—to Nora, to Nico. He drew a gun from his jacket and pointed it at them. "Don't move."

Nora started to run to Rose, but Nico held her back. "Wait!" he whispered. "He's got to be the one who tried to kill you before!"

"No! Rose!" wailed Nora. The only thing she could see was her angel grasped in the crabbed fingers of that evil woman. Nico kept holding her back.

"For God's sake, don't shoot!" cried Ariel.

Dirk's flat eyes didn't even glance behind him. "I shot you once. This time I'll fucking kill you."

"Dirk, get us out of here!" cried the old woman.

Nora saw her inch along the long wall with Rose until she came to a corner near the front door.

"Shut up, Amarisa," Dirk said softly. "I know what I'm doing."

"Move over there." Dirk waved the pistol at Nora and Nico in the direction of a doorway to what seemed to be the nursery. Then he stepped toward them.

Suddenly, Nora saw Ariel grab a large crystal ashtray from the coffee table, lurch the few steps to Dirk, raise both arms and smash it over Dirk's head.

Dirk howled and fell. His pistol skittered across the wooden floor. Nico pushed Nora behind him and rushed forward, his eyes fixed on the pistol, but Dirk had struggled to his feet. As Nico bore down on him, Dirk stood solid, balled his fist, yanked it back and slammed Nico in the face. He crumpled.

"Nico!" screamed Nora. She ran to him, cradling his head as he lay on his back, unconscious.

But then Ariel tackled Dirk from behind. They both landed with a crash on the coffee table. The shattering of glass had the old woman screaming. Dirk hit the floor first, bloody and unconscious.

Nora let go of Nico and grabbed the pistol. She ran across to where Amarisa huddled in a corner, Rose still clutched in her arms. Nora stood back and trained the pistol at the old woman's forehead. She'd never fired a gun but, with shaking hands, she managed to cock it. "Give me my baby, you bitch. Or I'll kill you." An image flashed in her mind. *Anneke. The gun. Pointed at the monster who held her daughter.*

Amarisa held a red-faced, wailing Rose in front of her. "You daughter of a whore! You don't deserve this child. You *owe* her to me—to my family!"

"Put her down!" Nora waved the gun a bit, her hands gripping the pistol even tighter. *God, could she kill this person?*

Amarisa didn't budge. Then she slowly lifted a kicking, squawking Rose so that the baby shielded her from neck to stomach. Then she raised and lowered her, up and down. "Are you a good shot?" she hissed. "Are you willing to risk killing your own baby?"

"Stop!" cried Nora. "How can you do this? I'm Abram's daughter! Give her to me!"

Amarisa still held Rose in front of her, raising and lowering her little body. "You aren't Abram's daughter," she spit. "He would never have let his child be raised by his own murderer— by a Nazi! But with this child, we survive—without her, we perish!"

Nora took a breath, aimed and shot. Amarisa's leg crumpled and she screamed. Before she could drop Rose, Nora leaped forward and wrested her away.

"No, no, you can't!" cried Amarisa, now curled in a black ball on the floor, her hands pressing on the bloody wound on her leg. "You can't take her. She's mine! She's everything!"

Nora raced to the other side of the room, out of breath as relief flooded her, and all but threw herself on a bench at the bay window. Rose was still howling. Nora tucked the soft blanket tighter around her. "It's all right, sweet girl. It's Mommy, I'm here." Rose fixed her blue eyes on Nora's and stopped crying.

Nora clutched Rose to her breast, thrusting her face into her neck, inhaling her delicious scent. She then frantically felt Rose all over. *Fingers, toes, all there!* Tears flooded down her face and onto Rose's. "Oh, Rose, my darling, my baby…"

She held her tight. She would never, ever, let her go again.

69

Now Nico rushed to her and put his arms around both of them. Nora saw Dirk lay near the couch on his stomach, sprawled on the floor, still unconscious, blood pouring from his side where it appeared that shards of glass had pierced his body. His hands were now behind his back. Ariel had somehow managed to bind them with his belt.

Clutching Rose, Nora strode over to the couch, where Ariel and Leah sat, their arms around each other, Leah sobbing. Nora stood directly in front of Ariel, glaring angrily. He tried to rise, but Nico shoved him down and stood over him.

"Please, don't hurt him!" Nora looked at the woman, now sheltered in her husband's arms. "We didn't harm the baby, we love her!"

Ariel stood, but Nico inserted himself between Nora and Ariel and shoved him back down. Nico pointed at him. "Sit—*now.*" His voice sounded deadly.

Before Ariel could sit, Nora stepped forward. "You bastard!"

ANTOINETTE VAN HEUGTEN

she cried. "Your aunt and father murdered my mother and kid-napped my child! Why didn't you do something? *Answer me!*"

Ariel sank into the couch. His eyes seemed to beg her. "No!" he cried. "Amarisa wasn't there. I took Rose, but I didn't kill your mother! I'm not a murderer!" Leah pressed her face into Ariel's neck as he drew her again into his arms.

Nora shifted Rose to one hip. "How *dare* you! You're going to rot in jail!"

"Please, please, let me explain! It was my father!" he pleaded. "He killed her—not me!"

"I don't believe you!"

"My father was obsessed," he said. "He believed Hans killed my uncle."

Nora stepped back, holding Rose close to her chest, still shocked that she actually held her in her arms. A thought came. *I still can't prove that Hans didn't kill his uncle.* "But that doesn't explain why he killed my mother!"

"Because he believed that Anneke was an NSB-er who be-trayed my uncle and the rest of our family. That because of her they were killed in the camps. That Hans was jealous of Abram and that was why he killed him, shot him down like a dog in the street."

He stared at the floor. "All his life my father searched to find them. A vendetta. He couldn't think or talk about any-thing else. It ruined his life."

Ariel raised tortured eyes to hers. "We did everything to convince him and Amarisa that it didn't matter what hap-pened back then. That they had to put it behind him and go on. But my father never could. When he finally found your mother—and I have no idea how he did—he carried out his insane plan. And now he's dead."

Nora shifted Rose to one hip, leaned down and slapped him viciously across the face. It sounded like the crack of a whip.

She put her face close to his. She wanted to rip his throat out. "You stole Rose! Do you have any idea what you've done? Are you out of your *mind?*"

Rose burst into tears. Nora shushed her and then turned to Nico. "Call the police—now. I want this murderer, this kidnapper, arrested." She pointed at Dirk, who now seemed semiconscious, but unable to speak. "And the same goes for that bastard."

Nora heard a clumping behind her and turned. The old woman was dragging her bloody leg as she moved toward Nora, her hands grasping at Rose. "Give her to me!"

"Get the hell away from us! I don't know what your role was in all this, but you'll never touch my child again."

Amarisa fell to her knees. "You have to give her back!" she pleaded. "She is my life. She is everything!"

"She was never yours," said Nora coldly. "And you'll have a different life—in jail."

Amarisa crumpled, wailing. Nora heard her muttering, as if she was already saying the prayer for the dead.

"Look at me." Ariel raised his tortured eyes. "Here is what is going to happen to you," she said icily. "They'll deport you and try you in the States. And if I have anything to do with it, you'll get the death penalty. Texas is famous for it."

Ariel lifted his hands in a pleading gesture. Leah started to speak, but Ariel shook his head at her. He fixed on Nora. "Wait, wait, I'll explain everything! Just listen, please!"

Nico stood by the phone stand, receiver in hand. He gave her a questioning look. She held up a finger. Not yet. She shot out her next words—each a bullet. "You have two minutes. Start talking."

In a rush, Ariel began. "I went to see my father a few weeks ago, but he didn't answer the door. He never went anywhere and had been in poor health. I was worried so I used my key and went inside." He drew a breath. "On my way out, I saw his travel itinerary on his desk. Your address was scrawled on it."

Nora didn't believe this bastard, but she would hear him out. And then she would see him punished. *As if anyone could ever be punished enough for what he and his father had done.*

Now terrified, Ariel spoke even faster. "I got on the first plane to Houston. I wasn't sure what he would do, but I knew that whatever it was, I had to stop him. When I got there, I went straight to your home. I could see he had already beaten your mother and was pointing a gun in her face."

Nora couldn't bear it. "And what did you do while your father—that *monster!*—killed my mother?"

"I couldn't do anything! I ran toward him, but I tripped on the carpet. By the time I got up, he had already pulled the trigger! It was awful—all that blood, your mother's face—"

"Stop it!" cried Nora. "I don't want to hear it."

"But you have to! I ran to him and he had a heart attack. He fell to the floor."

"You let him die!" cried Amarisa. "You took my brother from me, and now Jacoba. I wish you'd never been born!"

Ariel went on. "Just before he died, your mother told him that you were Abram's daughter and that your baby was Jewish. His dying wish was that I take Rose back to Holland and raise her as a Jew."

Nora felt no pity at all. "So you did what he said. You stole my child after your father murdered my mother. Can you imagine the hell I've been through these last weeks or didn't you give a damn? How could you *do* such a thing!"

Ariel opened his mouth to speak. Nora held Rose closer to her. "You coward! Why did you do what he said? Why didn't you just leave her there?" She throttled a sob.

"I heard a car in the driveway. I panicked! So I just took

the baby and ran. I knew that if I stayed, I would be arrested, that the police would say I killed your mother."

"Then why didn't you give her back?" asked Nico. "You could have left her at a hospital, a police station—somewhere she would be found. You are disgusting."

"I know, I know," he said, putting his head in his hands. "I was terrified. And then I thought about what my father said. That the baby was our family. That she belonged in Holland with us." He turned and glanced at Leah, tears in his eyes. "And we couldn't have children," he whispered. "I thought it was fate, a gift from God out of a horrible nightmare. I didn't think about her grandmother, about you. I didn't think about anything except not getting caught and of putting the child into my wife's arms." He looked at Leah, but she only had eyes for Rose. Nora saw the love in them.

"God forgive me," he whispered.

Nora stared at him, still feeling cold fury. "God may forgive you, but I won't." She walked back to the bench, sat and kissed Rose's soft forehead. She felt as if her heart rate was returning to normal. She turned. "You attacked me, stalked me."

"I was terrified you would find me. That I would be arrested. That you would find the baby and take her away from us."

"We didn't harm her!" cried Leah. "We took perfect care of her!"

Nora pointed at Amarisa, still crouched and moaning in the corner. She looked at Leah. "You go to hell."

Ariel and Leah turned to one another. Nora could hear their muted sobs from across the room.

Nico walked over to Nora and touched Rose's silky hair and round cheeks. His eyes locked upon Nora's. She saw the love there.

"Meet your daughter," she said softly.

Nico took the baby as if he were holding a precious but foreign work of art. As he held her close, he looked at Nora with delight. His eyes told her everything. That he had just fallen in love with his child. Nora smiled. She had dreamed of the two of them together.

Nico leaned down and whispered in her ear. "I'm going to call the police. You and the baby go outside and wait at the restaurant on the corner. I'll stay here until they arrive." He paused to touch the soft curls on Rose's head.

Nora started to nod and then hesitated. "Wait."

"For what?"

Nora kept her voice low. "I'm not sure. I have to think this through." She put a hand to her forehead for a moment. "I believe him when he says it was his father who was insane and killed my mother. Yes, he was there and he took Rose, but now I have her back and she's safe and unharmed." She took the baby from Nico's arms and felt the warm, heavenly weight of her.

"I don't understand what you're saying."

"I don't know, either, but what if Hans really *did* kill Abram?" she asked. "What do I gain from having this man arrested if the man I thought was my father got away with murder?" She paused. "And if what he says is true, then Hans was not only responsible for Abram's murder, but he also may have been responsible for betraying and condemning almost everyone in his family to death in the camps. Everything points to him. And we have no evidence to refute it."

"That still doesn't excuse him! He should go to jail for a long time."

"Nico," she said slowly. "If I am Abram's daughter, then that man sitting over there is my cousin. If I send him to jail because of events my own parents set in motion, how do I live with that?"

"But Anneke was not an NSB-er, Abram's sister told you that. That must prove that she didn't betray anyone."

"But she pretended to be one. Even if Hans was a murderer, I think she is also partially accountable. She never intended it, but without her, Hans would never have killed Abram."

"I still don't get this."

Nora kissed Rose's soft cheek and then looked up at him. "I want to take Rose home. She's all that matters. Don't you agree?"

Nico looked at both of them tenderly. "Of course that's the most important thing. But are you sure you don't want to prosecute?"

Nora looked at the ruined couple on the couch, the old woman crumpled on the carpet. "They've already been convicted. They don't need me for that."

70

Nora and Nico walked to where Leah and Ariel now stood. They were no longer sobbing, but both faces showed tracks of their tears.

"I'm going to take Rose home now," she said softly.

Ariel nodded. "You can call the police. I won't resist."

"I am not going to press charges."

Shock filled his eyes. "How can you do that! I took your daughter and caused you immeasurable pain. My father killed your mother."

Nora studied him. His black eyes were so like her own. "Because I didn't choose to be Abram's daughter and you didn't choose to have a father who was a murderer. Because I don't know what role my parents played in all of this long ago."

Ariel tried to speak, but couldn't. Leah collapsed onto the couch.

Nora pointed at Amarisa, still wailing on the floor, and at

Dirk, just now able to sit up. "They're your problem." With Rose in her arms, she motioned to Nico that it was time to go.

Ariel walked to Nora. "What can I say? I don't know how you can do this, but I thank you with all my heart."

Nora now looked into the face so similar to her own. "Because you are my cousin. And because enough harm has been done. It ends here. Putting you in jail won't bring my mother back." She looked down at her sleeping baby. "And because everything I have ever wanted is right here."

Ariel nodded and gently touched one of Rose's plump fingers. "Goodbye, my darling," he whispered.

Nora followed Nico to the front door. She and Nico left the house. They didn't look back.

71

Nora walked through the empty rooms of her mother's house, remembering Anneke's smile and the quiet, warm look her father always gave her. Rose lay in the bassinet Anneke had given her, sleeping peacefully. It was almost as if she felt her grandmother's presence and love, so deep was her sleep.

It had now been almost a year and a half since she had gotten Rose back. The house had finally sold. Reluctantly, Nora had come back to make sure the movers had cleaned out the place. Everything had been boxed up and put into storage months ago. Nora would return sometime later to sift through the remains.

Nico's divorce was final and they had begun their new life together by buying a house near the *Vondelpark*. For now, Nora just wanted to leave Houston behind forever and go back to Nico. She and Rose would be returning to Amsterdam tomorrow. She had an interview with a hospital for a position—recommended by her old boss. She felt excited at the prospect.

She took a slow turn through her childhood bedroom, the tiny bathroom and her parents' room—all empty. Her footsteps echoed on the wooden floors, already dusty. There was nothing so sad as a house abandoned. She walked into the kitchen and noticed a note on the counter. From the movers. They didn't know what to do with the items in the recessed cabinet in the master closet.

What did that mean? She walked to her parents' closet and flicked on the lights. It was bare. Only a few hangers hung on the wooden bars. She went to her mother's side, where she had kept her evening wear, seldom used. A discrepancy in the wall caught her eye. A crack, a thin black line, seemed to take on an odd depth as she surveyed it. She looked closer. A knob protruded from the woodwork. She gripped it and pulled. A panel swung open.

Deep red velvet lined shallow, recessed drawers, each divided into compartments. It would have been entirely hidden by Anneke's hanging clothes. *Another secret place. Another private world.* Slowly, Nora opened the panel as far as it would go, afraid of what she would find. But she knew instantly. They stood side by side, sunk in rich coronation velvet. Silver orbs.

Nora lifted the first gently from its nest. An intricate *A* inscribed on the front. She ran her finger over the detailed work. She knew what would be on the back. As she turned it over, the cool of the metal warmed to the curve of her palm. An identical *A. Abram en Anneke.* She unfastened the silver clasp from her neck and lifted her mother's locket to compare them. They were the same.

Nora pulled the drawers open. Thirty-four identical silver globes glowed softly, burnished flares against the claret vel-

vet. A holy shrine—Anneke's hallowed place, her final reli-
quary. Pieces of Anneke's heart commemorating each year
she had survived without Abram. Nora imagined her mother,
year after year, holding the silver stones, warming them in
her hands, never losing the touch of his hand, the love of so
long ago.

Nora sensed the intrusion of her presence. She was never
meant to see this. She closed the secret panel. She would come
for them later.

She walked back into her parents' bedroom and glanced
around. *Was there anything else she had missed?* She turned to
go and then realized that she had almost forgotten the shadow
box on the wall. It had always hung there and, after time, had
become part of the room, like furniture one never noticed.

Nora walked over and studied it. *The Anneke Rose.* That
was what her father had called it. Anneke had cultivated it
in her beloved greenhouse, her one passion. There she was
happy, her hands in the rich earth, nursing cuttings, singing
softly to herself.

Hans had built her a small room off the greenhouse. While
Anneke gardened, Nora would lie on a mattress in her nook,
reading and sleeping; sleeping and dreaming. Many summers
were spent this way, the two of them in companionable silence.

Each summer morning, Anneke would clip a tiny pink
rosebud and lay it on Nora's pillow. And every morning, Nora
would take her book and curl up on the bed, the rose a scented
bookmark, a daily token of love and thoughtfulness.

Nora stared at the intricately embroidered rose in the
shadow box. Pink—a soft, baby-breath blush of a rose. It
seemed so real that Nora could almost smell its pure, child-
like scent.

She lifted it from the wall and walked toward the door.

Then she heard something flutter onto the carpet. An envelope. Nora stared at it. Probably a bill from the framer, taped onto the back of the shadow box. She laid the box on the bed, sat and opened the envelope. She shook it upside down. A dried pink rose fell onto Nora's lap. Inside was a letter dated two months after Rose's birth.

My darling Nora,

How strange it is that I must write a letter to you instead of telling you these things as you sit in the other room, peacefully nursing my grandchild. I hope when you read this that you will not blame me for keeping my secrets from you, knowing I love you more than you can imagine.

I will not tell you the details of my life during the war. It was a time of hate, death and loss. What is important for you to know is your true heritage. I have struggled all these years trying to decide whether to tell you this at all, but as my daughter, I feel you have the right to know.

During the war, both Hans and I fought in the resistance. It was a terrible, terrifying, yet exciting time. I met another resistance fighter, a Jewish man named Abram Rosen. He was the love of my life, Nora. I know it must hurt you to know that Hans was not. He was a fine man who loved me. And you were the light of his life.

A shameful fact of my life is that my father was a Dutch Nazi, a cruel, brutal man. I pretended to be one to hide my resistance activities. In 1942, Abram was forced into hiding. I moved him constantly, terrified that he would be discovered. In April of 1945, just one month before the liberation, I discovered I was pregnant. Abram was thrilled about the baby. He just knew he would make it, that we three would make it—to freedom.

I had tried to keep my relationship with Abram secret from Hans, who was a childhood friend. He was horribly jealous. One night Hans and I had an argument about Abram. I told him I was pregnant and he went into a rage. I didn't know that he had been following me to the house where Abram was hiding. He ran out and I ran after him, knowing he would go there, terrified at what he might do.

Then it happened all at once. Hans and Abram fighting outside the safe house, the Dutch police running up behind me, my pulling Hans away from Abram. And then an officer shot Abram. Between the eyes. His last look was at me. I shall never wipe that from my mind.

Hans was blamed for killing Abram. He did not. I was blamed for leading the police to Abram. I did not. I learned only after Liberation Day who had betrayed my darling Abram. The killer told me himself.

My father.

He was suspicious of my absences late at night and had me followed. I never knew how he did it, but on that horrible night, he had the Groene Politie *track me to Abram's safe house. Then the fight. The shot.*

I was pregnant. My lover was dead. Life was over for me. I didn't care where I went, what I did. Everything was hopeless, lost, destroyed. I had a difficult pregnancy. After you were born, it was Hans who persuaded me to come to America. He knew he would be blamed for Abram's murder and that, as an NSB-er, I would be arrested, jailed.

Hans and I tried to make a good life for you. I hope we have. Now you have your own daughter to love. My only wish for you is that you find your Abram. If you do, never let him go.

I leave you this rose I made for you. I leave you the love that is here in my heart, as perfect as yours for Rose. Never mourn me. You are the child of a great love. Live your life as one.

EPILOGUE

———

Nora walked to the *Leidseplein* on a beautiful summer day. She saw Nico sitting with Rose at an outdoor café. She grasped the locket around her neck. She knew what was inside. She had placed photographs of her and Nico into the two oval spaces. Beneath them were the old pictures of Anneke and Abram.

Nico saw her and waved. Rose came running toward her, red curls bouncing, her mouth open in laughter. She walked to them, her hand molded gently around the new life that grew inside her. She walked to the man she loved, her daughter and a life filled with promise and joy.

It was as Anneke and Abram would have wished. Their love lived on.

★ ★ ★ ★ ★

ACKNOWLEDGMENTS

For my first editor, who is forced to live with me as I go through the tortured rituals that precede every novel and who reads every line of every revision. Without his unqualified love and encouragement, I would still be staring at a blank page. Thank you, my darling Bill.

For my family, for always being there.

For my brilliant agent, Al Zuckerman, and the agony he puts me through with every novel, pushing me to make every word, scene and chapter the very best it can be. I cannot imagine writing without you!

For Glenn Cambor, without whom I would never have become a writer and who has saved my life in so many ways.

For Beverly Swerling and her steadfast support and encouragement.

For my professor and mentor, Francis Bulhof, who long ago taught me Dutch and who patiently shepherded a naive girl through the scholarship maze that led her to the Netherlands.

Deep appreciation for my dear friend Marijke Clerx, my cousin, Liesbeth van Loon, and her husband, Yvo, for reading the manuscript and correcting my most flagrant errors in language and history. Thanks to Prof. A.G.H. Anbeek for his course in Dutch culture.

For my editor, Susan Swinwood, and the entire MIRA group, for their continued support. I take full responsibility for any historical errors regarding events depicted in the Netherlands during the war. My research was conducted over thirty years ago, when I spent a year in the carrels of NIOD *(Nederlands Instituut voor Oorlogsdocumentatie)*. I was fortunate to meet its founder, Loe de Jong, and to be assisted by the Institute's wonderful staff, who helped me comb through stacks of diaries donated by Dutch citizens after the war. Any errors in the Dutch language are mine, as it has been decades since I spoke with any fluency.

Finally, deep gratitude to my readers for their enthusiastic response to my first novel, *Saving Max*. I hope you enjoy this one, as well.

'We did what I suppose most people would have done.
We asked, "Where did they hope to go?
And what could we do to help?"'

– Ida Cook

Ida and Louise Cook were two ordinary young English women who lived quiet lives in London's suburbs, loved opera, and had the unshakeable courage to save hundreds of Jews from Hitler's death camps throughout the 1930's.

As a successful novelist for Mills & Boon, Ida used her sudden wealth to fund their dangerous undercover missions. Time after time they ventured into the heart of Nazi Germany, to smuggle those facing deadly persecution to safety.

Safe Passage is a moving testimony to two women who risked everything to save others and help them rebuild their lives in freedom.

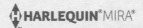

Dark secrets lie just around the corner

Holly Ansell's brother Ben has disappeared. Determined to find out what's happened to him, she visits Ashdown Park where she discovers an old mirror and Ben's research into the house that once stood there. Little does Holly know that Ashdown and the mirror hold so many secrets, scandals and the power of fate…

For fans of Barbara Erskine and Kate Morton comes this unforgettable time slip story about the power one lie can have over history.

In a family built on lies, who can you trust?

Audrey Bailey will never forget the moment she met Ralph Templeton in the sweltering heat of a Bombay café. Her lonely life over, she was soon married with two small children. But things in the Templeton household were never quite what they seemed.

Now approaching 70, and increasingly a burden on the children she's never felt close to, Audrey plans a once-in-a-lifetime cruise around the Greek isles. Forcing twins Lexi and John along for the ride, the Templetons set sail as a party of three – but only two will return.

On the night of her birthday, Audrey goes missing…hours after she breaks the news that the twins stand to inherit a fortune after her death. As the search of the ship widens, so does the list of suspects – and with dark clues emerging about Audrey's early life, the twins begin to question if they can even trust one another…

Everyone has secrets…

Sarah Quinlan's husband, Jack, has been haunted
for decades by the mysterious death of his mother.
But when Jack's beloved aunt Julia is involved in a
serious accident, Sarah begins to realise that
nothing about the Quinlans is quite as it seems.

Caught in a flurry of unanswered questions, Sarah
dives deep into the rabbit hole of Jack's past, but
the farther she climbs, the harder it is to get out.
And soon she is faced with a shattering reality she
could never have prepared for…

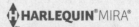
M444_MP

FORBIDDEN LOVE
IN THE TIME OF WAR

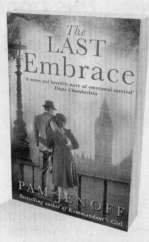

August 1940: World War II is about to break and
sixteen-year-old refugee Addie is finding love and
acceptance away from home in the arms of Charlie
Connelly. But when a tragedy strikes the Connelly
family Addie is left devastated and flees, first to
Washington and then to war-torn London.

Then, when Charlie, now a paratrooper, re-appears
two years later Addie discovers that the past is
impossible to outrun. Now she must make one last
desperate attempt to find within herself the
answers that will lead the way home.

M419_TLE

Loved this book?
Let us know!

Find us on **Twitter @Mira_BooksUK**
where you can share your thoughts, stay up
to date on all the news about our upcoming
releases and even be in with the chance of
winning copies of our wonderful books!

Bringing you the best voices in fiction

H HARLEQUIN®MIRA®

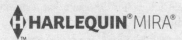